SIDEQUEST
ADVENTURES
The Foreworld Saga

SIDEQUEST ADVENTURES

ADVENTURES

THE FOREWORLD SAGA

—— BY ——

MARK TEPPO, ANGUS TRIM,
MICHAEL TINKER PEARCE, LINDA PEARCE

47N RTH

Text copyright © 2013 by FOREWORLD, LLC
"The Lion in Chains" originally published by 47North, October 2012
"The Shield-Maiden" originally published by 47North, November 2012
"The Beast of Calatrava" originally published by 47North, January 2013

Published by 47North, SEATTLE
www.apub.com

ISBN-13: 9781477848234
ISBN-10: 1477848231
Cover design by: Kerrie Robertson
Library of Congress Control Number: 2013942326

Whoso had seen that shattering of shields,
Whoso had heard those shining hauberks creak,
And heard those shields on iron helmets beat,
Whoso had seen fall down those chevaliers,
And heard men groan, dying upon that field,
Some memory of bitter pains might keep.

—The Song of Roland

Table of Contents

LION IN CHAINS
A TALE OF FOREWORLD

—— BY ——

ANGUS TRIM & MARK TEPPO

PROLOGUE

King Richard's return from the crusade should have been a glorious progression—he had, after all, managed to negotiate a peace with Saladin that allowed Christian access to Jerusalem—but the voyage home had been fraught with unpredictable weather. At sea, their boat had been driven off course, and when they had been forced to abandon the vessel, they had made landfall farther west than they had anticipated—in lands nominally controlled by the Holy Roman Emperor, a man who was aggrieved about Richard's conduct in the Holy Land.

Richard had, in fact, a number of enemies in Christendom, which made an overland journey north from Italy fraught with danger.

They stumbled into Gorizia, thinking they were farther east than they were, and were nearly caught by Meinhard, the nephew of Conrad of Montferrat, king of Jerusalem. Conrad had been murdered in the Holy Land, and many believed Richard was the architect of the assassination. Meinhard, as did others in Christendom, wanted Richard to answer to this charge, and he would have captured Richard had it not been for the dogged loyalty of a handful of Shield-Brethren, men of the *Ordo Militum Vindicis Intactae* who had insisted on accompanying Richard back to England. Richard's party escaped, and after several harried days of travel through the Alps, they reached Friesach, a town known for its silver mint. They were trying to outrun news of their presence in Christendom, hoping to remain anonymous, but the people of Friesach were too eager to be helpful, filled with a false sincerity that masked an underlying apprehension. Friesach was a trap, and Baldwin of Bethune, one of Richard's remaining knights, volunteered to remain behind, pretending to be the king, while Richard—along with William de l'Éstrang and the sole remaining Shield-Brethren—rode on toward Moravia.

But first they had to get across the Danube, the wide river that flowed past Vienna, the home of Leopold V, the duke of Austria.

There was a ferry east of the city that would take them across the river, and while William went to negotiate passage, Richard and the young Shield-Brethren knight found an inn in the village of Erdberg. Richard stumbled inside, leaving the knight to tend to their horses, and the king nearly wept with joy as the heat from the fire started to thaw the icy surface of his skin. The innkeeper brought him food and drink, and only after his belly was full and his clothes were starting to dry did Richard shake himself free of the cloying fever fog that had clouded his mind the last few days. *I just have to get across the river*, he thought.

Richard picked up his tankard and glanced around for the innkeeper, meaning to call for more ale. There was no sign of the man, and he realized that the few patrons in the inn were all trying very hard not to look at him. He knew he was not a pleasant sight: his plain robe and cloak were filthy, his beard and hair unkempt; he was both sweating and shivering. He knew he was taller than most men, but the weight of the fever on him made it easy to obscure his height. He had left the bulk of his money with Baldwin in Friesach, knowing that wealth only attracted attention. *How could they possibly know who I am?* he wondered.

As he set his tankard down on the table, he caught sight of the ring on his hand. He had tried to take it off several days ago, but his hands had been too stiff and swollen, and he hadn't been able to get the band past his knuckle. It was not the ring of a poor merchant. It was the ring of a king.

The door of the inn banged open and men, wearing the livery of the duke of Austria, marched into the room.

ONE

⬛▬

Henry VI, emperor of a vast portion of Christendom that stretched from the Low Countries in the north to Sicily in the south, was growing tired of waiting. Initially, having the king of England in a castle dungeon where no one would ever find him had been a delightful distraction. Henry had mulled over endless ideas about what to do with his captive, but the truth was that he couldn't simply leave the king incarcerated forever. The doddering old fool Celestine had already excommunicated Leopold for having captured the king of England in the first place, and Henry suspected the Pope would eventually get around to excommunicating him as well. Such expulsion could be reversed, of course, with the right sort of abasement to God and the Church, but Henry had enough crises to address already.

The duke of Saxony, Henry the Lion, was—once again—making trouble in the north. Lion, the lackluster younger brother of Richard, was spending too much time in Paris, making plans with Philip, the king of France. And now the bastard Tancred had crowned himself the king of Sicily. Land that was Henry VI's by right of marriage!

This was the eternal problem with ruling such a vast domain. An emperor never slept well; he could never be sure his borders were secure. And if he wasn't being vexed by sons of a previously vanquished enemy who had managed to raise an army to take back what had been stolen from their fathers, then it was some unexpected dearth of coin in his treasury.

Maintaining an empire was expensive.

Ransoming Richard back to England had been a masterful idea, but it was a plan that was taking much too long to come to fruition. That was the problem with insisting on such a fantastic amount—one hundred thousand silver marks—to ensure the release of the English king. It took time to assemble that much coin.

Henry had some reason for celebration, though. He had received word from his spies that England had finally assembled more than half of the ransom. Of course, he had also heard disturbing rumors that Philip was quite aware of England's progress in gathering the funds to rescue Richard. His spies suspected Philip was contemplating some sort of counterproposal.

Henry thought his spies weren't nearly devious enough in their estimation of what Philip was considering.

There was a sharp double rap on the door to his room, and his steward, Wecelo, entered. Wecelo was tall and thin, and his robe fit him badly enough that he reminded Henry of a wounded bird. Wecelo stepped aside, holding the door, and a second man entered.

The visitor was shorter and broader than Wecelo—neither of which was very difficult—and the man's face was burdened with a large nose that had been broken several times. As he reached the center of the room, the man dropped to one knee and touched his fist to his forehead.

"Ah, Otto," Henry said, "I have a delicate matter for your attention." Otto Shynnagel was not the sort of commander who swayed men with his beauty or bearing, but what he lacked in countenance and charm, he made up for in loyalty and single-mindedness.

"I am at your disposal, Your Majesty," Otto replied, remaining on one knee, though he raised his head and gazed intently at a spot near Henry's ankles.

"Several weeks ago, I sent several ambassadors to England, inquiring after the money that Queen Eleanor is seeking to raise for the safe return of her son. Last night I received word that the ambassadors were preparing to return to my court, along with a portion of the money."

"Yes, Your Majesty," Otto said.

"Queen Eleanor is sending a contingent of guards, of course, augmenting the men accompanying the ambassadors," Henry said. "The silver will be well guarded, though I suspect France might try to intercept the company as it returns to Speyer."

"And you wish me to intercept this ambush?"

"Not in the slightest," Henry said with a smile. "I hope the French are successful in stealing this cargo."

Otto's brow furrowed. "I do not understand, Your Majesty."

"Philip wants me to keep the king of England here until the fall. He wants another six months to conquer more of Richard's holdings in Normandy, and frankly, such aggression is not unwelcome to the Holy Roman Empire. But I cannot condone such action outright. Nor can I openly facilitate such an opportunity for France. But Philip thinks he can sway me with a counteroffer of an equal amount of silver—even though I know he does not have that sort of coin at his disposal. Where might he get such funds?"

"From English wagons," Otto replied, a hint of a smile on his lips.

"Precisely. If England fails to deliver this first portion of the ransom, then I am not beholden to return their king. Philip's offer suddenly becomes much more interesting to me, does it not? Such funds would be useful to us in our efforts against Tancred."

Otto squared his shoulders and nodded. "Of course, Your Majesty."

"But why should I let Philip steal this money and then try to give it to me anyway, while exacting concessions from me?" Henry asked. "I think it is much better for the empire if England lost their ransom and it was clear that the thieves were French, but the money was never recovered. At least, not by France or England. Do you understand?"

"I do, Your Majesty."

"I can certainly be horrified by this turn of events—this barbaric thievery by the French king—and, showing great generosity, release the king of England to address this most heinous injury against his country by the French." Henry allowed himself to smile. "My attention would be on Sicily anyway"—he waved a hand at Otto—"where my newly hired army was confronting Tancred."

"It would be an honor to lead that army," Otto said. He grinned openly now, a smile made lopsided by his flattened nose. "I will ready my men," he said, touching his fist to his forehead once more. "We will depart immediately."

"Very good," Henry said.

Otto stood, spun on his heel, and strode out of the chamber. Wecelo paused, hand on the door, staring at Henry with a noncommittal expression. "You are not informing Duke Leopold of our decision, are you?" Wecelo asked.

"Of course not," Henry snorted. "He'll want his half. I can't give him half of something I never received, can I?"

"That would be impossible, Your Majesty," Wecelo said.

"A pity about his excommunication, though," Henry said.

"Yes, Your Majesty. A tremendous pity."

"I suspect he'll manage to find a way to have it lifted. Taking the crusade, perhaps."

"For a second time," Wecelo pointed out.

Henry laughed, delighted with that realization.

◆ ◆ ◆

For a king in captivity, King Richard was well rested, well fed, and well groomed. He sat on a wooden bench near the pond in the center of the garden, a plank across his lap. A white swan glided slowly across the placid surface of the pond, leaving few ripples in its wake. The king's right hand was moving carefully across the plank, sketching the swan with a piece of charcoal. He wore a dark-green tunic trimmed with brown fur, and his hair and beard were neatly groomed. Hung on a gold chain around his neck was the official seal of England, and on his right hand was a silver ring with a heavy crimson stone.

Maria trailed a few steps behind Richard's manservant, a stiff-backed young man who, to her eyes, appeared out of place within the imperial court. They had spoken briefly when she had presented herself to see the king, and he spoke German like a native, but he didn't strike her as being from the local gentry. He hid his common origins well, but she was adept at sensing the tiny hesitations and imperfections that revealed a nonaristo-cratic heritage.

"Your Majesty," the manservant said without preamble as they reached the pond. The swan swiveled its head toward them at the sound of the servant's voice, eyeing Maria more. Knowing who was the interloper of the pair.

Maria curtsied as Richard looked up, and she noted that the manservant did little more than nod toward Richard. *A strange familiarity*, she thought. It was not unlike the relationship she had with Richard's wife, Queen Berengaria of Navarre, but she had attended to the queen for many years.

"Hello, Feronantus," Richard said, his eyes straying to Maria. "Who is that with you?"

"Maria of Navarre, on behalf of Queen Berengaria," Feronantus said.

"Ah, my dear wife, worrying about me." Richard's gaze dropped to the letter Maria was holding. "What news from Rome?"

he asked, his attention returning to his drawing, dismissing her before he even heard her answer.

"She isn't in Rome any longer," Maria said, her words coming more quickly and more distempered than she had intended. "Concerned about the enormous *ransom* demanded by the Holy Roman Emperor, she returned to Navarre to assist England—and *your mother*—in raising the funds."

Richard's hand stopped moving on the drawing; then, very deliberately, he smudged a line with the edge of his thumb. Maria held her breath, and the only noise in the garden was the sound of the swan rustling its wings.

"Is there anything else in that letter?" Richard asked quietly.

"She misses you, Your Majesty, and languishes greatly without your presence. She hopes, God willing, that you may be returned to her soon." Maria punctuated her summary with another curtsy. She had written the letter at Berengaria's request, and she knew there was no coded message beyond what lay on the page. While she had carried secret messages for the queen before, such was not the case this time. The queen had simply wanted someone she could trust to report on Richard's well-being at the Holy Roman Emperor's court.

Arrogant as ever was Maria's private assessment.

"God willing," Richard echoed. He looked at her again, and this time he actually studied her face. "Have we met?"

"No, Your Majesty," Maria lied.

Richard's eyes narrowed and she thought he was going to challenge her claim, but he set the piece of charcoal down and held out his hand. "Let me see the letter," he said.

She relinquished it to the king, and he broke the seal to peruse the neat lines inscribed on the parchment. "This isn't her handwriting," he noted.

"No, Your Majesty," Maria said.

"Yours?"

Maria nodded.

"Do you speak it, too?" Richard asked, referring to the language in which the letter was written.

"I have a passing familiarity with the language of your countrymen, Your Majesty," Maria said in English.

"You have less of an accent than I, and it is my mother tongue," Richard laughed. "Queen Berengaria has sent someone to spy on me."

Maria flushed, a reaction that only seemed to amuse Richard further. Feronantus looked mildly uncomfortable to be party to this entire conversation.

"So my queen has started to raise funds on my behalf, has she?" Richard said. "She is a lovely girl and means well, but does she know the enormity of the sum that the emperor has laid upon my release?"

"She would not be making this effort if it were a mere pittance, Your Majesty," Maria pointed out.

"No," Richard mused, "she certainly would not."

The swan, sensing a lull in the conversation, chose this moment to rise up, flapping its wings. It was a beautiful bird, and they all stared at its broad white wings.

"Such an enormous amount of money would be very tantalizing," Richard said in the wake of the swan's interruption. "Henry wants to exchange hostages, both from England and from here in Germany, as assurance that neither side reneges on the ransom terms. However, I have heard rumors around Henry's court that he is growing impatient. He has sent a delegation of ambassadors to my mother, in hopes of getting his hands on some of the coin sooner than later."

Maria nodded absently. Such rumors had been heard at Queen Berengaria's court as well. Gathering the ransom was taking a long time, and too many people—both high and low—were starting to dream about having such wealth.

"I do not trust Henry," Richard said. "Nor my brother John." He shook his head. "Nor the king of France. Too many men with access to mercenaries who would readily take orders for a bit of that silver."

"Aye," Feronantus said quietly, and Maria glanced between Richard and his servant, wondering what conversation between the two of them she had missed.

Richard sighed, and for a moment, his shoulders slumped. "This game has to be played," he said, adjusting his posture and setting aside his weariness. "It serves me little to depart from the emperor's court without the ransom being paid. My detractors will only increase their incessant braying about my honor, or lack thereof. Good Christian men will begin to doubt what I accomplished in the Holy Land." Richard shook his head again. "Too many died to ensure access to Jerusalem. I will not let their deaths be wasted. I will abide by the terms of my captivity—that is my chivalrous duty—but I cannot sit by and do nothing while others plot to disrupt my mother and wife's efforts on my behalf."

He flipped over his sheet of parchment and began sketching in broad strokes on the blank sheet. "They'll follow the river, won't they?" he said. Maria assumed he was talking to Feronantus, for she had no idea what he was talking about.

"Aye," Feronantus said, nodding. "If the emperor convinces Queen Eleanor to part with a portion of the ransom, they'll come by boat from London. To Walcheren and Middelburg, and then up the Rhine."

Richard's head bobbed up and down as he continued to work. Beneath his hands, a twisting course of a river emerged, along with a coastline that she recognized as England and the continent—France and Normandy. "How far up the river?" Richard asked. "All the way?"

"It depends on the weather," Feronantus pointed out. "If they leave England too late, there will be ice. It will slow the boats."

"Henry won't like the delay," Richard said. "He'll take the silver off the boats and bring it over land." Some of Richard's marks on the page were chevrons, and Maria guessed they were indicative of mountains. "If they travel on the north side of the river, that puts them close to Saxony, and the Lion of Saxony has no love for the emperor right now. On the south side of the river, they are closer to France."

"But not that close," Feronantus said.

"Close enough," Richard mused. "The jingling sound of all that silver will carry far, and I suspect the king of France will be listening very intently."

Feronantus shrugged, as if to say that such allure was lost on him.

"If that is the case, why would Philip wait?" Maria asked. When the two men looked at her, she blushed, but continued. "If I were to steal such an amount, I would not decide to do so on a whim."

"I would choose the time and place," Richard said, nodding. "I like your thinking, Maria of Navarre. It is a rare and wondrous gift. No wonder Berengaria sent you to visit me without the slightest inkling of what I am supposed to do with you. A solution presents itself readily enough, though, doesn't it?"

"What solution?" Maria inquired.

Richard finished his drawing and held it up for the pair to examine it. Just past the first major curve of the river, Richard had drawn a series of narrow hills. "Here," he said. "This is where I would lay an ambush. Plus"—he slapped a finger against the sheet—"I would force the issue. It doesn't need to be ice on the river; it can be anything at all. Just enough of a crisis that the captain of the silver train decides to go overland."

"That is a rather speculative observation," Feronantus said dryly.

"I know," Richard laughed. "Which is why I need to depend on you two to act as my eyes."

"Us?" Feronantus and Maria said at the same time.

Richard grinned. "And if I am correct, you will need to be more than my eyes…"

TWO

The Shield-Brethren chapter house in Mainz was located near the ruins of the old Roman *castrum*, which had been the first settlement in the valley where the Rhine and Main flowed together. There were a number of chapter houses scattered across Christendom, and most were little more than tiny hermitages—temporary housing for members of the order, with one or two permanent residents charged with upkeep. The one in Mainz was almost like a small keep. It had an outer stone wall and several outbuildings around a main chapel, and it comfortably held several dozen Shield-Brethren knights and various support staff. Outside of Petraathen, the mountain stronghold that was the order's home, the chapter house in Mainz was the largest Feronantus had seen.

He identified himself at the gate, and after relinquishing his horse to a squire, he made his way to the central building to speak with the quartermaster. On his left was a large training yard, and the initiates were running through a familiar drill. That much never changed: the training master trying to teach the young and the clumsy how not to die in battle.

To think he had been one of those untrained and untested lads a few years ago. It seemed like a dream. Like someone else's life. Before his initiation scars had even healed, he had been bloodied in battle.

As he reached the main building, he was met by an older knight and led inside to a narrow room that contained two long tables. Light streamed in from high slits in the ceiling, and a worn standard of the order's sigil hung on the wall to Feronantus's right. This was the communal mess hall, the chamber where the knights held their *Kinyen*. Seated at the table were several weathered men, and Feronantus judged them to be the chapter house's quartermaster and his senior knights.

He bowed, hands out and open, showing the rounded scar on either forearm. "I am Feronantus," he said, "knight initiate of the order. I joined the crusade with Frederick Barbarossa, but returned with Richard Lionheart."

"Greetings, brother Feronantus," said the man sitting at the near end of the table. His long gray hair was pulled back from his face, and his beard curled in thick strands as it had been plaited recently. "I am Geoffrey, quartermaster of this house, and I bid you welcome. Your name and deeds are known to us."

Feronantus dipped his head once more. "They are but minor tales," he said, slightly embarrassed by the elder knight's words. "Hardly worth recounting."

"Aye, that may be true," the older man said with a tiny grin, "but that does not diminish them." He signaled to the man who had accompanied Feronantus to the room. "Come and sit," he said to Feronantus. "Share your story with us."

Feronantus nodded. He had timed his arrival at the chapter house to coincide with the midday meal, anticipating that his arrival would precipitate some discourse before he could get to the real reason for his visit. Of the Shield-Brethren who had accompanied King Richard on his return from the Holy Land, he was the only one who had stayed with the king. When he was surrounded by the duke of Austria's men near the stable in Erdberg, he had not identified himself, and he and Richard had been taken to Dürnstein castle, a cold and remote stronghold where he had watched over the feverish king. Once Richard recovered, he had simply insisted that Feronantus—as a trusty manservant—remain with him, and that had been that. It had only been after the Holy Roman Emperor had brought both of them to the imperial court that he had managed to send word to the *Electi* at Petraathen, informing them that he still lived.

Why he stayed with the captive king, playing the role of the unassuming servant, was a decision neither he nor Richard ever discussed. It just felt like where he was supposed to be.

He had had many months to reflect on his intuition. His *oplo*—the order training master at Petraathen—had taught the initiates about the idea of *Vor*, the heightened awareness each Shield-Brethren knight sought to perfect in battle. While in the Holy Land, he had felt something that might be construed as the *Vor* during the Battle of Arsuf, where Richard finally bested Saladin and the Muslim armies.

The third time he had felt the strange fluttering feeling had been several days ago when he had met Maria, the handmaiden of Queen Berengaria.

✦ ✦ ✦

Maria returned to the inn shortly before the evening slipped entirely from the sky. Torches had already been lit along the winding street in a vague attempt to keep the winter shadows at bay. From the street, she could hear the raucous noise coming from the inn, and she braced herself for the sweltering heat and cacophony of a room filled with drunks. She had chosen this inn partially for its steady business—it was easier to remain anonymous in a crowded room—but that did not mean she relished braving the noisy and sweaty mass.

Keeping one hand clasped about the base of her hood, she slipped through the open door in the wake of a lumbering merchant, who stopped abruptly on the inside of the threshold and threw his arms up in the air as if he meant to embrace the entire room. Perhaps he did, for it seemed as if everyone turned and shouted a greeting to the rotund man at the same time. The noise was deafening, and the weight of the shouts shoved Maria against the inner wall. Gasping for breath, she forced her way through the press of bodies, trying to reach the narrow stairs that led to the sparse rooms upstairs.

The noise lessened once she reached the second floor, though she could feel the timbers quaking beneath her feet. *How long would they drink and sing and pound their tankards on the tables?* she wondered as she went to the last door on the left.

She knew the answer. Germans would go all night, given the opportunity; during her foray into the market, she had heard about a recent festival the city had celebrated. For some, the festivities hadn't ended.

She tried the door at the end of the hall and, finding it unbarred, opened it, slipping into the dark room. She leaned against the door as she shut it behind her, taking a moment to catch her breath. She did not care much for crowds, even when they were useful in obscuring her.

"It is quite a celebration downstairs," a voice said in the darkness.

She let out a tiny shriek and then composed herself as she recognized the voice. "Why are you sitting there in the dark?" she demanded, her tone made harsher by her apprehension.

"I was listening," Feronantus said. He moved slightly, and the stool he was sitting on creaked, letting her know he was on the other side of the narrow cot that split the room in half.

"You forgot to bring a candle up, didn't you?" she realized.

"Aye," he said, "I did. Wait a few moments. Your eyes will adjust to the gloom."

"I don't need to see anything," she retorted, still slightly peeved that he had startled her. "Nor do you," she pointed out as she fumbled for the latch, sliding it across the frame so no one could open the door from the outside. "What did the Shield-Brethren say?" she asked as she felt for the edge of the cot. While what she had said about candlelight was true, she would have preferred some light in the room, and she realized she was just as guilty as he for neglecting to bring up a stub of wax with a tiny flame.

"Very little," Feronantus replied. "Mostly, they listened."

"Will they give you aid?"

"Of course," he said. "They are my brothers."

"Will it be enough?"

"It depends on the size of the imperial guard, and how many French come to ambush them, and how many men the emperor sends to ambush the ambushers." He made a noise in his throat that she took to be a short laugh. "You never have *enough*," he explained. "You always wish for a few more."

Having found the cot, she crawled onto it and fussed with the ragged blanket provided by the innkeeper. The lodgings weren't much, but she had slept in worse conditions. Any night with a roof overhead was a night to be treasured, and she suspected there would be a number of them coming up where she would be sleeping in much less comfort. "I asked about freemen," she said as she tried to get comfortable. "We are too far north. We have to go south if we are to find men who would be amenable to our cause."

"It will take too long," he replied. "You should just find crossbowmen."

"I know," she sighed.

They had been avoiding the topic for several days. As they had traveled north from the imperial court, they had been listening to the gossip along the river. The emperor's ambassadors had gone down the Rhine two months ago, in a fleet of a half dozen boats, several of which had been filled with armed men.

If the French intended to successfully ambush this party on its return, Feronantus estimated the ambushers would need at least twice the number of German soldiers. Making a difference in that battle meant gathering no small force in very little time. Feronantus, being a member of the *Ordo Militum Vindicis Intactae,* could call upon his order for assistance, but the question remained: How many knights could he assemble?

And if they couldn't field Shield-Brethren, who else were they going to find?

English longbowmen had been Richard's suggestion, *not crossbowmen,* when Maria had intimated a lack of understanding the distinction.

The trouble was finding such men within the Holy Roman Empire.

◆ ◆ ◆

For months, the agents of the Scaccarium Redemptionis, the exchequer of ransom, had been delivering silver to the crypt beneath St. Paul's Cathedral, in the heart of London. Hubert Walter, the Bishop of Salisbury, was in charge of raising the ransom for King Richard, and his men—hand-picked for their devotion to the Crown—weighed and marked the incoming silver, filling casks and crates with coin and ingots.

On a daily basis, Hubert delivered a report to Queen Eleanor, detailing the previous day's receipts and updating his projections as to how long it would take England to raise the ransom. Recently, his news had not been good, and when the emperor's ambassadors arrived in London, Hubert and Eleanor pled the case for a partial delivery of the ransom. One hundred thousand silver marks was not an amount that could be raised quickly—as was evidenced by the difficulties the exchequer of ransom was having—and more important, the sheer weight and bulk of such an amount was cause for concern.

The imperial ambassadors, being prudent men who had no desire to be the object of every bandit and rogue nobleman across Christendom, agreed with the queen's suggestion. Hubert immediately ordered the chests of silver beneath St. Paul's to be emptied into smaller containers for transport. Each barrel required four men to lift it onto the bed of a wagon, and each wagon required double the team to pull it through the streets of London to the docks at Queenhithe. There, a half dozen ships waited to receive the thousands of pounds of silver.

Hubert personally oversaw the transport of the silver from St. Paul's, riding beside the lead wagon. The carts moved slowly through London, the wheels grinding against the stones of the streets. Even though Hubert had tried to maintain a level of secrecy over the course of the wagons, it was impossible to disguise the armed escort that accompanied the caravan. They had barely left the square near St. Paul's before the streets became choked with Londoners who wanted to watch the historic procession.

Hubert couldn't blame them. The exchequer of ransom had levied a tax of more than a quarter of the total wealth of every individual in England. They felt they had a right to see where that money was going.

He was more than a little relieved when the wagons reached Queenhithe. King Richard was a charismatic man—well loved by his subjects, for no reason other than the stories told by wandering minstrels were always entertaining and patriotic—but it had been many years since he had been back to England. Walter had wondered—to himself, but never to anyone else, especially the queen—if Londoners were going to realize they were paying many times over to get Richard back as they had paid to have him leave in the first place. Was he really worth that much to England?

The leader of the imperial ambassadors was a reedy man named Willehalm Zenthffeer. He made little effort to disguise his derision in regard to English efficiency, and Hubert was looking forward to handing over the silver and wishing the imperial ambassador Godspeed and all the luck in the world in getting the weight of silver to Speyer in a timely fashion.

Hubert was, in fact, looking forward to being done with this whole business of taxing the citizens of the English crown. He wished, not for the first time, that Richard had listened to him in Acre. That the king had come back with his army, instead of sneaking off like he had. That he had listened more readily to those around him during the campaigns in the Holy Land. That he weren't as stubborn and arrogant as he was brilliant and manipulative. In a tiny corner of his heart, Hubert hated Richard, but he also knew he would always serve his king. Unreservedly and without complaint. Just as he knew Richard would reward such devotion and service.

Get me out of here and you can name your position, Richard had told him the last time Hubert had seen him in Speyer, eight months ago.

I am a bishop already, Hubert had argued, *and I have gone on crusade with you. What else is there?*

It had been a foolish question, the answer to which both he and Richard already knew: *archbishop of Canterbury.*

All he had to do was bring the king home.

As the wagons rattled to a stop behind Hubert, Willehalm limped out of the cluster of imperial soldiers ranged across the docks. "Is this all there is?" the imperial ambassador sneered, idly glancing at the line of wagons.

"It is," Hubert sighed. *Nearly ten thousand pounds of silver*, he thought.

THREE

Feronantus was met at the gate of the Shield-Brethren chapter house by Rutger, one of the initiates he had met yesterday. Rutger clasped his forearm in the traditional greeting of the order; both men could feel the hardened edges of the initiation scars on the forearm of the other man.

"Were we at Petraathen together?" he asked Feronantus as they walked across the yard toward the main house.

Feronantus shook his head. "I don't recall," he said. Rutger appeared to be a few years younger, and those few years made quite a difference at the stage when the initiates were training for their trial.

"It was too late for us to join the crusade," Rutger said. "I went north, to Týrshammar, for a few years."

"Týrshammar," Feronantus echoed. "Near Gotland?"

"Aye," Rutger said. "It's on an inhospitable rock. The wind blows all the time, and the winters are even more miserable—and longer—than they are here."

"It sounds idyllic," Feronantus said. "It is no wonder they raised a citadel there."

Rutger laughed briefly. "There are stories about the men who come from the North," he said.

"There are always stories," Feronantus said.

Rutger nodded, chewing on the inside of his cheek. "That there are, brother." He smiled. "I enjoyed the one you told last night. I wish I had been able to join you in the Holy Land. How glorious that must have been, to be a part of King Richard's return."

They reached the door to the main house, and Feronantus paused. "It rained a lot," he said, "and we didn't get much sleep. It wasn't exactly glorious."

Rutger brushed past him and pulled the door open. "You haven't been to Týrshammar," he said. "You will look at everything differently after a winter there."

Inside, Geoffrey and the other knights from the previous day were waiting, along with a number of the other Shield-Brethren who were at the chapter house. The communal room was crowded and overly warm already.

"Greetings, Feronantus," Geoffrey said, clasping Feronantus's hand in the same way that Rutger had. "I was surprised to discover this morning that you had not lodged with your brothers last night. Is there some explanation for this lack of civility?"

"I was not alone last night," Feronantus said bluntly, and his words drew reactions from a few of the assembled men.

"Men of the order do not congress with whores," Geoffrey said.

"Nor was I," Feronantus replied, fighting to hold his anger in check. It was highly irregular for him to spend the night in the same room as an unmarried woman of age, more so one who was a personal attendant of Queen Berengaria, but the common room had been overflowing with revelers and sleeping outside the door would have drawn too much attention to them. He had sat quietly in the dark until he had heard Maria's breathing become slow and regular, and only then had he stretched out on the floor and gone to sleep. He had woken first this morning and had left the room as quickly and as quietly as he could imagine. No one saw him enter or leave the room, and other than their brief conversation when she had returned last night, there was little record of his ever having been in the room.

Yes, it had been crude and unchivalrous behavior on his part, but one of the many things he had learned while in King Richard's company over the past year was that proper decorum could get you killed. Every time they were discovered during Richard's flight across Italy and the Alps, it was because the king had acted too much like a king and not an itinerant merchant or nameless knight returning to his homeland.

Geoffrey cocked his head to one side, studying Feronantus intently. He had flatly denied Geoffrey's insinuation without offering any other explanation, and he could tell the quartermaster was puzzled by his lack of exposition.

The problem was there was no easy way to explain Maria. In many ways, he was glad she had departed earlier this morning. Traveling alone with her was a constant source of confusion; they needed to be able to focus on their respective duties without distraction. The Shield-Brethren might believe his plea for assistance, but they would have difficulty understanding why she would have been joining them.

"I will be staying with you from here on," Feronantus said, giving the quartermaster a means to disregard the issue of the previous night's lodging. "Though, I hope we will not be staying here overlong."

"Yes," Geoffrey said, taking a step back and pushing his tongue into his cheek. "King Richard's concern about the ransom may be nothing more than the fertile imagination of a man who has been imprisoned too long. And if we march on the imperial caravan, could it not be construed that we are making an aggressive move of our own?"

"Only if they attack us before we have a chance to explain ourselves," Feronantus replied.

"And what explanation would we give them? The same one you gave us yesterday? Do you have any letters from Richard to support your story?"

Feronantus shook his head.

"The imperial ambassadors will be very suspicious of anyone offering aid and protection during their journey. As would I, if I were in the same position. How can we convince them our motives are pure?"

"Maybe we should wait until the French attack them," Rutger suggested.

"*If* the French even attack. In the meantime, where are we? Riding alongside the caravan?" Geoffrey asked. "Do you not see how that could be even more insulting to the emperor?"

"I think the emperor cares more about the money actually arriving than how it is protected during its journey," Feronantus pointed out. "I do not care how insulted his ambassadors may be. If there is no French plot, then we have simply ensured that the English ransom is delivered. If there is a French plot, then our aid will be useful and respected."

One of the other knights spoke up. "Queen Eleanor supported our order in the previous crusade. We sought to pay our debts by aiding her son. Would not that include doing whatever is in our power to assist in his safe return to England?"

"This is a game between the emperor, the king of France, and King Richard," Geoffrey said. "We do not wish to antagonize any one of the three by choosing a side."

"Even if one of them were an aggressor against fellow Christians?" Feronantus asked.

"That is a matter of perspective, boy," Geoffrey snapped. "You were in the Holy Land with King Richard. You saw the mess he caused."

"He won back access to Jerusalem," Feronantus said. "The other princes wanted more glory. They wanted to sacrifice more of us. By making peace with Saladin, King Richard saved many lives. He acts while others stand around and shake their swords and plot against each other. You may not like the message I have brought to you from King Richard, but the gist of it is that he seeks to prevent bloodshed. Why are we quibbling about aiding him? We are not assisting King Philip in stealing England's coin. The emperor has not promised us a share of that money if we assist in ensuring that it arrives safely. Nor is the emperor offering us a portion of this money to be his sword arm in whatever action he desires to take in Italy. It may not be our place to condone the actions of a king or an emperor, but it is our place to make sure that what is promised actually happens."

"We have to protect them from their own base desires," Rutger said.

That comment won him a few guffaws from the other knights and a stern look from Geoffrey. Rutger stood fast by his words, though, and Feronantus laid his hand on the other man's shoulder in support.

"King Richard could have asked us to help him escape," he said, "for is he not protected by the decree of the Pope that all crusaders be allowed to return home after they have served the Church in the Holy Land? But he hasn't, for that would be beneath the dignity of a king and a righteous knight. The emperor seeks to put him on trial for his actions in the Holy Land—actions that our order participated in. Are we not on trial as well? We aren't protecting the money for Richard's sake, or to take a side in this conflict between these three men. We're protecting the money because it is our duty to do so."

After some deliberation, Geoffrey nodded. "Very well," he said, "but we are not going in such numbers as to make the imperial escort nervous. Is that satisfactory?"

Feronantus bowed his head. "Aye, brother, it is. We seek to supplement their company, not threaten it."

"I will lead it," Geoffrey continued. "And you are coming," he said, pointing at Rutger. "You will be in charge of the *base desires* of our mounts."

"Shoving hay in one end and shoveling shit away from the other is the cycle of life, Sir Geoffrey," Rutger said. "It is an honor to be included in such a critical role."

"Perhaps when you speak less rashly in the future, I might be inclined to offer you a more elevated position," Geoffrey said to Rutger. He clapped his hands once, forestalling any further discussion. "Pack your heavy gear," Geoffrey said to the remainder of the men in the room. "There is no reason for us all to be as foolish as Rutger."

◆ ◆ ◆

Maria rode south from Mainz. It might have been quicker to follow the Rhine, as she and Feronantus had after leaving Speyer, but that would have felt too much like doubling back on their existing route, and she knew she would not be able to find freemen like she needed there. She had to reach Strasbourg, at least, and probably go farther. Maybe even into France. She had come to Speyer from Queen Berengaria's court in Poitiers, and so knew the route she had to take.

She wore a plain robe and cloak and kept her hair tied back and hidden beneath a hood, trying to minimize the fact that she was a woman riding alone, but she could only do so much to hide her shape and size. She had worn men's clothes in the past, and while it had been an effective disguise, it was a difficult charade to maintain. Her best assets at this time were speed and the invisibility afforded by the judicious use of silver coins. Many a farmer was happy to feed both her and her mount for a few shards of silver. Country folk were very good at not asking too many questions and forgetting they had seen her as soon as she passed beyond the next hill.

She would reach Strasbourg in a few days. She knew several inns there with garrulous staff, and they could tell her where to find English freeman. Richard had said that his army had been scattered during its return from the Holy Land. She had wanted to press him as to why this was the case, but heeding Queen Berengaria's admonishment to curb her tongue in the presence of the king, she had said nothing.

Besides, she knew why. She didn't need to ask him. He had a history of leaving people behind.

The Shield-Brethren knight, Feronantus, on the other hand, was not the sort to abandon anyone. Richard's chivalry was too feigned, too much the sort of courtly behavior effected by troubadours and young men. Feronantus was the opposite, and he intrigued her. During the few days they had traveled together since leaving the imperial court, she had discerned little about him (and he, in turn, had asked few questions about her—and his lack of curiosity was almost as interesting as his reticence). He spoke German fluently, suggesting that he had grown up in the empire; he knew French and Latin and a bit of Arabic—all of which was conversant with what she knew of his order's training; and while he didn't seem to be educated, he was clearly intelligent. She could discuss literature and philosophy with him, and while he would not necessarily know of the works she mentioned, he was able to engage her on their contents. On martial matters, she had no doubt he was exceptionally trained.

She saw why Richard sought to keep him near. He was quiet, dutiful, and unassuming; yet he listened carefully, was very aware of his surroundings, and completely confident in his ability to deal with any sudden conflict.

She had felt very safe traveling with him, and for part of the first day of her ride south, she felt exposed without him riding beside her. After midday, however, she set aside such romanticized notions and reasserted her own training.

Richard had been right about her, though she had not been sent to spy on him. Queen Berengaria had other goals in mind.

FOUR

The sea trip from London to the island of Walcheren on the coast of the Holy Roman Empire was typically an uneventful crossing, though to minimize exposure on the open water, Willehalm Zenthffeer ordered the fleet to hug the English coast for most of the day following their departure from Queenhithe. Storm clouds were boiling along the eastern horizon on the second morning, and even though the captain of the lead ship expressed concern about turning the ships out into the North Sea, Willehalm gave the order anyway.

During the evening meal the previous night, several of the other ambassadors had expressed their concern about the weight of silver each ship was carrying. Hubert Walter, the queen's exchequer, had made it clear to them several weeks ago the approximate sum that was being given to them, and Willehalm could tell the number had not really sunk in. Not until the wagons started arriving at the docks and the soldiers had started unloading the barrels. It had taken most of the morning to load the ships.

Six ships. Each laden down with a full crew and cargo. Each carrying enough silver for any one of the ambassadors to buy a title and land in Spain or Italy—as well as a private army to protect their new holdings. All that silver made them nervous, afraid that someone would try to steal it. Willahelm privately thought they were all fools, for not one of them had given any thought to taking it themselves.

As soon as the ships made the turn to starboard, the storm pounced on them, shrouding the six ships with dark clouds. Winds blew the sails taut, making the masts creak and the rigging sing, and the decks were awash with rain. For a few hours, there had been concern that one of the smaller ships would be swamped by the high waves, but her captain managed to get the ship's nose pointed into the brunt of the storm.

It blew them off course, and they finally reached Middelburg a day later than they had been expected. Another day would be lost making repairs and adjustments for taking the ships upriver. Once the ships were secured at the docks, Willehalm went ashore to find out what the weather was like on the Lower Rhine.

And to get a decent meal. The food in England had been abysmal. His stomach had grumbled incessantly the entire time he had been in London, and his bowels were still unsettled.

He took a carriage to an inn several streets away from the noise and stench of the docks. His purse was bulging with silver. He had opened several barrels on each ship prior to leaving England, just to make sure that England wasn't sending his emperor barrels full of sand and rock. Spending it on a good meal and a bottle of wine were part of his privilege.

Partway through his meal, he was approached by a man who claimed to speak for the king of France. Willehalm had the innkeeper bring another glass to the table, and he poured the man a measure of wine.

Then he listened intently to the man's proposal, and when his visitor explained how a French invasion would result in an eradication of all things English, Willahelm glanced down at his plate of decidedly non-English food.

Willehalm smiled.

✦ ✦ ✦

An hour's ride east of Strasbourg, Maria came upon a small village caught in the throes of some celebration. The main cluster of houses was set along the verge of a broad forest that blanketed the long valley. There was a handful of farms and fields prior to reaching the village green, and Maria judged that the number of families living in this village was less than three dozen. And yet, it appeared that several times that number were staggering around the main square. On the southern edge of the village, she found a long swath of open land that had been marked off by stakes topped with red strips of cloth.

On the far side of the field, she spotted tall posts with white circles on them.

Archery targets.

There was a field filled with horses, and a pair of dirty-faced boys who appeared to be in charge of watching the animals. Saddles and tack were neatly stacked along the fence. The boys eyed her with some suspicion as she dismounted—taking in, no doubt, the dry mud on her boots and the disheveled disarray of her hair (which she had not brushed out in the last few days), but their moods changed when she tossed each a silver coin. They broke into gap-toothed smiles and jostled each other in their enthusiasm to unsaddle and brush down her horse.

"What celebration is this?" she asked, wishing that Feronantus were with her. His German was much better than hers.

"End of harvest," one boy said.

"Ember Days," the other replied.

Maria nodded sagely as if she understood what the boys were saying. The Church had been slowly transforming all the local customs as its priests raised their churches and exhorted the local peoples to worship Jesus Christ. This confluence of rites led to confusing aberrations—not quite pagan, not quite Christian, but understood and celebrated nonetheless. All that mattered, really, was that an excuse had been enjoined for festivities, and those festivities included games of skill and martial prowess.

She wandered through the village, smiling and nodding as drunken men bumped into her. Some of them leered, a few pawed at her, and most of them were intoxicated enough that they were easily avoided. She followed the cheering and jeering, and eventually managed to reach the edge of the field where an awning had been raised over a low platform.

Tables and chairs were scattered across the wooden stage. At the near end, chairs were clustered around a narrow table across which men tested the strength of their arms against one another. At the far end, there were no tables, and the chairs were all facing the field. Sprawling in these chairs were the men competing in the archery tournament.

There appeared to be three groups: local hunters, who wore rough, homespun clothing and who were disgruntled about having to compete with strangers; a quartet of Germans, who all wore finer clothing and who appeared to be not as in command of the tournament as they'd expected to be; and a final group of three, who wore unadorned clothes that were of the same quality or better than the men from the city but which had been worn much longer. The last three were also more unkempt, more boisterous, and more drunk than any of their competitors.

A serving woman struggled past Maria, and she quickly intercepted the woman, dropped several coins down the front of her low-cut gown, and plucked both of the jugs of wine she was carrying from her hands. She flashed the woman an understanding smile and shoved her way through the crowd to the platform. Wine sloshed out of one of the jugs onto her cloak, and the wet stain only made her illusion more complete.

She crossed to the archers and started pouring wine into empty cups. One of the locals eyed her suspiciously, trying to place her, and she turned her back on him quickly, moving on to his partners. The men from the city were readying their bows and arrows for the next round of shooting, and she took the opportunity to fill their cups without having to worry about being accosted by them. Behind her, one of the three complained loudly about having to wait for more wine, though if she would shake her ass a bit more he wouldn't mind waiting longer.

He spoke English, expecting that she wouldn't understand what he was saying.

She poured carefully, dwelling overlong on her task, and was nearly finished when a boot was firmly placed against her behind. "Move," the English speaker growled in German, firmly pushing her out of the way. Startled, she complied, realizing she had been blocking his view of the archers.

The Germans were using crossbows, and she understood why the locals were agitated. The crossbow had better range and more power than a hunting bow. Less skill was required to shoot the crossbow, and she surmised that the village's magistrate had, for reasons that were most likely financial in nature, opted to allow the Germans to compete in the village's festival games with the heavier weapons. She glanced about, wondering if the English were using crossbows as well, and noticed several long staves strung with taut lines of hemp. Longbows.

And the attitude of the competitors suddenly made sense. The locals were grumpy that crossbows were being used, putting their talents at a disadvantage, but the crossbowmen were also losing to a trio of drunk Englishmen who were using traditional bows, albeit ones that were nearly twice as tall as the hunting bows.

One of the Germans raised his crossbow to his shoulder, laid his cheek against the stock, and squeezed the trigger. The weapon jerked in his hands, and the crowd fell silent for a second, everyone intently staring at the wooden post on the other side of the field. A distant *thwok* echoed back—the sound of the bolt burying itself in the wood—and the crowd cheered.

Maria peered at the post. There were several rings drawn on the white circle, and on the edge of the innermost ring, there was a dark blot—the end of the crossbow bolt protruding from the target.

The German grinned at the other competitors and then began the laborious process of drawing back the string on his crossbow. One of the Englishmen, the fair-haired one with a neat beard and an easy grin, made a disparaging remark about how the audience was going to age a day before the German finished reloading his weapon. One of the other Germans barked an insult in return, but his words were lost beneath the general laughter that swept through the crowd.

The German with the crossbow ignored both the jibe and the crowd's response. He raised his reloaded weapon to his shoulder and shot a second bolt. It struck the target in the middle of the second ring.

The fair-haired Englishman made a rude noise, eliciting further glee from the audience.

The German's third shot pierced the center of the target, and the audience reacted with an extended silence. It was broken by a clapping sound from the fair-haired Englishman. "Nicely shot," he called to the German. "I admire a man who can shoot under duress."

The German crossbowman had the grace to incline his head and thank the Englishman for his compliment.

The long-legged Englishman had said nothing after admonishing Maria to get out of his way, and as the Germans returned to their chairs and their cups of wine, he unfolded himself from his seat. He strode over to Maria, pausing before her to inspect her face closely for a moment, and then he handed her his cup. She stared back at him, noting his crooked nose and his flashing green eyes. His hair was long and fell across his face, and his beard was a tangled mass of brown and red. He was an attractive man, and while he seemed to be aware of his beauty, he was not arrogant about his looks.

Unlike King Richard, for instance.

Suddenly flustered by his gaze, she accepted his cup. Her fingers brushed his, not entirely by accident, and she found herself offering him a shy smile as he put his hair back with his hand and turned to select one of the three longbows.

It was nearly as tall as he, and pulling three arrows from a cloth bag filled with them, he walked to the same spot from which the German had shot his weapon. He stuck two arrows in the dirt in front of him, and laying the third across his bow, he turned to his companions. "How long did it take Gerhardt to shoot all three of his bolts?" he asked in German.

"Several minutes," the stockier of his companions replied. He had a heavyset face with a deep cleft in his bare chin, wide shoulders, and thick forearms. He reminded Maria of a bear.

"An eternity," the fair-haired one said with a laugh.

"Indeed," said the longbowman. "Would you be so kind as to count to twenty?" he asked the German crossbowman who had just finished shooting.

"Twenty?" the German responded, somewhat confused.

"I'll do it," Maria heard herself saying.

The longbowman looked at her. "Even better," he said with a grin. "An innocent observer. Count to twenty, please. As fast as you can."

Maria nodded. She took a deep breath as the longbowman turned to face the distant target. She began counting, the numbers spilling from her lips as fast as she could say them.

The longbowman convulsed, seeming to collapse around his tall bow as he raised it, and then stretched his body out again—his back straight, his chest thrust up and out. The string of his bow sang, and she gasped slightly between "three" and "four." His right hand dropped, grasping the fletching on one of his remaining arrows, and he repeated the same motion again. "Eight," she said as the hard echo of the first arrow reached the crowd. There was no other sound than the creak of his bow, the tightening strain of his string, and her voice, calling out the numbers. *Ten. Eleven. Twelve. Thirteen.*

"Fourteen," she said and stopped. He had released his third arrow already, and in the wake of her voice came the sound of it hitting the target. The noise was different from the other two. There was still the heavy report of the arrow striking the wood, but it was preceded by splintering noise. A brief crackle of wood breaking.

The longbowman didn't even bother to examine the target. He turned his back on the field and walked over to her, plucking his wine cup from her hands. "Thank you," he said simply, raising the cup in salute and then taking a long drink from it.

Around him, the crowd was starting to make noise. Isolated murmurs of wonder at first and then, like a spark landing on dry kindling, a whooshing noise as the audience erupted into loud cheers. Maria glanced past the longbowman, peering at the target.

At first, she couldn't make out where the longbowman's arrows had landed, but then she realized all three arrows were buried deep in the wood, much deeper than the crossbow bolts had gone. All three were clustered in the center of the target. One above the center, one below, and the third had shattered the German's crossbow bolt as it had pierced the very center of the target.

"A most impressive display," she said.

He shrugged as if it were nothing out of the ordinary.

"Tell me," she said, raising one of her jugs to refill his cup. "Do your friends shoot as well?"

"No," he said with a large grin, "but not for a lack of trying."

"Ignore him," said his broad friend who had risen from his seat and wandered over. "He only shoots like that when he is drunk. Most of the time, he can't even draw his bow."

"You are jealous, John," the longbowman replied good-naturedly, "because it only takes a few drinks for me to regain my skill. No amount of wine or practice will ever make you that good."

John clapped the other man on the back, smiling broadly at Maria. "He is a liar and a cad," he said to her, "and you should not believe anything he says."

"I do not have to if he can shoot like that," she said.

"See, Robin," John said, "she is only interested in what you can put on the table. She does not wonder of your expertise in other domestic areas."

"I wonder about a great many things," Maria said, "but right now, I am wondering if there is more to your party than the other man over there."

"Who? Will?" John looked over his shoulder at the third long-bowman. "He'll do, in a pinch."

Ignoring John, Robin asked, "How many others?" all trace of levity gone from his voice. He appeared to be quite sober suddenly, and his gaze was fierce and focused.

"Enough to save the king of England," she said, switching to English, ensuring that she had their attention and that no one else could understand what she was saying.

✦ ✦ ✦

The fire from the burning boat turned the water of the Rhine orange and yellow. Its railings and the lower third of its main mast were blackened, and tiny flowers of flame still danced around the upper portion of the thick pole. Tattered streamers of ash-streaked sail lingered near the very tip of the mast. The ship leaned to port, its hold filling slowly through the open holes in its hull. It would sink eventually, quenching the fire that slowly devoured its wooden frame. From the top of its half-burned mast, a flag bearing the imperial seal hung limply.

The ship had been cut loose from its moorings at the Wesel docks when the fire had threatened to leap to other boats. On the dock, a line of armed men separated the swarm of locals from five other ships, flying the same flag, and a scattered mess of heavy barrels that had been rapidly off-loaded from the burning ship before it had been scuttled. The magistrates of Wesel, as well as the local militia, were attempting to maintain order, but the fear of fire about the other ships had created a smoldering panic onshore that was not dying very quickly.

Otto Shynnagel leaned against a stone wall of a storehouse, watching the confusion. The ship that had been fired and scuttled was one of the treasure ships from England. Judging by the fury of activity that preceded the vessel being shoved back from the dock, he suspected the crew had managed to off-load the ship's cargo, but now they were faced with having one-sixth of the imperial ransom sitting openly on the Wesel dock. Whoever was in charge of the treasure ships was certainly going to be worried that someone might discover what cargo he was transporting.

Who knew what would happen then?

Otto was curious as to how the fire had started. It seemed unlikely that a French spy could have gotten on board the ship. Had the fire truly been an accident? If he hadn't been warned to watch out for such activity, he would have lamented the bad luck that had befallen the caravan, but he wouldn't have suspected sabotage.

He thought the imperial ambassadors would be trying to acquire another ship, and he was surprised when a wagon arrived and was ushered through the line of soldiers. Sailors began loading the cart, and when more wagons arrived, the sailors began off-loading barrels from the other boats.

Otto didn't understand why they weren't going to continue by boat. Had the fire spooked them that badly? He thought about the routes they might take. They would travel along the eastern side of the Rhine. Would they cross the river at Duisburg and head for Kaarst, Bergheim, and Kerpen? It was a less-traveled route than along the path of the Rhine, but it would be quicker as the crow flew.

It was also closer to France.

It all started to make sense to Otto. The emperor had been right. The French were trying to steal the silver, and they had someone working for them in the imperial party. Someone making sure the caravan was heading right into an ambush.

FIVE

The rider met them along a muddy track outside of Cologne. His horse was covered in sweat, and the animal staggered awkwardly when the rider slid down the saddle. Feronantus eyed the horse sadly, wondering if its rider had pushed it too hard.

The rider was a slight man named Domarus, who, unlike the rest of the company, had brought no maille with him. He wore a rough leather vest and bracers on his arms, and he carried only a bow, arrows, and a long knife. His saddle was nothing more than a leather frame and a blanket with a single strap around the horse's barrel.

He was a scout, and he ranged far ahead of the larger, slower-moving party.

"They're not on the river," he reported to Geoffrey and the rest of the company. "I heard from several sources that there was a fire on board one of the ships when they reached Wesel. Four days ago. They unloaded and set off overland. On the other side of the river."

Rutger groaned and Feronantus shook his head. No wonder they hadn't seen any sign of the imperial party. They were on the eastern side of the Rhine, while the Shield-Brethren were looking for them on the west side.

Geoffrey remained unconcerned. "What about Koblenz and the gorge? Will they cross to this side there?"

Feronantus did not know enough about the geography of the surrounding area, and he could only assume the Rhine passed into more mountainous terrain near a place called Koblenz. It sounded like the sort of place that would force a wagon party to make a significant detour. The question was, which direction?

Rutger shook his head. "They wouldn't wait that long. They'd cross earlier, or not at all. But if they didn't, that would mean passing through Mainz and Worms."

"Easy to acquire more guards along that route," Geoffrey said. "But they would also not be able to pass without scrutiny, which would slow them down."

"And they'd stop at Worms," Rutger said. "The emperor has a palace there. There'd be no reason to take the ransom all the way to Speyer."

Geoffrey looked at Feronantus. "What do you think?" he asked. "You are the one who sees subterfuge afoot. If I were leading the wagons, I'd stick to the safe routes—more people friendly to the emperor, more men who could be called upon to join me."

Feronantus looked over his shoulder at the two dozen knights ranged behind them along the road. "I think it is odd that a complement of imperial guards who are all very much aware of the enormity of their cargo would lose their vessel to a fire."

"Accidents happen," Geoffrey pointed out with a shrug.

Feronantus stared at the Shield-Brethren quartermaster, trying to ascertain if the man was willfully unaware or simply testing his resolve and his ability to think carefully. It was obvious to Feronantus that the fire in Wesel had not been an accident. He knew it as clearly as he knew the sun would rise in the east. Was it the *Vor* that guided him, or was it just that obvious?

"They're on the western side of the Rhine already," he said.

"How can you be sure?" Geoffrey asked.

Feronantus caught Rutger watching him carefully. "I am," he said. It was too complicated to explain, but he could see all the pieces of his argument clearly. It made sense in his head. He had no doubt.

◆ ◆ ◆

In the first hour after the fire had started aboard the treasure ship, Willahelm had been concerned that someone might stumble upon the dead sailor in his cabin. But once the fire burst through the deck and began rampaging through the hold, he was no longer concerned that his part in the inferno that swept through the ship would be discovered. The sailor—one of the three navigators—had been sent by the captain, and there had been no time to learn anything more from the man. He glanced at the pile of oil-soaked blankets on the floor of Willahelm's cabin and knew instantly what the imperial ambassador had been about to do. He tried to bolt for the door, and his cry of alarm turned into a rattling gurgle when Willahelm's knife entered his back. Willahelm threw the man's body on the oil-soaked pile, tossed a lit candle at the pile, and shut the door of his room as soon as he heard the growl of the oil igniting.

The next hurdle was convincing the imperial guard and the other ambassadors to cross to the western shore of the Rhine. He had anticipated more discourse concerning his suggested route, but the other ambassadors were in such shock at the idea of sabotage that they eagerly agreed to his levelheaded proposal. *The western route was less traveled*, he argued. They could move quickly and would not be slowed by other caravans and crowded towns. *Look at what had happened at Wesel*, he said, *it was so very difficult to guard their cargo when surrounded by so many people.*

Of course, it was actually easier for them to be ambushed along the western route, especially when the French did not have to cross the Rhine in order to attack them. They could commandeer the wagons and be in Leige before the emperor even knew his treasure had been stolen.

In Leige, he would take his share of the treasure and hire an expensive carriage to convey him and his wealth to Paris, where the king of France would personally thank him for providing the coin to finance an invasion of England.

It was such a lovely thought, and it made him inordinately happy during the tedious days following the accident at Wesel. First, they couldn't find enough wagons, and then there were problems with the oxen. Throughout the continued delays, Willahelm maintained a calm mien and a steady perseverance that the other ambassadors found comforting.

If only they knew, he thought.

Mid-afternoon on the fourth day after leaving Wesel, a shout went up the line, and Willahelm sat up in his saddle, peering ahead at the rider charging at them along the dusty road. It was one of their forward scouts, and his surcoat was stained with blood.

"Ambush!" The cry spread through the caravan, and all around him, the imperial guard galvanized into defensive action. The drovers on the wagons began to whip their oxen harder, but they did not know where they were actually going, and in the following minutes, the wagon caravan descended into chaos as the oxen tried to flee and the imperial guard tried to drive the wagons into a more defensible unit.

And then the ambushers were among them.

Willahelm caught sight of men wearing blue-and-white surcoats. The drover on the wagon beside him screamed as two arrows struck him, and he tumbled off the plank of his wagon. The oxen, unaware they had lost their master, charged onward, and the wagon jounced as the wheels on the near side went over the fallen wagoner. Barrels shifted in the back, and one spilled out of the wagon, breaking as it hit the road. Silver scattered across the road, glittering in the afternoon light like a spray of water.

Willahelm was dazzled by the silver, and he didn't realize he had been struck by an arrow until he coughed and felt something wet spatter from his lips. He looked down at the shaft protruding from his chest, pawing at it lightly as if it were not real. He heard a roaring noise, like thunder, and he glanced up in time to see something coming at his face. *A small bird*, he thought, wondering what it was doing flying in the midst of the battlefield, and then his vision splintered into a spray of glittering water.

My silver, he thought. It was slipping away from him. Falling out of his unresponsive fingers...

SIX

The road wound along the base of a narrow bluff, edged with pink-and-gray stone. A scraggly forest of pine and oak blanketed the northern end of the bluff, and individual trees poked defiantly out of the slope. On the eastern side of the road, fields that had been farmland a generation ago were being reclaimed by wild grasses and the isolated groupings of young saplings, eager to spread their branches without being hemmed in by older trees. A haze of dust lay over the valley.

Domarus had spotted the silver caravan earlier, hurrying back to alert the rest of the Shield-Brethren company. When they had spotted the rising dust, they had spurred their horses into a gallop, hoping they were not too late.

Feronantus rode in the second rank, behind the lancers. His helmet and the men in front of him limited his field of vision, and he was nearly upon the caravan of wagons before he could see the confusion into which they were riding. The wagons were in disarray; several were off the road entirely, moving in haphazard directions as their oxen teams wandered without drovers to direct them. One wagon was overturned, its team slaughtered. Scattered groups of men—some wearing blue-and-white surcoats, some wearing imperial colors—fought with one another. It seemed there were more men in blue and white.

"Alalazu!" The cry rose around him as the Shield-Brethren host engaged the caravan attackers. The rank of lancers, forming into a wedge, burst through the cluster of riders at the front of the caravan. Feronantus, with Rutger on his left, clashed with the few riders who had not been unhorsed by the lancers.

Guiding his horse with his knees, he slashed with his sword, cutting through the surcoat of a man holding a mace. He felt the tip of his sword rattle off maille, and he raised his shield as the mace-wielder retaliated, slamming the heavy head of his weapon against Feronantus's shield. He grunted, feeling the impact through his arm, but it was better to take the hit on his shield than anywhere else. His maille might protect him against swords and arrows, but a crushing blow from a blunt weapon like the mace would easily break bones.

Feronantus peered over the edge of his shield. As his opponent raised the mace for another blow, Feronantus leaned forward, thrusting with his sword, and the tip of the blade caught the other man just below the jaw. He flicked his hand to the side and felt his sword slice through flesh, catching for just a second as it cut through the leather strap of his opponent's helmet. As Feronantus's horse jostled the other horse, the mace-wielder tumbled out of his saddle, blood spurting from his throat.

Out of the corner of his eye, Feronantus sensed another man coming from his left, and he drummed his heels against his horse as he ducked behind his shield. As his horse surged forward, he swept his shield outward, and he felt a sword scrape across the surface. He lowered his shield, twisting his body to the left so as to bring his sword to bear against his new opponent, but there was no need. The man had been concentrating on hitting Feronantus and had failed to notice Rutger, whose sword caught him in the side of the head, cleaving through the leather of his helm as well as his skull beneath.

He had no time to thank Rutger, though, as a crossbow bolt punched through Feronantus's shield, the bolt piercing his surcoat and lodging in his maille. He didn't think it had gone all the way through, but he knew that he might not even realize how badly he had been struck until after the battle. He caught sight of the crossbowman and directed his horse at the man. If he succeeded in reloading the weapon, Feronantus might not be as lucky a second time.

The crossbowman knew he was in race for his life, and he struggled to pull back the heavy string and get another bolt loaded. The man tried to not look up as Feronantus drove his horse at him; his hands shook as he fumbled with the bolt, trying to lay it down on the stock of the crossbow. He pulled the trigger before he had even raised the weapon all the way to his shoulder, and he looked up in time to see Feronantus's sword arc toward his face.

Feronantus felt the shock of his sword hitting bone at the same instant he felt his horse stumble. The animal collapsed, and he leaped out of the saddle. His sword was wrenched from his hand, but he held on to his shield. The ground rushed at him, and for a moment, he was back in the darkness underneath Petraathen. The cold water rushing around him, the weight of the aspis pulling him under the surface. *Never let go*, his oplo had instructed him. *Never let go of your shield.*

He hit the ground, shield first, and rolled over it and to his feet. His chest heaving, his helmet slightly askew—blocking his left eye—he took stock of his surroundings. The crossbow bolt had struck his horse, and it had stumbled and fallen. Judging from the way it was thrashing on the ground, one of its legs had been broken. But the crossbowman was down, Feronantus's sword jutting from his chest.

The general melee had moved off to his left. For a moment, he was out of the fighting.

Feronantus retrieved his sword, gave his horse a merciful death, and then started toward the wagons.

◆ ◆ ◆

"There are three groups fighting," Otto's scout reported. "The imperial guard, some other group, and men wearing the red rose."

"Shield-Brethren," Bertholdus growled. He was Otto's second-in-command. A sword cut to the neck had permanently damaged his voice, and the scar was a vivid line across his throat.

Otto nodded in agreement. "King Richard's dogs," he said. He jammed his helmet on his head. "Let's just kill them all," he said to Bertholdus.

Bertholdus smiled and raised his arm to signal the rest of Otto's mercenaries. When he brought his arm down, the host charged, streaming out of the forest at the base of the bluff.

◆ ◆ ◆

The field of battle was a chaotic mess. The imperial guard was fighting the men in blue and white, who—it seemed to Feronantus, judging by the language he heard some of them using when they shouted to each other—were French mercenaries. Some of the imperial guard recognized the red rose emblem of the Shield-Brethren, but there were still a few altercations between imperials and Shield-Brethren until it was clear that they were allies. At which point the French realized they were surrounded, and their efforts turned more to flight than conquest.

Then, as individual French fighters were throwing down their weapons and fleeing, a fourth group burst out of the forest and charged toward the bloodied fields. The new group attacked the fleeing French, and the imperials cheered the arrival of reinforcements, but Feronantus didn't see their colors. His stomach knotted as he recalled Richard's theory of betrayals and counter-betrayals.

"Where's Geoffrey?" he shouted at Rutger, who was still astride a horse.

Rutger shook his head. His shield was missing, and a sleeve of his maille was stained red.

"They're not allies," Feronantus shouted.

"They seem friendly enough," Rutger said. "They're killing the French."

"They won't stop with the French," Feronantus snarled. "Find Geoffrey. Rally our brothers."

As Rutger turned his horse, Feronantus ran toward a nearby wagon and clambered up onto the plank. From his vantage point, he could see the approaching host more readily. He couldn't count their number quickly, though he guessed there were more than four dozen. They wore no colors, and they carried no standard.

The cold awareness of the *Vor* churned in his guts. These men definitely weren't reinforcements. They were Henry's private mercenaries, and as he watched, a pair of men, running in front of the rest of the host, fell upon a Shield-Brethren rider. One of the two dragged the knight out of his saddle, and the other one stabbed the fallen knight again and again with his sword.

"We're under attack," he screamed, his voice tearing.

The host, hearing his alarm, howled in response.

Shivering, Feronantus leaped off the wagon. If the Shield-Brethren had sustained no losses, they were still outnumbered two to one. But he knew some of his brothers had fallen. He had no idea how many imperials were left, but he doubted they had much stomach for more fighting.

He, too, was tired. He had started to feel an ache in his chest where the crossbow bolt had struck his maille, and there was blood dripping from the bottom of the right sleeve of his armor.

He didn't recall getting hit in the arm, but it had happened. His sword felt heavy.

He tightened his grip on his weapon.

The odds were bad, but that didn't mean he was going to give up. The Shield-Brethren never gave up. They never lowered their shields.

SEVEN

—◆—

"This doesn't look good," Will said, shading his eyes and peering down at the melee in the valley below.

Robin dropped two bundles of arrows next to him. "Which ones are the good guys?" he asked.

"We are, remember?" Will said.

Behind them, John finished stringing the last of the tall English longbows and tossed it to Robin. "Does that mean we're supposed to kill them all?"

Maria stood on the other side of Will, scanning the valley below, trying to make sense of what she was seeing. The silver wagons were scattered, and the field was littered with bodies, all wearing a number of different colors and emblems. Many of the dead appeared to be imperial guard, but there were a number wearing blue and white as well. She spotted a smaller group wearing long white surcoats over coats of maille. Their surcoats were emblazoned with a red rose.

Her heart beat quickly, both thrilled and saddened at what she saw. There were Shield-Brethren dead on the field. But there were more of them still standing. She wasn't too late.

"The men in white with the red emblems on their chests," she said quickly.

"They'll make for easy targets," Will said.

"No," she countered. "Those are my friends."

Robin laid an arrow across his bow and performed the still-odd motion of drawing the string back. "And the others?" he asked, peering down at the melee.

"Not friends," she said firmly.

Robin released his first arrow.

◆ ◆ ◆

Somehow Feronantus wound up shoulder to shoulder with Rutger. They had a wagon at their back, and Rutger's left arm hung useless at his side. Feronantus was having trouble maintaining his grip on his own sword. No matter how hard he squeezed, it kept twisting in his grasp. The pommel was red with blood, and he could feel more of his life running down his arm.

Three of the mercenaries stood opposite them, armed with swords and shields. They were gauging the Shield-Brethren pair, deciding how best to kill them. Two of their companions lay nearby; they had been overly eager and had taken steel to the throats as a result. The remaining three were a bit warier.

Feronantus leaned against the wagon, and he could feel Rutger resting his weight, too. They were both tired and injured. He had lost track of how many men he had engaged, nor could he remember if they had all died. The battle was a blur, almost like a dream, but his muscles quivered and ached with all the exertion.

"This is it, I suppose," Rutger said in a hoarse voice. "I can probably take care of the one on the left. Can you get the one on the right?"

"Aye," Feronantus whispered.

"That one in the middle, though, he's going to be a problem," Rutger said. "Do you think he knows it yet?"

"Not yet," Feronantus said.

As soon as the trio realized one or more of them was going to live, they would rush the pair of Shield-Brethren. They would take their chances.

The man in the middle suddenly threw up his hands. He still had his sword and his shield, and it was such an odd motion that everyone stared. Gradually, he dropped his arms, letting go of his sword and lowering his shield, too. Only then did Feronantus notice the bloody arrowhead protruding from his chest.

The other two mercenaries turned and looked behind them, trying to spot the archer. Feronantus pushed off from the wagon, intending on taking the fight to the mercenaries, but before he could close the distance, the man in front of him was knocked off his feet. He slid across the ground, nearly tripping Feronantus.

The third man grunted as he collapsed, too.

All three had been brought down by long arrows that had gone through maille, leather, and flesh as if all three were nothing more than thin cloth.

"The Virgin watches over us," Rutger said.

Feronantus looked up at the nearby bluff, spotting the line of men along the edge. "She brought English longbowmen," he said.

✦ ✦ ✦

With the arrival of the bowmen, the mercenaries who had come out of the forest realized they were losing, and they scattered. There was no point in pursuing them into the forest. It would take too long to hunt down individuals, and there was the more pressing concern of securing the wagons.

Most of the imperials were dead, and the few who survived were wounded and would have to be left behind at the nearest city where doctors could be found. Some of the drovers were unharmed, having lain down flat beneath their wagons, pretending to be dead. The French ambushers were dead or gone, and a handful of the mercenaries were still alive. Some had surrendered; a few had been forcibly taken.

Geoffrey and six other Shield-Brethren knights were dead. Most of the rest had been wounded in one fashion or another, but most of their injuries were superficial—they were used to gathering scars.

One of the mercenaries was a dark-haired man with a knotted scar across his throat. Feronantus gauged the way the other prisoners were maintaining their distance from him, and suspected this man was one of their commanders.

"What is your name?" he asked, and the man replied by spitting at him.

Rutger backhanded him with a mailled fist, and when the man spat at Feronantus again, there was blood in his spittle.

Feronantus turned his attention to one of the other prisoners. "What is his name?" he asked the cowering man.

The man shivered and stuttered. "Berth…Bertholdus," he said.

"Is he your commander?" Feronantus asked.

"Yes," the man said. "No," he amended.

"Who paid you?" Feronantus asked.

The man looked past Feronantus, his eyes drawn to the silver still lying in the road, glittering in the late-afternoon sun. He muttered something that Feronantus could not make out.

Bertholdus glared defiantly at Feronantus, and Feronantus was glad the man was bound. Otherwise, he suspected Bertholdus would attack him bare-handed.

"They were promised a piece of treasure," Rutger said. "Weren't you?" he asked the prisoner who had been talking.

Bertholdus laughed harshly, and the other prisoner flinched. "Shut up," the cowering man screamed.

"It doesn't matter," Bertholdus growled, fixing his hate-filled gaze on Feronantus. "The man who bought their services is dead. They were promised a pittance of what is in those wagons, and only now do they realize what fools they were." He looked at the other prisoners. "You were stealing from your emperor. Do you understand now how worthless your lives are? If these men don't kill you, the emperor will put such a price on your heads—"

"We aren't going to tell the emperor," a voice intruded. It was a woman's voice, and the sound surprised Bertholdus enough that he shut his mouth.

Feronantus looked over his shoulder and saw Maria. Trailing behind her were three scruffy-looking men—one broad, one fair-haired, and one with long hair and a piercing gaze. "Maria," he said, finding himself pleased to see her again.

She smiled at him, and he felt suddenly awkward at the sight of her equal delight at seeing him. Behind her, the long-haired man scowled.

Maria stood beside Feronantus and regarded the prisoners. "We have been charged by the king of England himself to ensure that this caravan reach the imperial court. We do not care who you are or what your grievance is with the emperor. The Shield-Brethren are merciful, but they are not fools. Try their patience, and no one will say a word if they slit all of your throats and leave your bodies for the wolves."

Rutger glanced at Feronantus with a raised eyebrow.

The prisoner who had spoken earlier whimpered and Bertholdus glared at Maria, but when she held his gaze, he deflated. His shoulders drooped and he lowered his head.

Maria turned to Feronantus. "We should gather those who can travel and disperse the silver from the damaged wagons among those who can ride. We need to be gone from here by nightfall."

She touched his arm briefly and then turned away, walking toward the trio of Englishmen nearby.

"Who put her in charge?" Rutger asked quietly.

"She did," Feronantus replied.

"Who is she?"

"I'm not entirely sure," Feronantus admitted.

◆ ◆ ◆

John nudged Robin. "I think she likes him," he said, nodding toward Maria and the pair of knights.

"Shut up," Robin snapped, and Will laughed gently.

Robin ignored his fair-haired friend. "Are all these wagons filled with silver?" he asked Maria as she rejoined them. "I thought you said we were saving the king of England." He glanced around. "He's not here."

"He's being held captive by the Holy Roman Emperor. These wagons are the first portion of the ransom that is to be paid for his release."

"Ransom?" Robin growled. "What ransom? Where did it come from?"

Maria hesitated before replying. "I do not know," she said, "but I assume it was raised by England."

"By *who* in England?" John asked.

Maria glanced up at him and said nothing.

"Wait a minute," Robin said. "We just attacked a bunch of imperials, French, *and* German marauders—in Germany—so that a shipment of silver, taken from English citizens, could be delivered to the Holy Roman Emperor? So that King Richard could be freed?"

"Oh, shit." Will sighed. "Here we go."

"The same King Richard who abandoned us in the Holy Land?" Robin continued. "He left all of us behind. His entire army. Many of us died for him. Died so that he could negotiate a dismal peace treaty with Saladin. We got nothing. We were coming home with nothing. And our leader—our king—had offended so many of our Christian allies that he had to sneak back home. He left us on the beach at Acre. Do you know what we had to do to get back to Italy?"

"No," Maria said softly, "I do not."

"And you think that we're just going to stand here and let you give this treasure to the Holy Roman Empire?"

"I do," she said. She stood still, gazing at Robin, waiting for his response.

Robin sputtered, unable to form words.

"Let it go, Robin," Will said gently. "She"—he shook his head—"it doesn't matter. Just let it go."

"You're not the only ones who have been maligned by the king," Maria said. "I serve Queen Berengaria, his wife, whom he also abandoned in the Holy Land. I know well of the betrayal that you speak. Richard may be an arrogant and foolish man who thinks much too highly of himself, but he is the king of England, and England stands by him." She gestured at the wagons behind them. "There is all the evidence you need."

"You lied to us," Robin ground out.

"I told you the truth," she countered. "As much as you needed to know."

"I don't like being lied to," Robin snapped.

"I won't do it again," she said, meeting his gaze, and he was somewhat taken aback to realize she meant it.

"Go home, Robin," she said, her voice becoming gentler. "As you said, you've attacked Germans and French while on German soil. Don't do something foolish and make England hate you, too. Go home; be with your kin."

"She's right, Robin," John sighed. He laid his large hand on Robin's shoulder. "Let's just go home."

"Fine," Robin said. "We'll go." He shrugged off John's hand and pointed at the scattered coins in the road. "But we're taking some of that with us."

"Take as much as you each can carry," Maria said. "I'm sure your king will understand."

Robin smiled grimly at her. "If he doesn't, he can come collect it. Personally."

EIGHT

"Check."

Henry glared at the chessboard. It was the third time Richard had threatened his king. The English monarch's style of play was confounding in both its irreverence and cunning. Richard had little regard for the safety of his pieces, but each white piece tantalizingly dangled in front of Henry turned out to be a trap. He had almost lost his queen twice already, and staring at the pieces on the board, Henry realized that he was definitely going to lose her this time when he moved his king to safety.

He was spared the loss by the appearance of Wecelo beside the table. "The wagons from England are here, Your Highness," his steward said.

"They are?" Henry said, and then he caught himself. "Yes, of course they are," he said in a much calmer voice.

Richard was smiling at him, and Henry fought the urge to knock the chessboard aside. "We can come back to this game later," he said.

Henry tipped over his king. "It's not that important of a game," he said, rising from his chair.

"No," Richard said, that infuriating smile still on his lips. "It isn't, is it?"

Henry made a strangled noise in his throat and stalked out of the room, his steward and the king of England trailing behind him. Henry tried to figure out what could have possibly gone wrong with his plan. Had he not been clear enough with Otto? Had Otto missed the caravan? Had the ambassadors stayed on the Rhine all the way to Speyer? There were too many questions, and he forced them all aside. He would have answers soon enough.

He strode out of the castle, blinking heavily as he emerged into the clear winter day. There had been frost on the ground and rooftops this morning, a sure sign that winter was rapidly approaching. He peered at the wagons clustered in the great yard of his estate. There were more than he'd expected, and they were all bursting with barrels and crates.

He stared at the men who stood beside their horses. They weren't wearing his colors.

"What's this?" he exclaimed.

"It would appear to be an inordinate amount of silver," Richard said, coming up behind him.

"I can see that," Henry snapped. He waved a hand at the men. "Who are these men?"

One of them strode forward. He stopped before Henry and dropped to his knee in an appropriate bow. His white surcoat was stained with dirt and something darker, and he was wearing maille beneath it, but Henry recognized him. It was the man who had been with Richard at Dünstein—the man the king had claimed was his personal attendant. "I am Feronantus, knight initiate of the *Ordo Militum Vindicis Intactae*," the man said. "And my brothers and I are delivering the shipment of silver from Queen Eleanor of England."

"What?" Henry said. "Where are my ambassadors? Where is my imperial guard?"

"It is with great sadness that I tell you that they are all dead," Feronantus said. "We came upon your party as they were being attacked by bandits and marauders. We did our best to save them, but alas, we were too late."

"Bandits?" Henry couldn't believe what he was hearing.

"Yes," Feronantus said. He raised his head and looked up at the emperor. "*German* bandits."

Henry shut his mouth quickly, swallowing his response.

Richard leaned over, chuckling. "Just because I am your prisoner," he said quietly in Henry's ear, "does not mean I am a fool. Check, and mate, Your Highness."

✦ ✦ ✦

After taking a long and relaxing bath, putting on a new gown, and having an opportunity to get all of the tangled knots out of her hair and re-braid it, Maria presented herself at Richard's quarters.

The king was seated by the window of his room, a writing desk across his lap. He looked up as she came in, and he idly motioned for the servant to leave them before returning his attention to his letter.

Maria wandered over to a nearby chair and sat, folding her hands in her lap.

"Everything worked out?" Richard asked as he finished signing his name to the letter.

"For the most part," she replied.

"And Berengaria's portion of the ransom?"

"Redistributed to English hands," she said.

Richard nodded. "I will suffer this ransom to be paid for the sake of peace between the Holy Roman Empire and England, but I will not suffer my wife having to pay any portion of it."

Maria hesitated. "Should I tell her?" she asked eventually.

"Of course not," Richard snorted. "Whom did you give the money to?" he asked.

"A freeman named Robin, of Locksley."

"And what is he going to do with it?"

"I don't know," she replied. "He was…"

"What?" Richard asked when she trailed off.

"He was a charming man," she said, "but somewhat prone to indignation." She weighed whether she should say anything more and decided she had said enough.

"Do you think he'll spend the money foolishly?" Richard asked.

"No," she replied.

"Wisely?"

"No," she said after a moment.

"Hmm," Richard said. "Perhaps you should go to England and offer your assistance."

"I should?"

"Yes, I think you should," Richard said. "I have received word that my brother John is spending too much time in Paris, letting the king of France fill his head with nonsense. My mother has enough on her mind that she doesn't need to worry about my brother getting it into his head that he might be a better king of England than I."

"What do you expect me to do?" Maria asked.

"Distract John," Richard said. "I'm sure you can think of some way to get under his skin. Talk to this Robin of Locksley; change his mind about what he should do with the money."

"Are you asking me to start a rebellion in England?"

Richard shook his head. "You? No," he said. "I am asking *you* to do no such thing."

Maria shook her head. "The queen warned me to be careful of your devious nature," she said.

"Of course she did," Richard said with a grin.

Maria stood, smoothing the front of her gown. "Your Majesty," she said, curtsying, "I regret that I cannot stay longer here at Speyer."

"I am saddened by the idea of your departure as well," Richard said. "I bid you a safe journey."

"And I hope that you may be reunited with your homeland soon," she said.

Richard made a small noise in reply, and his gaze drifted toward the window. She took this as a sign their conversation was over, and she curtsied one last time before leaving Richard to his contemplation.

"Oh, Maria." Richard stopped her as she reached the door. "Take Feronantus with you. Now that Henry knows he is no longer a simple servant, there is no point in him staying here, is there?"

"No, Your Majesty," Maria said. She pressed her hand against her breast. "I don't see any reason he should stay."

"He's good company, isn't he?" Richard said.

Maria was glad the king couldn't see the flush rising in her cheeks. "Yes," she said quietly, "he is."

- END -

THE
SHIELD-MAIDEN
A TALE OF FOREWORLD

—— BY ——

MICHAEL "TINKER" PEARCE & LINDA
PEARCE

ONE

Light from the rotund moon reflected off the ocean on the outboard side, allowing them to keep the longship oriented. Land was the darkness on the other side of the *karvi*, the sleek and narrow longship. It was closer than the ship's captain preferred, but Kjallak Arvidson had overridden his concerns. If they were too exposed on the water, they might be sighted by the Danish marauders they knew were somewhere behind them—a veritable fleet of four longships. There were only a dozen men on the *karvi*—less than a third of the number the boat could comfortably hold—and they could not afford to get caught. The *karvi* had a very shallow draft; it could hug a shoreline safely. If they were spotted, they could beach the boat easily too, and head inland.

Of course, in that case, their journey would take longer, which was why Kjallak had risked taking to the sea.

His men dozed on their benches, their oars raised and locked. Kjallak sat in the stern, staring out at the moon-dappled water. Beside him, Halldor, his second, leaned against the raised tail of the ship, snoring occasionally.

The wind was behind them, and it pushed gently against their sail. There was a current too, and the combination of wind and water propelled the boat at a steady pace. It felt like a good omen.

Kjallak had risked sailing at night in order to make up for the time they had lost a few days ago when a northern storm had driven them aground. They were expected in Visby and were already overdue.

A tremor ran through the hull of the *karvi*, and Halldor stirred beside him. Kjallak stared ahead, peering through the dim night, but he saw nothing beyond the pale planks of the longship. He heard the captain's voice, calling out to the lookout in the prow of the boat, and he winced slightly when a small light sputtered to life. The lookout had lit a lantern, and he cringed at the idea that they were making themselves so visible on the open water.

He stood and walked carefully down the center of the boat. Around him, the men started stirring on their benches, shaken out of their nocturnal stupors by the tremors.

"What is your man doing?" he hissed at the captain when he reached the forward benches. "We can be seen."

The captain held up a hand, all his attention devoted to listening to the night and the ocean. Kjallak held his tongue and listened as well, trying to hear what the captain was hearing. He felt the stern of the boat drift outboard slightly.

"Oars," the captain shouted suddenly, startling Kjallak. "Get them in the water!" The captain leaped up, darting for the rack midship where the oars and poles were stored. "Outboard side," the captain commanded.

The boat shook again, the tremor much stronger this time, and Kjallak staggered, falling back against the nearby bench. The *karvi* groaned beneath him as it came to a complete stop in the water. The lookout was shouting something, waving his lantern down near the railing.

The men got their oars in the water, and they pulled frantically. They had no rhythm; each was pulling out of time and tempo with the man next to him. The captain shouted at them to get it right.

The boat spun slowly around its bow, turning until the stern was pointing at the moon. The captain finally got the sailors organized, and the boat struggled free of whatever had seized it. As the prow swung around, redirected by the sailors and their oars, the narrow *karvi* listed to the inboard side.

"Some of her seams are done up; we need to put in to shore," the captain said, stomping over to Kjallak. His mouth was turned down as if there was something more he wanted to say, but he only shook his head and shoved past Kjallak. "Raise your lantern, boy," he called to the lookout. "We need to see where we're going before we all drown."

"It is ill luck," a voice said behind Kjallak, and he turned to look up at his second, who seemed unconcerned about the listing angle of the boat.

"Aye," Kjallak said. "We've had our share of it."

"It will turn," Halldor said simply.

Kjallak was used to his second's taciturn—and yet seemingly endless—optimism, but he didn't have the same temperament. "I hope so," Kjallak sighed, wishing—for neither the first nor the last time—that he and Halldor weren't so dissimilar. "It'll take two or three days to re-peg and tar the hull. If we're lucky and there's a hold nearby, we might be able to get some horses and go overland."

"Add a day to your reckoning," Halldor said, shaking his head. "Tomorrow is the equinox. There will be a *blöt* and feasting. If we arrive at a hold, we will be guests, and there will be no avoiding it."

Kjallak frowned. *Another delay*, he thought. *Was this entire journey cursed?*

TWO

➤

Sigrid Pettirsdottir rolled across the dusty yard behind the long-house. She kept her grip on the haft of the lang ax and swept the butt at her opponent's legs even as he followed up the blow from his shield that had knocked her to the ground. He dodged her counter, giving her just enough time to get her feet under her and raise the ax in the high guard. The pair circled warily, each looking for an opening. She was sweaty inside the quilted linen armor-cote, her hair itching under the felted wool lining of the spangenhelm. She ignored all that, though—her eyes remained locked on the centerline of her opponent's body, just below the neck.

Äke Fair-Haired was a seasoned warrior half again her size, armed with a practice sword and a heavy round shield that covered him from mid-thigh to shoulder. Äke moved with care, his eyes remaining locked to her frame too. Her bearded lang ax was blunted—a practice weapon like his sword—and even though it wouldn't shear through his maille, a heavy blow from the ax could crack bones.

Her foot caught momentarily on a tuft of grass as she circled, and the hitch in her movement was the mistake Äke had been waiting for. He punched his shield at the center of the lang ax's haft and stepped forward to her right, his sword licking out toward her shoulder. It was a good attack and should have been successful, but Sigrid had anticipated him—her stumble had been a ruse to draw him in.

As he thrust forward, she stabbed the butt of the ax into the edge of his shield, rotating it in his grasp. The rim of the shield struck him in the chest, throwing his sword blow off, robbing it of its speed. She moved into the blow, catching it on the haft of her weapon and passing his sword over her head. Bringing the butt of the ax across his chest as she stepped in to check him with her hip, she threw him to the ground hard enough to drive the breath from his lungs and send his helmet rolling across the yard.

Stepping out of reach, she grounded the butt of the ax and leaned on the head, catching her own breath as the cheers and laughter from the other Sworn Men watching them washed over her. Äke half laughed, half gasped himself as he lay flat on his back.

"Aye, the lang ax is a man's weapon," she teased when she had the breath to spare. "I can see that now. It's certainly done for one man today."

Äke sat up, shaking his head ruefully. "Fairly spoken," he said, "and well tested, *skjölmdo.*"

Sigrid grinned as she stripped off her helm. It was the first time he had spoken of her as a warrior—a Shield-Maiden—instead of simply referring to her as *girl.* It had been nearly a year since she had taken her vows to the Jarl, her father, and while the Sworn Men accepted her presence in their ranks, their respect was more elusive. Äke, though, was First among the Jarl's Sworn Men, and the others looked to him for guidance and leadership. If he spoke of her differently, then the others might follow suit.

She offered Äke her arm, and he took it, hoisting himself to his feet. He held on to her arm for a moment, though, standing close to her. "It is but one bout," he said, his voice quiet but firm. She tensed, feeling a familiar flush start up her cheeks. "That is what others will say," he continued. "Do not let their words unsettle you. It does not matter. One bout is enough on the battlefield, yes?"

"Aye," she agreed, swallowing her anger.

Äke grinned at her. "It was a good throw, *skjölmdo*. You could have done much worse to prove your point." He released his grip and clapped her on the shoulder. "Gods," he said loudly, addressing the crowd, which was drifting away. "I am thirsty. Is it time to start drinking yet?"

Sigrid let a tiny smile crease her lips. The hold was celebrating the beginning of spring, and most of the Sworn Men had little to do until the games started later in the day. That very indolence was what had led Äke to make his comment about the lang ax earlier, as well as her own challenge to settle the matter on the field.

Some of the Sworn Men raised their voices in agreement with Äke, and the First of the Sworn Men banged his sword against the metal center of his shield to incite their enthusiasm to an even greater volume.

Shaking her head, Sigrid slipped her helm under her arm and grabbed the lang ax. She didn't follow the Sworn Men. It was barely midday; there would be more than enough time for drinking later.

◆ ◆ ◆

Sigrid gasped as she pulled her head out of the rain barrel. It might be the first day of spring, but the nighttime air was cold, and the days were still too short for the sun to warm up the water in the rain barrels. She shivered as she shook out her auburn hair to shed the excess water. She stripped off her linen sark, then dipped it in the barrel and used it to scrub her torso. She made no effort to hide herself; she had long given up feeling self-conscious about exposing herself so. As a Shield-Maiden, she was like the other warriors under the laws of the land, which meant she was a man in all the ways that mattered. She acted as they did; bathed the way they did; slept the way they did; ate, fought, and demanded respect like they did. To shirk any part would be to acknowledge that she felt she was different from them; any such acknowledgment would be a perpetual reminder that she was *less* than they.

Still, she did not undo the cloth that bound her breasts under her armor-cote until she had shrugged into a clean sark.

For even though she lived as a man in many ways, she did not enjoy all their freedoms. They were allowed to bed the thralls as they saw fit, and she did not participate in such rutting equally. There was a practical reason, after all: a pregnancy would take her from her duties for months at a time. Though, in truth, she didn't fancy the men among the thralls. They were not in the same demand as the women, naturally, nor was she the type to take a woman to her bed.

Conversely, she would not be bartered off to marriage like the other daughters of the Jarl. Rather, she could choose a husband of her liking, though in this too she did not enjoy perfect freedom. The other Sworn Men could marry as they would, and their Jarl would award them a place. But as a woman warrior, she was expected to establish her household and prove that her income could support a family. She would also have to provide her husband a *hauswif* to fulfill her duties in the household while she was occupied with her work.

Fortunately, she had already made arrangements on that score. Now all she had to do was find a man worthy of her.

She pulled on a clean pair of wool trews, and—tossing her balled-up, soiled sark to a thrall—she gathered her things and entered the hold's longhouse. After she stored her weapons and armor-cote, she was helped into a tunic of russet linen by Cem, a pretty Celtic thrall who had tended for her since they were both children. Nodding her thanks, Sigrid belted on her pouch and saex knife.

The saex had been a gift from her father when she swore her oath of service to him. As the thrall combed her unruly mop of hair, Sigrid examined the weapon with care, checking for signs of rust or dullness in the edge. She couldn't help admiring the knife. The stout, single-edged blade was the length of her forearm, and the handle was of ivory from the tusk of a walrus, bound at the shoulder with silver wire to prevent the handle splitting. The ivory was incised with the figure of a dragon, its crest, limbs, and tail intertwined about it so fancifully that the nature of the beast was nearly obscured. While clearly decorative, the carving also served the purpose of improving the grip. The handle was surmounted by a riveted silver plate pierced by an iron staple for a lanyard to secure the blade to her hand when working. Satisfied with the blade's condition, she slid it into the silver-mounted sheath suspended horizontally below her belt.

The fact that her blade was of a higher quality and workmanship than the other blades given by the Jarl at the oath ceremonies was overlooked by the others. What man could fault a father for indulging his daughter?

Even one as headstrong as she.

As Cem worked out the knots in her hair, Sigrid sighed and closed her eyes, letting her mind summon up the last conversation she had had with her father, not three days past.

◆ ◆ ◆

"What you ask, daughter, is not something I can give you. It is simply not possible." Pettir Olafsson paced back and forth across the private room that he shared with Sigrid's mother. Age had stooped him slightly, and his beard and hair were more silver than white. His left leg pained him when it was cold, and his pacing back and forth was a means of keeping the stiffness at bay. Though it was, by no means, the sole cause of his consternation this evening.

"Were it my expedition, I would certainly consider your request," her father continued, "but for you to leave this hold and go out under another man's command—a man whom you do not know and who does not know your skills—that is out of the question."

"Why?" Sigrid demanded. "Have I not taken the same oath as your Sworn Men?"

"Yes," Pettir sighed, "of course you have. But—"

"But you do not go *avikinga*," Sigrid said, finishing his statement by turning it into something else. "If I wait for you, I will never make my own way. Ulf and Skeggi have your leave to seek their fortune in other lands. They and I are of the same age, though they have no more experience than I."

"Ulf and Skeggi are not my daughters," Pettir snapped, and seeing her expression, he threw up his arms. "Yes, there. I said it. Is that what you wanted to hear?"

She took care to keep her temper in check. It would not do for her to fall into hysterics at a moment like this. "I don't deny that I am your daughter," she said carefully. "But when I braid my hair, it isn't so that I look pretty for the young warriors who come to your hold, seeking to petition you. I braid it so that my spangenhelm fits firmly on my head. When I cut my nails, it is not so that I may sew better, but so that my grip on my sword is more firm. I may be your daughter, but I have also sworn a vow to fight for you, for your hold."

"Aye," Pettir replied. "That you did."

He looked as if he were going to say something else, but Sigrid continued before he could speak. "You have the same obligation to me that you have to the rest of your Sworn Men. You owe me the opportunity to make my fortune." She crossed the room and laid her hand gently on her father's arm. "I know, in many ways, I will always be your little girl, but I am a woman grown, Father. I would marry at some time before age or injury renders me unfit, and I cannot do so without means of my own. How else am I to do so except by going *avikinga?*"

Pettir shook his head. "Oh, to have such bad luck that we live in quiet times," he said. "When you swore your oath, I had resigned myself that you would go to war with us when the levy was called. That you would fight among friends and kin. But"—he shrugged—"who could have known peace would break out?"

"If I had known, perhaps I would have remained your little daughter and let you marry me off," she said.

He favored her with a knowing grin. "Would anyone have had you?" he said, putting his hand under her chin and raising her face. "You had a fierce reputation, daughter."

I learned it from you, she thought, staring intently at her father. He nodded, knowing full well what she was thinking.

"*Skjölmdo* do not, as a rule, go *avikinga,*" he sighed, a thoughtful expression creeping across his face. "Truth be told, I would not say the same to your aunt. This life is too quiet for her. She will mount an expedition of her own in the next year or so, I suspect, if she can finance a ship. I have little doubt she will find men willing enough to go with her."

Sigrid's hand tightened on her father's arm.

Her father's sister, Grimhildr Olafsdottir, was a Shield-Maiden. After her sons were grown and her husband taken by winter fever, she had joined herself and her daughter, Malusha, to her brother's household. It was at her hand that Sigrid had learned the arts of war.

"Let us discuss this, though, if and when such an eventuality arises," her father said, extricating his arm from her grip. "Though, if you must pray for war to break out," he added, leaning in and lowering his voice, "do so quietly, please? I, for one, am enjoying spending my winters at home, in front of a roaring fire, my hand gripping a mug of mead rather than the hilt of a sword."

THREE

As Cem was finishing with Sigrid's hair, another thrall peeked in on them. "Visitors," the thrall exclaimed, and then disappeared before either Sigrid or Cem could ask a question. Sigrid felt Cem pulling her hair harder than necessary as the thrall hurriedly tried to brush out the last recalcitrant snarl.

"Cem," Sigrid said, stopping the other woman with a touch. "Leave it."

Cem blushed, stepping back and dropping her gaze to the floor. "I am sorry," she started.

"It is fine," Sigrid said as she rose from the stool. "Let us go see who has come to visit. It is undoubtedly more exciting than my hair." She understood the allure of visitors: they would bring news of lands beyond her father's land-hold, and maybe even new stories and sagas. The thirst among the hold's folk for new stories was nigh unquenchable.

Together, Cem and Sigrid hurried to the main hall of the longhouse, where her father, the Jarl of the hold, would receive the visitors. The room was already crowded when they arrived, and Sigrid, being taller than most men, had an unobstructed view. Cem, on the other hand, stood on her toes, craning to see.

At the far end of the room, Sigrid's father, her mother, several of the Sworn Men, and the hauscarl were greeting a dozen men. The spokesman for the visitors was a lean older man, well dressed and decked out in a richly embroidered dark blue linen tunic under a long coat of gray herringbone wool worn against the spring chill. He carried a hand ax in his belt and a narrow langsaex hung under his left arm. His younger companion was a veritable giant, and Sigrid estimated that he was wearing what must be three stone of iron scales for armor. An enormous sword hung on his belt, and a round shield was slung at his back. The rest of the men stood behind in two ranks of four each, all in maille and spangenhelms, armed with sword and shield and spear.

"Shield-Brethren," someone said at Sigrid's side, and she turned her head to find Äke standing beside her. He was dressed in a sweat-stained sark—what he had been wearing under his armor-cote—and his legs were bare. He noted her gaze and shrugged as his eyes ran over her tunic and brushed hair. "I was having an earnest discussion with Ejulf and Solvi," he said by way of explanation for his attire.

"Debating the proper use of a lang ax, no doubt," she replied.

"Precisely," Äke insisted. He noticed her looking at the fresh stain on the front of his sark. "I was parched," he said. "Fighting is thirst-making work."

"So is talking about it," she said dryly. She nodded toward the men at the other end of the room. "Why are they here?" she asked. The Shield-Brethren, members of an ancient martial order known as the *Ordo Militum Vindicis Intactae*, had a citadel on an island off the southern tip of Göttland. Týrshammar was its name. The order had its origins far to the south, somewhere in Christian lands. The sagas spoke of an even older fortress, high in the mountains, called Petraathen. Named after a Greek goddess— She Who Fought First.

Sigrid had always liked the idea of a warrior goddess who, like Freya, fought in the front ranks of her devotees. As it should be.

"I heard something about a boat," Äke said.

Sigrid shushed him, straining to hear what her father was saying. He was inviting the Shield-Brethren to join them for the *blöt*: the celebration of the bountiful grace of Ostara that would provide for their lands over the coming six months. The leader of the Shield-Brethren accepted the Jarl's hospitality gracefully, but Sigrid sensed from the tension in the leader's shoulders that he was chafing at the delay such hospitality would exact upon him.

It was then that she realized the tall one was staring at her. She stared back—not in a challenging way, but more to acknowledge his attention. His lips formed into a thin smile, and he inclined his head in her direction.

"Your hospitality is well known," the leader of the Shield-Brethren was saying, "and it would be our honor to accept."

"It is my honor to offer my house and hold to you," her father said, bowing. The formalities finished, he grinned at the Shield-Brethren. "You're just in time too," he added. "The games are about to begin."

✦ ✦ ✦

In the early spring, it was the hold's custom to conduct a festival for Ostara, the goddess who broke the icy grip of winter and allowed the lands to be fertile once more. There was an invocation, complete with a sacrifice and a ritual plowing of the first field, and while the food for the feast was being prepared, the families of the hold participated in games of skill and stamina. This was the time of year when the boys, and occasionally girls, who had reached puberty competed to show they were worthy of training in the arts of war. There were footraces to show speed and endurance, contests of wit and agility, the throwing of axes and spears, and feats of lifting and carrying. Scores were tallied throughout the day, and by evening the winners were known. At the night's feasting, the winners who chose the warrior's path dined with the Jarl's Sworn Men. It was their first taste of the life of professional warriors; for many, it was more intoxicating than any amount of mead.

Halldor remembered winning in his own hold's games. He knew the thrill these boys would be feeling; though the memory of that heady feeling in his heart and head was tempered by all that happened to him since. The training. The fighting. The blood—his and his enemies'. Would he make the same choice, knowing what he knew now?

He imagined he would, and that realization made watching these games somewhat bittersweet. These boys wanted so desperately to become men, and they had no idea the price to be paid for that desire.

Some of the hold gathered to watch their kin compete in the games; others gathered in the yard of the palisade or spilled out of its gates. Tales were told, songs sung, and the adults played their own games: throwing darts or quoits, or wrestling to the boisterous cheers and jeers of the onlookers. Tables of finger foods had been set out in the yard. Thralls handed out prunes, dried cherries, flatbreads of wheat and barley with honey or preserves, dry sausages, and fresh goat cheese under the watchful eye of a stern older woman in a stained apron.

Halldor's stomach grumbled noisily at the sight of all that food. He had been eating cold rations for a week—as had all the Shield-Brethren. Regardless of Kjallak's consternation about their delay, Halldor knew the company's leader was pleased about the Jarl's hospitality.

Horns of ale and mead were being readily passed among the crowds as well, though the Shield-Brethren would drink more sparingly than they would eat. The All-Father, the One-Eyed Traveler who watched over all wayfarers, cared little for drunkards, and none of the order wished to burden their journey further by inciting Odin's displeasure.

As he stood near a long table, idly accepting food from a thrall who was eager to stuff him as full as possible (a plan which he was heartily enjoying), he let his gaze roam across the yard. He didn't realize he had been looking for the tall woman he had seen in the longhouse until he spotted her approaching. He was man enough to note the young woman's natural grace, combined with an economy and precision of movement that bespoke a warrior's training. He found the combination intriguing.

"Are you enjoying our *blöt*?" she asked as she reached the table. Halldor noted she did not have to crane her neck to look up at his face as much as most did.

"I am," he replied. "It reminds me of my own boyhood."

"A time not too far removed," she noted.

He laughed. "Far enough," he said. He set aside the plate he had been holding and bowed. "I am Halldor Sigvatrsson. I am from"—he waved his hand toward the east—"from a hold you have, undoubtedly, never heard of."

She returned his bow. "I am Sigrid Pettirsdottir," she said.

"Ah, your father is the Jarl." Halldor nodded. "Yes, I can see the resemblance, though you have your mother's hair."

Sigrid raised a hand and touched her hair, and Halldor noticed the calluses on the side of her hand. They were similar to the ones he carried.

"Your presence at our celebration is not merely to trip through the halls of memory or make merry of the season, is it?"

"No," Halldor said. "We had an unfortunate accident with our boat. Not far from a fishing village that resides in that narrow cove a few miles down the coast."

"I know the one." She nodded. "And I know of the waters thereabout. Tricky, but not treacherous. Unless your captain is either blind in one eye or you were…" She trailed off, gauging him carefully.

He laughed off her suspicion. "*Avikinga*? Us? The Shield-Brethren are not holdless marauders. Do the *skald* actually tell such fanciful stories of us?" He shook his head. "We ran afoul during the night," he explained.

She nodded thoughtfully, as if she might be inclined to believe his story but was withholding judgment for a moment. He caught an impish glee in her eye, though, as she turned her head and looked over at Kjallak, who was patiently listening to a Sworn Man with pale hair and a thick beard that had been groomed and braided. "Your master is anxious, though he hides it well," she said. "And I suspect it is not entirely due to Äke's lengthy story."

"Is that who he is speaking with?" Halldor asked. He examined the man talking to Kjallak. "I saw him with you in the great hall earlier, did I not?"

She regarded him plainly. "I was standing with a number of folk from this hold," she said. "Your wandering eye is keen to have noticed me among the others."

Halldor was a little taken aback by her direct manner. "You are tall," he said and then stopped as he realized he was stating something very obvious. "My apologies," he continued, feeling a flush rise in his cheeks. "Forgive me if I have said or done something to offend you."

She shook her head, though he could not tell if she was responding to his words or to her own thoughts. "It may not be my place to offer you and your master advice, but I am certain it has not escaped your notice that we do not have such horses to spare for you and your men," she said, changing the subject.

"Aye," Halldor said awkwardly, still somewhat befuddled as to how he had managed to express himself so poorly.

"While my father would have sent word to the farmholds to gather mounts, your arrival coincides with many of those same folk being here for the festival. It will be much easier for my father to request horses from them. It is quite fortuitous, don't you think?"

"I…yes. Yes, it is."

"I am certain my father's hauscarl is among the farmers now, making known your needs. Your master will have horses on the morrow, and what better way to spend the day than with entertainment and feasting?"

"I can imagine no better way," Halldor said.

Sigrid looked at him again, staring at his face, and though her attention was not unwanted, he still felt awkward. She offered him the briefest of smiles again and then bowed once more before taking her leave.

Halldor tried his best not to stare after her, and he managed to resist the temptation for a few moments.

"Who was that?" he heard Kjallak ask.

"The Jarl's daughter," Halldor said distantly. He tore his attention away from Sigrid's departing form and looked at his elder. "She—" He cleared his throat. "The Jarl is making arrangements for horses," he said.

Kjallak glanced after Sigrid. "Is that all she said?"

Halldor caught a twinkle in the eye of the older woman who was watching the tables of food. She glanced away quickly when he glared at her. "Aye," he said, "that was the gist of it."

◆ ◆ ◆

At the outdoor feast following the games, Halldor and Kjallak were seated at the high table with the Jarl and his wife. They were joined by a striking older woman, nearer to fifty years of age than forty, who was introduced to them as Grimhildr, Pettir's sister, along with a willowy woman with dark hair and eyes named Malusha, who was Grimhildr's daughter—the Jarl's niece.

Grimhildr was a tall, spare woman who wore a tunic and long coat of rich wool. Her elaborately tooled boots reached high up her calves, and heavy raw-silk trousers were bloused into them after the fashion of the Rus far to the east. Large beads of amber and chains of silver and gold hung about her neck, and her wrists were bedecked with many bracelets, her fingers each sporting one or more rings. Her saex knife's sheath was similarly rich in its decoration, and she wore a sword slung low on her left hip.

Malusha, on the other hand, wore a light gray linen dress, the neck and wrists of which were trimmed in elaborately stitched patterns. Over this she wore a dark blue woolen apron with silver medallions, covered with hammered runes, securing the straps over her shoulders. Kjallak showed no sign of confusion as to the difference in attire between mother and daughter. "*Skjölmdo*," he said to her after pleasantries had been exchanged with the Jarl and his wife, Fenja. "It is a pleasure to meet you. I had been speaking with one of the Sworn Men earlier today, and he was telling me stories of your charge."

Halldor had been glancing around the room on the pretense of making sure the other Shield-Brethren were taken care of. They were scattered across several of the tables reserved for the Sworn Men. He counted heads, noting that the winners of today's games were intermixed with the Shield-Brethren and the Sworn Men, a pairing that made him smile. He caught sight of Sigrid, and she looked up and smiled at him just as Kjallak's words penetrated his thick head. *Skjölmdo. Shield-Maiden.*

"Aye," Grimhildr said. "I am rather proud of her, in fact; she shows extraordinary promise."

Halldor's attention was pulled away from the other tables by the arrival of the thralls with trays and plates of food.

The choicest bits of the ox that had been roasting all day came to their table, and then the warrior's table next, and so on. Halldor had seen the beast earlier—suspended on a thick pole of green wood over a long pit filled with coals—and knew there was an enormous amount of meat to be had from an animal that size. He suspected there would be no shortage of meat, and his eyes widened as the thralls continued to bring trays of food to their table. There were roast boars and goats, salmon and herring—fresh, smoked, or pickled!

After the meat came a sweet soup made from dried fruit; bowls of spring greens with vinegar or cooked in bacon fat; roasted or boiled turnips and beets; flatbread with gravy, honey, or preserves; and—as a rare treat, indeed!—boiled eggs. There was mead as well, of course, flagons and horns of the thick, honey-flavored drink, and Halldor was suddenly concerned that he couldn't eat enough to be a dutiful guest. There was just too much food!

And no sooner had the thralls finished laying out the feast, than people began to get up and move about the room, completely disregarding the distinctions of the arranged tables. As Kjallak and Grimhildr fell into comfortable conversation—old warriors sharing stories of distant exploits—Halldor was subjected to a steady stream of available young women who subtly hinted that they might be available to *him* that very evening. In fact, the thralls weren't subtle at all, making their intent plain even to the extent of whispering often quite explicit offers in his ear.

He did his best to remain amiable throughout, keeping in mind that he was a sworn initiate of the Shield-Brethren. While the order did not require celibacy of its knights, he did not know the Jarl's household well enough to chance offending some family member or another by bedding one of the eager—and quite persistent!—thralls. As soon as he could manage without being offensive, he excused himself from the throng and made his way toward the clusters of fighting men, whose company was much less fraught with…

"The maids do like a new face, don't they?"

Halldor recognized the man as the one Kjallak had been speaking to earlier in the day. *Äke*, he remembered, the First of the Jarl's Sworn Men. "Aye," he replied. "I am like a rare flower." Äke threw back his head and let loose a full-throated laugh. Halldor joined him, though he did not think his comment that uproarious.

"I am Äke Fair-Haired," the other man said when he had recovered from his bout of humor.

"I am Halldor, son of Sigvatr."

"A Shield-Brethren knight," Äke said.

Halldor nodded. "That I am."

"The *skalds* sing stories of men like you," Äke said, sipping from his horn.

"Do they?" Halldor said, his attention wandering. He spotted Sigrid near one of the bonfires that provided the light and heat that kept the night at bay. "She is *skjölmdo*," Halldor said, figuring he might as well fess up to what he had been looking at.

Äke laughed, pressing his teeth against the bottom edge of his horn. When he lowered it, his beard sparkled with mead. "Aye, that she is," he said.

"It would seem to me that a woman would be at some disadvantage as a fighter; they lack the upper body strength and weight of a man. Though I suppose that matters little if they are trained well," Halldor said thoughtfully. "*It is not the arm that wields the sword, but the body*," he mused, quoting from the lessons that had been drilled into him at Týrshammar. "*The body is moved by the feet, and the hand follows the foot.*"

"Aye," Äke said, a touch ruefully. "Size may be telling, but it is not the entire story." He rubbed his ass, making a show of wincing.

Halldor took Äke's measure carefully. He was taller and heavier than Sigrid and his arms were longer. Maybe a full handspan longer. "Truly?" he said, his curiosity plain in his voice. "Ah, now there is a story I must hear."

"I hardly know it," Äke said, looking chagrined. He took a long pull from his horn. "Early this morning, I merely said that the lang ax was a man's weapon, and next I knew she took one up and called me out. I took my shield and a practice sword and we squared off. I moved in when she stumbled and next I knew I was flat-out in the dust." He glanced over at Sigrid, his face reddening with embarrassment. "That *girl* never stumbles. I should have known better."

"So she fights with the lang ax?" Kjallak asked.

Äke snorted. "No, she was taught to fight with the hewing spear. I've never seen her fight with a lang ax before. It didn't matter. She picked it up and sussed it out right quick."

"She's that good then?" Halldor asked.

Äke looked thoughtful a moment. "In some ways she's the best I've ever worked with," he said. He pointed a finger at Halldor. "Mind you," he continued, "I'll thump you good if you ever tell her I said so, Shield-Brethren or no."

"I have forgotten already what it is you have told me," Halldor assured him, though he most certainly had not.

Äke belched before continuing. "She never puts a foot wrong, and her sense of timing and distance is just as good. I tell you, I was a warrior when she was just a gleam in the Jarl's eye, and I am First among his Sworn Men, but I never take for granted that I could defeat her in a fight."

Halldor stopped a passing thrall and took the flagon of mead from the young woman. He refilled Äke's horn and tapped the flagon lightly against it. "Let us drink then," he said, "to the hope we shall never have to face her on the field of battle."

"Aye," Äke said, shaking his head and lifting the full horn to his lips.

Halldor raised the flagon to his, though he did little more than sip from the wide-mouthed container. Over the rim, he looked at Sigrid, a subtle prickling at the back of his skull.

The sensation was not new. If he was mindful, it would steal over him while in battle, though he had felt it the previous night. It had stirred him awake, in fact. Shortly before the boat had sprung its seams.

✦ ✦ ✦

Temperatures plummeted as soon as the sun fell from the sky, and despite the fires, the warm clothes, and copious amounts of mead, the nighttime air began to seep through clothing and chill the skin and bones beneath. Some of the heartier souls filled the yard inside the palisade, where more bonfires burned and the walls reflected and contained the heat. Instruments were brought out, kegs tapped, and soon music and dancing filled the space.

The core of the party—the Jarl and his family, the Sworn Men, and their guests—retired to the great hall of the longhouse for a hot drink and to hear the tales told by a *skald* who had traveled to the hold for the occasion. The common folk would pass through as space allowed, clustering into the hall to hear bits and snatches of the *skald*'s songs before returning to the yard for more merriment.

Sigrid took advantage of the coming and going of the thralls and the commoners to slip out of the great hall herself during the applause and cheers that followed one of the *skald*'s stories. The cold air was refreshing after the smoky great hall of the longhouse. The combined misty breath of the revelers picked up the light of the fires, making the air almost glow over the crowded yard. The sound of flutes, horns, fiddles, and drums echoed across the space filled with dancing bodies.

As she neared the tables—a few still laden with the remnants of the feast—she was surprised to find her cousin Malusha idly nibbling on some dried fruit. The younger woman looked up at Sigrid, smiled, and lifted up two horns of mead as if she had been waiting for Sigrid.

Sigrid accepted the horn from her tiny cousin. "What?" she inquired, noting that Malusha's grin had not diminished.

"Help me, cousin," Malusha implored, fighting hard not to laugh. She pointed past Sigrid. "Is that the sun, rising early, or..."

Sigrid glanced quickly over her shoulder and spotted the giant Shield-Brethren, his blond head bobbing above the crowds. His hair reflected the firelight in a way that made it appear to glow. Sigrid tried to grab Malusha, who was already dancing back, staying out of reach. "Do not leave me," she hissed at her cousin.

"Never," Malusha laughed. "But I know when to make myself scarce too." Sigrid's cousin vanished into the shadows of the long-house, the trilling sound of her laughter fading after her.

Sigrid considered running after her for a moment, but when she heard Halldor call her name, she held her ground. Raising her horn, she rapidly drank half its contents, her throat tight against the sudden influx of mead. Nearly choking, she forced herself to slow down.

"Do you dance?"

She swiped the back of her hand across her mouth before she turned. "Dance?" she asked, trying to make her lips turn upward into a smile.

Halldor's face glowed in the firelight, or perhaps the apple color in his cheeks came from the mead—Sigrid wasn't entirely sure. "Yes, dance," he said, waving a hand toward the merriment going on near the palisade. "It is what people do when they are celebrating. They dance; they drink; they—"

He broke off, and Sigrid was impressed that he could manage to eke out another shade of red in his face.

"And what part should I dance? The man's or the woman's?"

"Aye," Halldor said. "I have heard that about you. Though, while I still have my wits about me, I can attest there is no confusion in my mind."

"Made up your mind already, have you?" Sigrid replied.

Halldor took her tone the wrong way, and his face crumpled as he brought up his hands defensively. "No, no," he said, "I only spoke of dancing."

A hearty peal of laughter slipped out of her, and he blinked in surprise, uncertainty writ across his features. Starting her training as young as she did, she had little practice in the womanly arts of flirtation and fewer opportunities to miss them, and maybe it was the drink making her bolder than she might be otherwise, but she found his awkwardness disarming.

"I wasn't," she said. "Speaking of dancing, that is." She took a long pull on her horn, giving him time to think about what she was saying, and when it seemed as if he hadn't quite got it, she said, very deliberately, what was on her mind—what Malusha had known she was thinking. "All things being equal, I'd kick your heels out from under you and have you right here in the yard."

Halldor gaped at her for a second and then threw his head back and laughed, his voice ringing with honest delight at her nerve. "Äke told me you'd give as good as you got in a scuffle," he said. He raised his hands again. "Peace, *skjölmdo*, I yield. Thank the gods I only came at you with words; I would fear for my life if we crossed steel."

And well you should, she thought, intending to say those words as she stepped forward, meaning to poke him in the chest with a stiff finger as punctuation for her words, but also as an excuse to stand closer to him. But her finger never touched him. His eyes never left her face, but he grabbed her finger before it had even crossed half the distance between them. He squeezed her digit—not unkindly— and then, realizing what he had done, he let go and stepped back.

"I am sorry," he said quickly. "Did I harm you?"

"No," she said, quite puzzled. Her hand was still upraised, finger extended, but he was out of measure now.

Measure.

She was thinking about her finger as a weapon, and Halldor as an opponent.

He rubbed at the side of his head as if it bothered him, and when he looked at her again, all the levity was gone from his eyes.

"What is it?" she asked.

"Something's wrong," he said.

As the words left his mouth, a cry came drifting out of the longhouse—a long, terrified wail. Sigrid shuddered as she heard it, and she quickly brushed past Halldor, heading for the longhouse. "My mother," she snapped at his unasked question.

FOUR

Halldor followed Sigrid as she rushed into the longhouse. A headache was blooming in the back of his head, a combination of the mead dulling his senses and a sudden increase in his heart rate. Thralls and Sworn Men were milling about, both in front of the longhouse and in the great hall inside. He caught up with Sigrid as she pushed her way into the great hall, and together they forced their way through the crowded confusion.

The fire in the long hearth that ran down the center of the room had burned down nearly to a bed of coals, and the light it threw off made for many shadows in the corners of the room. He spotted several Shield-Brethren; though they stood alert, hands on hilts of weapons undrawn, they were not ready for battle. They had been given no orders.

At the far end, near the half wall that separated the Jarl's private quarters from the rest of the hall, he spotted Kjallak, Grimhildr, and a few other Sworn Men. Sigrid broke away from him as they approached: she moving to speak with Grimhildr; he, to Kjallak. Kjallak's expression was a welter of emotions: concern, apprehension, anger.

"What has happened?" Halldor asked.

"The Jarl's wife, Fenja, was suddenly stricken during one of the sagas," Kjallak said. He waved a hand at the closed partition to the Jarl's quarters. "The Jarl is trying to comfort her now."

"Are we under attack?" Halldor said.

Kjallak glared at him. "Why do you think that?" he snapped.

Halldor glanced briefly around the room before returning his attention to Kjallak. He hesitated to say anything in front of the others. Fortunately he was spared having to explain his question by Sigrid.

"Mother had a vision, didn't she?" Sigrid said.

"Aye, she did," Grimhildr replied, even as she watched Halldor closely. "She saw sails off the coast. Coming out of the darkness. Landing at the village."

"This isn't the first time she has had such insight?" Kjallak asked, picking up on the inference in Sigrid's statement.

"No," Grimhildr replied. "Though she has not had such insight for some years."

Kjallak's expression grew thoughtful, and Halldor laid a hand on the other man's shoulder and shook his head slightly. "Danes?" he asked Grimhildr, keeping everyone's attention on the present concern.

"Danes," Grimhildr said. She turned to Sigrid, who had fallen mute after her first question. "Gather the Sworn Men," she said. "Get them in their gear." She looked at Kjallak. "If we wait too long, they'll fire the town before they march on the hold. We can probably drive them off, but losing the fishing village at this time is dangerous. If I'm wrong, the men will get some exercise and training." She grinned wolfishly. "They don't get enough exercise, in my opinion."

The door to the Jarl's quarters creaked open, and Pettir slipped into the hall. He appeared to have aged in the last hour: his hair hung around his face, lank and colorless; his skin was pale, covered with a sheen of sweat. "Three ships," he said, speaking to

Grimhildr. "She talks in her sleep. *Three ships. Wolves on the beach. And fire; everything is on fire.*"

"Go," Grimhildr hissed at Sigrid, who had not torn herself away. The tall *skjölmdo* shrugged, as if stirring herself from a bad dream, and hurried off to assemble the Sworn Men.

✦ ✦ ✦

After making sure the runners knew the message she wanted them to carry, Sigrid hurried to her own sleeping closet to dress for battle. She quickly changed into a pair of heavy woolen trews and short, knotted wool socks, then bound the trousers tight around her lower legs with winengas, long strips of woolen fabric that protected her lower legs against thorns and brush.

Slipping out of her tunic, she shrugged into her heavy, quilted armor-cote and maille. The maille, fifteen pounds of flat riveted iron rings, each the size of her fingernail, was tricky to slip into but well worth the effort; it could stop arrows and turn any but the heaviest cuts. It covered her from shoulder to mid-thigh and protected her upper arms with demi-sleeves. She raised her arms, and Cem, who had appeared out of nowhere while she had been struggling to get her maille on, pulled tight the lacings that held the armor snug to Sigrid's body.

That done, she allowed the girl to sling her belt with the sheathed saex knife around her hips and buckle it. Slinging the baldric that carried her langsaex about her, she settled the weapon in place below her left arm, took up her hewing spear, and strode quickly out of the longhouse.

The half dozen Sworn Men not manning the palisade or gates were assembled in the yard. Their equipment was by no means uniform, but each wore a helmet or spangenhelm and carried a round shield and a spear. Some also bore hand axes or langsaexes, and two—Äke and Thorbjorn—wore long, double-edged swords at their sides.

Grimhildr stood with the Sworn Men, resplendent in her war harness. Her maille shirt had full sleeves and hung to her knees. Her knees and lower legs were protected by iron greaves, and her spangenhelm had a full aventail of maille protecting her neck and throat. Like Sigrid, she had a hewing spear in one hand and a round shield slung across her back.

Pettir emerged from the longhouse, and as he reached the yard, he was joined by the Holmgard, a militia of able-bodied men who had been in attendance at the *blöt*. They were armed with whatever they had brought with them—langsaex or spear—though each did have a round shield and an iron helmet with a nasal guard from Pettir's stores. While they were individually responsible for the defense of their own land-holds, it was the Jarl's responsibility to see them adequately armored when they fought on his behalf.

The smell of dust, oiled steel, leather, and humanity filled the yard, and Sigrid frowned as she made a quick count of their forces. Not counting the Shield-Brethren and the men they must leave to defend the hold, their number was less than forty. Her breath hitched in her chest as she considered how many Danes three longships could carry.

They could be outnumbered several times over.

Her father spent little time galvanizing the men. They still had to march to the village, and there might not be any Danish invaders. There was no reason to get the men more excited or nervous than they already were. There would be time enough for all that if it came to fighting. With a shout, he signaled for the gates in the palisade to be opened, and the company set out with the Sworn Men and the Shield-Brethren leading the way. The Shield-Brethren marched in two ranks of six behind Kjallak and Halldor, while the Jarl's men moved in loose order, strung out along the road. They moved quietly enough, with little talking among themselves. The loudest sounds came from the tramp of their feet on the hard-packed road and the rustle and scrape of their gear.

Sigrid was assailed by a mix of contradictory emotions. On the one hand she was filled with a fierce elation: she was finally to put her long training to the test—marching and fighting with the Sworn Men as an equal! On the other hand, her stomach churned, twisting and biting as if she had a beast in her belly. *Am I afraid to die?* she wondered at first, but she dismissed that thought readily enough. If she fell in battle, she would dine in the halls of the All-Father. What, then, was it? As she looked at the other faces around her, seeing similar lines of apprehension and concern etched in sweat-slicked skin, she realized these were her kin. Not all of them were blood, but they were family. She had grown up with most of them, and if there was to be battle, some of them would not return home. Fighting bravely in battle was one thing, but she did not want to disappoint any of her comrades. Or her father. Could she strike a blow that would end a man's life?

Fighting in the yard with the others was dangerous—accidents could, and did, happen—but it was not the same thing as earnest battle. Her aunt had assured her time and again that, in the heat of battle, her training would take hold and she would strike without conscious thought.

So be it, she thought. That was the purpose of training. She would either act or not. The rest was up to the gods.

Sigrid exhaled, letting go of the breath she had been holding, and her stomach unknotted. She was *skjölmdo*. She was ready.

◆ ◆ ◆

As they neared the village, they began to pass women and older men laden with household goods herding their young children before them. A rider had been sent ahead to warn the villagers, for while the Danes would usually spare the women and children, they did not always, and regardless, they took slaves as often as not.

The moon was still in the sky, and its pale light allowed the Jarl's party of warriors to look upon the village as they approached. The village was not walled, though there was a berm of rammed earth surrounding the landward sides. Halldor counted a dozen cottages strung out along the shore, several wall-less sheds, and a long and low shape festooned with fishing nets hanging from the eaves. He surmised it was a smokehouse, shared by all the villagers. Bobbing offshore were tiny shapes that seemed to be floating erratically, and he realized they were the town's fishing boats, put to sea so as to keep them safe should the Danes set fire to the cottages. In the distance, he could see the slender shape of one boat that remained on the beach—their *karvi*, still needing work done.

Houses could be rebuilt, as could boats. But the villagers would need means to catch food more than they would need roofs over their heads. Halldor recognized the brutal simplicity of their thinking; his own family had done the same once upon a time.

A small group of men approached, several of them holding torches. They were not enough of a war party to concern the Shield-Brethren or the Jarl's Sworn Men, and as they got closer, Halldor could make out details of their gear. They wore helmets of leather or iron and carried axes and spears. It was a meager force, but Halldor knew their hearts would be strong. This was their home.

"What news, Byrghir?" the Jarl called out as the villagers reached the berm. He spoke to the man most likely to be the leader of the small community.

"Jarl Pettir," Byrghir replied, after making an effort to bow. "I sent sharp-eyed and fleet-footed boys to see what could be seen. They have spotted four boats, no more than two miles up the coast from this cove."

"Four," Kjallak muttered, shaking his head.

"Grim odds, Kjallak," Grimhildr said, voicing what was on their minds. Her teeth flashed in the moonlight. "That many could march on the hold if they so desired."

Pettir motioned to Kjallak and Grimhildr, and the pair joined him on the other side of the berm to talk with the villagers. Their conference was hushed, though the Jarl tended to gesticulate with his hands as he spoke while Kjallak and Grimhildr were less expressive but no less intense in their discourse.

"Four?" Sigrid asked, wandering up next to Halldor.

"Maybe as many as one hundred men," he said.

Sigrid made a tiny noise in her throat, and Halldor could not blame her. He felt confident that he, Kjallak, and the other Shield-Brethren could account well for themselves, but at what cost?

"Are they discussing abandoning the village?" Sigrid asked, swallowing heavily and jerking her chin toward the huddled conference.

"Perhaps," Halldor said, thinking that such a plan was very likely under consideration. On the other hand, a strong show of force at the village might send the Danes scurrying back to their boats. They were *avikinga*—seeking profit, pure and simple; if the cost looked to be too dear, they would seek easier plunder elsewhere. They would find the village was already alerted to their presence, which meant the choicest slaves might have already been taken inland. Though, if the Danes were desperate for supplies, they might fight, regardless.

"If we stand and fight—and they break us—they'll make for the hold," Sigrid said, echoing the same thoughts that were running through his head. It was prebattle chatter, idle talk that served to keep other—grimmer—thoughts at bay. "A much riper prize than the village."

"The *only* prize," Halldor said.

"Aye," she agreed. "Even if my father gave up the village, what would it offer to the Danes? The boats are gone; the fishermen are safe. There is nothing here but scraps and timber." She looked at Halldor, her face suddenly pinched. "Your boat," she said, nodding at the long, slender silhouette.

Halldor shrugged. "Hopefully it will be spared, but it is of little use to us now in any event."

He squinted in the torchlight, trying to discern Kjallak's mood in the dim light. The Jarl had told Kjallak that this fight was not theirs, and he would understand if the Shield-Brethren decided to not take part in it. But until their boat was fixed or they found mounts for all his brothers, they were bound to this land. If the Danes overran it, their chances of reaching Visby would be greatly diminished.

And besides—it was the right thing to do.

FIVE

A decision was soon reached, and the trio returned to the host. Kjallak nodded to Halldor, a subtle signal that Sigrid did not follow, and with a few gestures, Halldor informed the other Shield-Brethren of the plan. They melted off the road, vanishing quickly into the shadows cast by the trees. He and Kjallak went last, and Halldor hesitated a moment longer to glance at her. He seemed to be on the verge of saying something, but he tapped the hand holding his spear against his chest instead. She replied in kind—two warriors wishing strength of heart and hand to the other.

"We stand here," Pettir yelled, expressing his intention to the Sworn Men and the Holmgard. The gathered men answered with upthrust weapons and a mighty bellow. Hearing the sound, the Danes would know the hold was aware of their landing and that there was a force waiting for them. They would know they faced a fight; that they could not venture toward the hold until they had faced the Jarl's men at the fishing village. Such was her father's intent, of course.

"The Sworn Men will hold the center," he shouted, "and the Holmgard will stand on either side." The men sorted themselves quickly by family groups to either side of the Sworn Men; he did not need to tell them to bring the shields to the front, the spears behind. "Byrghir," he called to the village leader. "Do not let them flank us. Throw whatever you can lay your hands on: spears, rocks, torches. Fish, even, if they are spoiled and rotten enough." The villagers shouted their approval of his plan, and the men roared again, their voices rising with laughter. "When these Danish dogs beg for scraps at the feet of their betters in Valhalla," Pettir continued when the cheering subsided, "let them tremble as they tell their fellows of the fierceness of our folk. As to the rest, let us send them back to their leaky boats like whipped curs!"

With that Pettir moved off, talking to a warrior here and there. Sigrid watched him with admiration even as she checked her own weapons. He appeared supremely confident, cheerful even, as he moved among the men. He seemed to have an instinct for which man needed steadying, who would respond to a jest or good-natured insult, when to share an anecdote about a past battle. He shaped them with words like a master potter at his wheel, turning them from a mob of armed men into a fighting force. He seemed completely relaxed, unconcerned that within the hour they would be facing several times their number of professional fighters.

A group of women and teenage boys well behind the shield wall that closed the gap in the berm caught her attention. The women were bringing up apron-loads of fist-sized rocks to leave in piles. The boys and some of the women were limbering up and sorting the rocks. One of the boys suddenly whirled something around his head and let fly. Moving almost too fast to see, the rock flickered over the heads of the fighters and vanished into the darkness.

A sling was a slow weapon and accuracy was difficult in the best of conditions, but a good slinger could hurl a fist-sized rock as far as a bow could shoot. While they would be little more than a nuisance to the Danes, even a lucky stone could stave in a helm or crack a shield. At the very least, being hit by a flung stone would be a distraction. *Every little thing helped,* she thought, unexpectedly moved by the dedication and bravery of these boys—not yet old enough to fight alongside the men, but still eager to defend their homes. As the first light of dawn brightened the sky, women moved among the fighters, passing out cups of hot fish soup. This was their last act before most of the women would depart for the hold, but a few—too old or infirm to fight or run—would stay to do what they could for the fighters. They would be poor candidates for rape or enslavement, and at very least they could give the Jarl's men water or bind wounds when or if chance allowed. They too sought to help.

An inarticulate roar of many voices rose in the distance, and the sound of horns echoed in the predawn twilight. The roaring grew until she could make out individual voices, mostly battle cries and invocations of the gods. Then she could make out a dark moving mass punctuated now and again by the dim flash of pale light on spearpoint or helm. At last the mass resolved into mailled men, spears or axes in hand, round shields slung at their backs, and long swords at their hips. At two hundred paces they stopped and began to form their lines. Sigrid wondered at the irony that their foes should invoke the same gods to attack and plunder that her folk did to defend.

Pettir, Grimhildr, and Äke moved along their lines, steadying their men and making last-minute adjustments. Now they could do nothing but wait and see what their enemy would do. Sigrid wondered at it herself. The Danes could send a small force to engage the defenders and send the rest to try to flank them. They could send forces on up the hill to take the hold while the bulk of its defenders were engaged here, or even send a delegation to parlay and demand tribute. Or they could come straight into the teeth of the defenders to smash them by brute force. Sigrid thought that they had the numbers to try the latter tactic with good odds of success.

Apparently the Danish commanders agreed.

"From their battle order it looks like they are coming straight for us," Thorbjorn commented. There was no emotion in his voice, as if he were speaking of a fact as simple and inconsequential as the sun rising.

"Good," Sigrid said. "It will save us from having to chase them down across half the country." For all her earlier apprehension and anticipation, she found herself bored and tired, and she understood Thorbjorn's lack of enthusiasm.

Thorbjorn laughed at her comment, as did a few other men nearby. "Gods," he sighed, "I just wish they would get on with it."

At length it seemed that the Danes were ready, and at the sound of a horn those in the front ranks unslung their shields. It was a signal to the Jarl's men, and each side began to yell at the other, pitching insults back and forth across the early morning air, striking their weapons against the metal bosses of their shields. The din rose to an unintelligible roaring in her ears that seemed to go on forever. Then a horn sounded again, and the Viking force began to advance. They did not march in time with locked shields; rather they seemed to flow forward, a group or individual leading now here, now there. At a hundred paces they raised their shields, bellowed their war cries, and charged.

At almost that exact moment, she heard stones whirring overhead. Gaps appeared momentarily in the mass of charging men, but they closed as fast as they opened. At a shouted command, the Jarl's shield wall opened up and spearmen ran through to hurl their heavy throwing spears before retreating back behind the shieldmen. Wherever a spear struck, a gap opened and the line faltered as the ranks behind had to dodge their fallen comrade. For the most part the spears did not kill, she noted, but when they stuck in a man's shield, it became unwieldy, and he had to stop to dislodge it or cut it off. As the Danes closed the distance between the two groups, she had but a moment to realize that this tactic would cause ripples in the shield wall of the approaching Danes. The wall would not be a solid mass.

What followed was chaos. The men that hit the wall first were cut down immediately, as several defenders struck at each Dane. Then the main mass of the attackers flowed up against them, and the shield wall was forced to give a step—then two—while it adjusted to the weight of the attack. Sigrid stood behind the shield wall with the other spearmen, thrusting her seven-foot spear past the men of the line whenever she saw an opening. She had only a brief moment to note what it felt like when the four-inch-wide blade of her spear sliced through a man's face. She felt the impact ripple up her arm, transforming into a shiver that raced up the back of her neck. *This is what it feels like...*she started to think, but then another face flickered at her through the shield wall and she thrust her spear at it as well. And another.

And another.

Their attackers were packed against the wall so tightly they could hardly fight, but their mass was enough to force the Jarl's shield wall back. Slowly, one step at a time, the shield wall retreated. The Sworn Man in front of her dropped, opening a hole in the line that she thrust through instantly, taking the man that had felled him in the belly before the other Sworn Men closed the gap. Another man fell—she dimly tried to recall his name, but her mind was no longer focused on such minutiae. All she could see was the gap in the shield wall he left behind.

She stepped forward, shifting her grip on the spear to one hand and holding it before her vertically like a shield as she snatched out her langsaex. Her focus collapsed even farther, even as her awareness expanded, and she felt like she was in the yard, fighting Äke again. Knowing what was coming next without thinking.

The Danish attackers seemed to have fallen asleep on their feet. Their motions—the set of each foot, the way they held their weapons—were slow and exaggerated. She watched them coldly, aware on a level far below thought of their movements and knowing how little she had to move in return. A slight turn of the wrist and a blow that would have killed her missed by a hairbreadth; a small twist of her blade allowed it to scrape along the rim of a shield to its target instead of being deflected; the thin space between the helm and the armor where her blade could slip through and pierce flesh. Despite the uneven ground, the uncertain light, the bodies, and fallen weapons, she never doubted her footing. Everything around her was frozen, and she moved through the battlefield with infinite precision and grace.

Do you dance?

Yes, the thought came to her distantly, as if someone else were having the conversation—in another time and place. *Yes, this dance I know.*

At some point she left her langsaex jammed through the chest of a mailled warrior. At another she left her saex knife in a man's groin. Wielding her hewing spear with both hands again, she danced through the battle like a wraith, omniscient and untouchable.

The shield wall crumpled, and she fought on. She felt a savage spike of joy when the wedge of Shield-Brethren scythed into the Danish flank. Sometimes she allowed weapons to slide past her guard to grate along her mail or pierce her flesh if it would not cripple her, but in turn gave an advantage. When she saw her aunt beleaguered and failing, she threw her spear without care of the fact that it was her only weapon. The spear took the man that would have killed Grimhildr through the throat and drove him into his companions. Grimhildr recovered her footing, and her blade flashed in the morning light as she took to the offensive against the Danes.

Sigrid stared at her empty hands, and she had barely begun to ponder what she should fill them with when a Dane came at her, lang ax raised over his head. She lunged under his blow, setting her hands on the haft of his weapon and twisting it free of his grip as she threw him heavily to the ground. She reversed the lang ax in her hands, striking the fallen Dane in the face—almost as an afterthought—before continuing her relentless and unstoppable dance of death…

◆ ◆ ◆

She had been lost in the rhythm of the lang ax: striking with the head, haft, and butt; feeling the impact of each on metal, flesh, and wood; hearing the pounding drum of her heart. And then, without notice, the rhythm stopped, and her lang ax swung through empty air. There was no one left to fight.

The Danes had been broken. They were retreating under a hail of spears, rocks, and curses.

She stood still for a moment, listening intently to the fading rhythm that had been coursing through her. Her chest rose and fell in time with that martial music, and as she realized the sound was nothing more than her own heartbeat, she sank to her knees, her breath changing into quaking gasps. She leaned heavily on the butt of the lang ax, suddenly unable to keep herself upright. The morning sun shone down on a field covered in gore, and she was stained with blood as well, from head to boot. There were bodies—and pieces of bodies—scattered all around her. Ripping off her spangenhelm, she doubled over, spewing the contents of her stomach onto the already fouled earth.

At length, Sigrid became aware of another presence, and her body tensed, thinking it needed to fight again, but the person wrapped strong arms around her. A rough voice, feminine and familiar, spoke in her ear. "It's all right now, child. Let it out," Grimhildr said softly. "Let the battle go. It takes most like this the first time."

Sigrid's stomach stopped heaving, but the shakes would not leave the rest of her as quickly, and her aunt held her tight until the last quivering sigh fled from her aching chest. Grimhildr let go, and Sigrid struggled to her feet, wiping her mouth with the back of her wrist.

Äke stood nearby, bloodied and helmetless, with a gash along the side of his head, and the upper half of his ear missing on the left side. He had a skin of mead in his hands, and he offered it to her. "Rinse your mouth out with this," he said, "but mind you don't swallow any or you'll be right back at it."

She did as he told her, rinsing her mouth and sloshing the honey wine through her teeth before spitting it out. He was right. As much as she wanted to swallow the sweet mead, her legs quaked at the thought, and her stomach flipped.

Grimhildr offered her a different skin, one filled with water. "Slowly," she instructed. "Let each sip settle before you take the next."

Sigrid returned the first skin to Äke and took a tiny sip from the second. Her stomach rebelled at first, but the water was cool in her throat, and she could feel the tension in her lower body fading as the water fell into her stomach. She took another sip, slightly larger than the first, and her stomach received it gladly.

"Better now?" Grimhildr asked.

"Aye," she said, looking about. "Moreso after I get out of this gods-damned muck."

Äke shook his head in wonder. "By the All-Father," he said. "You make quite a mess, don't you?"

SIX

Kjallak perched painfully on an upturned bucket, his left leg thrust out before him. From where he sat on the berm, he could see the fishermen milling about on the shore as the fishing boats were beached once more. The cottages were safe as was the beached *karvi*. They had beaten the Danes back.

He heard Halldor call his name, and he spotted his second approaching from the beach. He adjusted his position on the bucket, easing the pain in his hip. "Ho, Halldor," he said, "I am taller than you for once."

Halldor squinted up at him from the base of the berm. "Your seat looks precarious, Kjallak," he said. "Do you dare to take both hands off that bucket?"

"Later, perhaps," Kjallak said, keeping his tone light. "What news?"

"The good news is that our vessel is unscathed," Halldor said, waving in the general direction of the strip of beach where they had pulled their *karvi* ashore. "The bad is that the villagers claimed back their pitch pots before the battle. Many of them were set afire and thrown at the Danes."

Kjallak grunted. "I bet they were surprised."

"Aye, they probably were," Halldor said. "It will be a week, at least, before they will have enough to re-tar the hull."

Kjallak glanced over his shoulder, nearly tipping his bucket over. "And the Danish boats?" he asked, once he had resettled himself, ignoring the flare of pain from his left hip. The spear tip that had penetrated his maille had also scraped across the bone. He could see the lazy curls of smoke up the beach behind him. "Did they burn them?"

"Aye," Halldor nodded. "Two of them."

Kjallak sighed. He would have been surprised if they hadn't. The Danish forces had been decimated enough that they had no need for all four boats, and they had put two of them to the torch as they had fled so that the Jarl could not pursue them.

Nor, unfortunately, could the Shield-Brethren take one of the boats to replace their damaged vessel.

"The Jarl will see that we get horses," Halldor said. "It would be best for us to continue with that plan."

Kjallak made a face, thinking about sitting on a horse with his injury. "Aye, we'll proceed overland. We are already late. It makes little difference now." He sighed and let his gaze roam over the stained battlefield on both sides of the berm. "We have done a fair service to the Jarl this day. To all of Göttland. Those Danish bastards will be rowing hard for home."

By his estimate, nearly sixty Danish bodies littered the field south of the village. Thralls and villagers moved among the corpses, first stripping them of the more obvious valuables and then loading the bodies onto narrow, hand-drawn carts. A massive pyre was being assembled along the beachfront of the village.

Enemies or no, the dead deserved to go to Valhalla, though they would go without their arms and armor.

"Did you tell him?" Halldor asked.

"The Jarl?" Kjallak shook his head, knowing what his second was talking about. "There was no need. We stood and fought with him. It does not matter."

"He lost good men. Men he might not have lost otherwise."

"This is a raw land, Halldor," Kjallak said firmly. "There are too few of us in Týrshammar. We cannot take on the responsibility of protecting every hold and house. Besides, there is no way of knowing if these Danes were the same."

"There were four ships, Kjallak," Halldor pointed out. "The same number as were pursuing us."

"We cannot know if they were the same ships," Kjallak repeated, his voice stern. Halldor stared back at him, and Kjallak wondered again if he was high enough that Halldor couldn't see the blood staining his maille.

"How many injured?" Kjallak asked, changing the topic. Trying not to wince as he shifted his weight on the bucket. "How many of ours did we lose?"

"None," Halldor said. "Three, *at least*"—and Kjallak wondered at the stress Halldor put on the words—"are injured badly enough that it will be several weeks before they are ready to travel."

Kjallak nodded. "The Jarl lost a goodly number of his Sworn Men," he said. After a pause, he asked: "Did she survive the battle?"

"Who?" Halldor said. His face was turned away, and so Kjallak could not see his expression.

"The little—well, she isn't so little—the *skjölmdo.*"

"She did," Halldor said. He nodded toward the battlefield. "Did rather well too, according to the Holmgard."

"Did she?"

"Aye," Halldor let a grin slip across his face. "We saw the shield wall break as we came, the Danes overrunning the Jarl's men. The only reason they held at all was because of Sigrid. If we were the hammer, she was the anvil upon which we broke the Danes."

Kjallak's eyes grew wide in disbelief. "*Sigrid?* Her not yet twenty and never been in battle?"

Halldor had a strange expression on his face, one that Kjallak could not judge. "If we're to believe the stories the Holmgard tell, she killed more than a dozen Danes all by herself."

Kjallak stared at him suspiciously, but his suspicion rapidly melted into disbelief before becoming thoughtful consideration. Halldor had a peculiar sense of humor, but his expression was too intent—too serious—for this to be a jest.

"Berserker?" Kjallak asked.

Halldor shook his head. "According to those who witnessed her fighting, she showed none of the signs. And, as soon as the fighting was done, she stopped."

Kjallak nodded, still thinking. Berserkers were known for fighting on when the battle was over until they dropped from exhaustion, often injuring their own companions. "A potion?" he asked. "A method of setting aside her mind?"

Halldor shook his head to both.

"What, then?"

"*Vor,*" was Halldor's reply.

Kjallak frowned. *Vor?* In a fighter that young? That untested? *And* a woman? The idea was preposterous.

Most fighters at some point in their lives, either in practice or in battle, experience a moment where everything comes together, a moment of perfection where they can achieve the near impossible. It might last but an instant and might come to them only once, but this was the basis of *Vor*—the fate sight. The *Ordo Militum Vindicis Intactae* had long trained its knights to enter this state willfully in battle—extending it as long as they could sustain the focus—allowing them to fight with astonishing effectiveness. Several of the men in his company had shown promise—Halldor, the best among them. They were disciplined, exceptionally well trained; it was due to their ability to touch *Vor* that none of them had fallen in the battle.

But to kill a dozen men in the chaos of general battle? That seemed impossible. Even for an adept one who had been taught the inner mysteries.

"A gifted initiate? And a woman besides." He shook his head in disbelief. "It has never happened."

"It has," Halldor reminded him. "Once."

Kjallak's frown deepened. "There is much that is disputed about the founding of the Rock," he said, referring to the nickname the order gave to Týrshammar.

Halldor inclined his head, indicating that he didn't disagree with Kjallak. "But no one disputes her presence."

"Yes, well, and it was a bloody time for all," Kjallak snapped, disliking the direction of this conversation. "I'll not discount the possibility," he said, "but I'll not base any decision on idle battlefield reports from untrained eyes."

"We should look upon her ourselves, then," Halldor said quietly.

Kjallak couldn't stop the shiver that ran up his spine. Halldor had that iron calm about him, much like he had on the boat when it had been damaged. A resolute confidence that came from knowing something with complete conviction.

He knows, Kjallak thought.

His hip ached.

✦ ✦ ✦

Sigrid's wounds were minor, and in short order she was washed, bound, and poulticed as needed. The various cuts, bruises, and punctures had started to ache, and that coupled with the lack of sleep and morning's exertions left her exhausted. She drifted in a pain-haunted daze where they had seated her by one of the many fires lit to warm water for cleaning wounds and cooking.

She roused from her stupor when a platter was set before her: soup made from the leftover gravy and ox meat with chopped vegetables, a chunk of dense, black bread, a wedge of cheese, and a large mug of mead. She didn't have to be told twice to eat, for she was suddenly ravenous and thirsty both. She felt a momentary surge of nausea after the first few bites, but she simply swallowed and rode it out until it subsided, and then forced herself to continue eating.

Pettir had established this shelter as his command post, so Sigrid was in a good place to hear the aftermath of the battle managed. This meant first and foremost organizing the fighters still hale to follow after the Danes and ensure their rapid departure. Next, the Jarl's own people had to gather and treat their injured if their wounds were not mortal. They also gathered and cataloged the personal possessions of their own dead and returned them to their families.

The bodies of their enemies had already been looted, and all their possessions would be put into a pool to be distributed by Pettir, with the lion's share handed out to the families of the dead and the rest divided between Pettir and the fighters. Pettir would retain half of this store, and the remainder would be distributed equally among the men. Lastly Pettir would distribute special awards from his own share to those who had distinguished themselves in battle.

Certainly Sigrid was in line for a special award, and none could claim favoritism in this case. The surviving Shield-Brethren would also come in for special consideration for their role, and not just because they were guests and volunteers. They had fought with an effect out of proportion to their numbers. From what she heard from the Holmgard, it was their attack on the flank that had ultimately broken the Danes.

Äke was the one who told her about the casualties among the Sworn Men, and she lost her appetite upon hearing the news.

Skeggi and Ulf would not go *avikinga* come the spring after all. Sweet, funny Thorbjorn would never again lighten their days with his humor and japes. Gyrdh's young bride-to-be—her own childhood friend and playmate Hilary—was widowed before she was even wed.

Tears welled in her eyes as she thought of them—her brothers in arms and men she had known all her life.

Äke droned on, his voice as empty and lifeless as his report: in the end, fully half their order of battle was dead or expected not to live out the day.

"How..." she struggled to find the words to express what she was feeling. *How could people bear such losses? How could they go on when friends and family were taken from them, and many of them so young...*

"We will honor those who have fallen, Sigrid," Äke said, his eyes bright with tears. "We will live because that is the gift they have given us." He leaned over and picked up the mug she had been drinking from. He solemnly poured a measure on the ground, the mead spattering his boots, and then he drank deeply. He gave the mug back, and she poured out a similar measure, fighting back the tears that still yearned to spill down her cheeks. "We shall raise a toast to them tonight," she whispered. "And they will toast us as well, from the tables in Valhalla."

"Aye, that they will," Äke said. "The fishing boats are safe, and the scouts report that two of the four Danish boats were fired before they could get into deep water. We sent more of them on than they took from us."

◆ ◆ ◆

The folk assembled on the beach west of the fishing village as sunset approached. The able-bodied had amassed a huge pyre stacked with the bodies of the Danes. It had taken the entire day to gather enough wood and used most of the hold's oil to ensure that it would light quickly and thoroughly. Once lit, it would burn for days, tended by thralls and the villagers. Their own dead were laid on planks atop their foes, dressed in their best finery and armed with their favorite weapons.

As the sun brushed the edge of the sea, Pettir strode forward bearing a burning brand. Next came Kjallak and Grimhildr, each lighting brands of their own from his, followed by Halldor, Äke, Sigrid, and several others. They spaced themselves about the pyre, and as the sun touched the horizon, a horn sounded. They each cast their torches onto the pile of wood and corpses. The oil-soaked tinder caught quickly, and within moments the fire was a roaring tribute to the fallen, a light nearly as bright as the setting sun.

"Father of All, hear me!" Pettir proclaimed. "We send you this night our kin, fathers, brothers, husbands, and sons. Honor and keep them forever within your halls until finally they fight at your side in the Twilight of Days."

He accepted a cup of mead from a thrall and poured its measure on the ground before continuing.

"Ancestors of my people, hear my words and rejoice! Tonight our beloved kinsmen will join your ranks. Honor them and keep them well, for they have defended your children and brought glory to your people!" As he finished, women came forward, casting sheaves of early grain into the roaring fire—a tribute to Ostara, on whose day the battle had been fought.

"Honored Dead, hear my words and carry them with you into the Halls of the Father! Hold your heads high before the gods and your ancestors; you have fallen in defense of your land and loved ones, and there is no greater honor than this! We will hold you in our hearts and memories until that day when we once again stand at your sides, shoulder to shoulder and shield to shield, in the Twilight of Days."

There was no further sacrifice after this. Too many had given their blood to the land, and that was sacrifice enough.

Pettir, followed by those that had lit the pyre, strode through the crowd, heading for the berm that surrounded the village and the road beyond. He would walk, head held high, all the way back to the hold. Though they would grieve for those that they had lost, they would carry on—this was the debt they owed to their dead.

There would be another feast at the hold, one simpler than the one of the previous night, but it would be attended in greater earnest as they celebrated their victory and honored the fallen. Sigrid knew those who had remained behind at the hold—including those who had fled there from the village—would have been busy throughout the day, making preparations. They would not slaughter another ox, but there would be roast pig. Leftovers from Ostara's *blöt* would be gathered and reheated or extended as needed.

Sigrid found her appetite returning as she walked back to the hold. Her stomach made eager noises at the promise of more food.

"You are a healthy, passionate young woman, and a warrior to your core," Grimhildr said as she came alongside Sigrid.

"Pardon, Aunt?" Sigrid said. She had been lost in her own thoughts.

Grimhildr smiled, a hungry grin that spoke knowingly of what thoughts were racing through Sigrid's head. "Tonight," the older woman said, "in the wake of battle, you may find that you want a man as you have never wanted one before. It is the body's way to celebrate survival with an act of creation. It is natural and wholesome, but you must resist it if you can." She clicked her tongue and her smile returned. "And forgive yourself if you can't."

"I…cannot imagine being taken in by such thoughts today, Aunt," Sigrid said.

Grimhildr laughed and shook her head. "Choose your battles wisely, *skjölmdo*," she said. "Not all of them are fought with langsaex and shield."

Sigrid caught sight of Halldor, his head and shoulders above the other men around him, and she found herself blushing.

◆ ◆ ◆

She managed to avoid both her aunt and the man whom Grimhildr had undoubtedly been referring to during the feast at the hold. She ate sparingly and drank less, finding her body suffused with exhaustion. Nearly every muscle ached, and she could not comprehend how many of the men were drinking and eating in greater quantity than they had the night before. It was as if they were trying to eat not only for themselves but for those who had fallen as well.

At length, as she was beginning to nod off, Pettir stood and offered one final toast to the defenders. He waved his hand toward his thralls, and the day's bounty was brought forward. The men cheered as the Jarl began to distribute the plunder. First each of the surviving fighters was gifted with a small sack filled with rings and bracelets of silver and gold and a few gems or coins. Next came the time for special recognition for the heroes of the day, starting with the Shield-Brethren.

Pettir gave to Kjallak a beautifully ornamented torque of silver and gold. A saex knife of similar quality went to Halldor, and each of their men received a heavy armband of gold. Grimhildr was given more rings than she had fingers, as well as numerous chains of gold; Äke received a fine maille shirt.

"Sigrid," Pettir called out. She blinked heavily, staring dumbly at her father. She didn't understand why he was calling her name. Grimhildr shouted her name as well, and it was taken up by the others. She struggled to her feet, and pushed forward by the weight of the shouting around her, she walked to the high table.

"Sigrid, blood of my blood," Pettir said when the cheering died out. "This day you have shown yourself a hero to equal any in the Sagas! Without you even the Shield-Brethren would not have saved us. When the shield wall fell we thought all lost, but you fought with such skill and ferocity you took the heart of the Danes and broke their will to fight. This victory belongs to you more than any other."

She had expected to feel pride at his words, but her heart was in her mouth, and all she felt was an intense desire to run back to her table and hide beneath it. Pettir took her hands in his, holding her in place. He caught her attention, and as she looked into his eyes, she saw the truth of his words. "If I lived a thousand years and had a thousand children I could not be more proud than I am at this moment," he said.

"Father," she demurred, trying to pull away. Her embarrassment was even more acute. He let go of her, but only to place something in her hands. She gasped at the sight of the scabbarded langsaex.

Obviously one of the Danes had traveled far, for it was a langsaex in the style of the Rus far to the east. The hilt was like a narrow sword hilt in worked gold covered in knot work, and the scabbard fully framed in that metal with matching decoration. The horn handle had been incised with interlocking swirls in a style of decoration that she had not seen before.

"By the runes on its blade, this is Leg Biter," her father said. "May it never fail you or our people in time of need."

The men cheered, the voices thundering in her ears. She could not hear the words she mumbled to her father, but he nodded knowingly and grasped her head tightly to kiss her once on the forehead. Her face burning, her eyes stinging with tears, she stumbled back to her seat.

The others crowded to congratulate her, and she nodded distantly when someone asked to see the blade. It was handed around, and everyone agreed it was a fine prize. The horn handle was well shaped, and the decoration carved into it made for a secure grip. The blade was long and well balanced. It was a superb weapon, one meant for an impressive warrior.

At this point, their praise turned to her, and such attention made her ill at ease. She wanted nothing so much as to simply be left alone; at length she made her excuses and fled the feast, her new langsaex clutched to her breast.

SEVEN

━━

Sigrid woke with a groan. She felt like there wasn't any part of her without its own particular ache. She rolled out of her cupboard and almost kept going right to the ground. Straightening painfully, she fumbled into her trews and slipped her shoes on before staggering to the commode. She had washed yesterday after the battle, but doing so again, even in the ice-cold water from the rain barrel, made her feel better. She spent some time stretching and limbering up, and by the time she was dressed and entered the great hall, she felt almost human.

The hall, however, looked like a battlefield in truth, minus the gore and severed body parts. There were people scattered haphazardly, sleeping or passed out, on nearly every horizontal surface. The Shield-Brethren were already awake, though even they looked a bit frayed around the edges. Halldor acknowledged her entrance with a halfhearted wave of the spoon he was using to eat his breakfast porridge. Thralls moved about the room clearing things away and occasionally rearranging the sleepers to make them more comfortable—or simply to clear their paths so they could accomplish their work.

A thrall brought her a bowl of porridge with dried fruit and honey. Feeling a need to be away from people, she took the bowl into the kitchen yard and plunked down on a bench to eat. She was a sensible girl and not naive in the least. She knew that she was reacting to the battle, the killing and deaths of her comrades. In time she would find a new sense of herself and adjust, but for now, just for this moment, she wished to be alone.

Her privacy lasted little more than the time it took to eat her porridge. Äke walked into the yard with his own bowl and winced as he lowered himself next to her on the bench.

"Some say that the mercy of the gods is to allow us to forget what battle is like, but I think it's that we forget what it is like *after* which is the true mercy." He paused only long enough to shovel some porridge into his mouth. "How is your head and heart this morning, Sigrid?"

"Sore," she mumbled, wishing he would shut up and go away. She could feel him looking at her.

"We should practice," he said after a moment of examining her.

"Practice?" She raised her head and stared at him. "Why? Have you not had enough fighting?"

He shrugged. "I said nothing about fighting," he replied. "*Practice*," he repeated. "It is the best thing for you—head and heart. It will keep you from stiffening up, from being bound by the memory of the battle." He tapped his spoon against the rim of his bowl. "There are so few of us left," he said. "The Holmgard are not Sworn Men. Just because we have fought and won does not mean we can sit on our asses and grow fat. We have much to teach—"

"Shut up," Sigrid said. She shoveled the last bite of her breakfast into her mouth and then slammed the bowl down on the bench between them.

Äke smiled at her. "Get your gear," he said. "I'll be in the yard."

◆ ◆ ◆

Her armor-cote had been so blood soaked that the thralls had despaired of ever getting it clean, but after enough soaking and scrubbing it at least no longer smelled of sweat and gore. It did cling damply to her, hindering her movements and, more tellingly, irritating her.

Äke had already started drilling the Holmgard when she returned to the yard. Many had not participated in the battle and so were fresh enough, but they *had* participated in the toasts last night and more than one looked to be in foul temper and out of sorts.

Sigrid felt awkward and uncomfortable, and the weapons felt foreign in her hands, but she fell in with the others and managed to keep up with the drills. When Äke broke them into pairs for sparring, she found herself facing him. He started slowly, but she just could not seem to get into the rhythm of it. He kept slamming his shield into the knuckles of her sword hand, and he knocked her down more than once. After he hit her on the side of the head with the flat of his lang ax, he signaled a stop.

She ripped off her spangenhelm and threw it down, glaring at him. "I'm done," she snapped.

He said nothing, staring blandly at her through the slits of his helm. She dropped her shield as well, growing more frustrated as he said nothing. "What did you expect?" she snapped, more angry at herself than him by that point.

He shrugged. For a moment, he appeared to be about to say something, and then he shrugged again and turned away.

She threw her langsaex down as well, completely frustrated by him and the whole drill.

With a bellow of rage Äke spun, his ax flashing toward her head.

✦ ✦ ✦

"It's my own damn fault," Äke gritted through clenched teeth. "I shouldn't have surprised her like that…"

"Shut up and bite this," Grimhildr told him as she shoved a leather strap between his teeth. She grabbed him around his torso, holding him steady, while nodding to Halldor, who was gripping Äke's right arm in both hands.

"I'm going to count to three," Grimhildr said. "Are you—"

"Three," Halldor said, pulling and twisting the Sworn Man's arm.

Äke bellowed as his shoulder slipped back into place with an audible crunch. The Sworn Man spit out the strap and glared at Halldor. "She was supposed to count," he snarled.

"Is your arm better?" Halldor asked.

Äke blinked and gingerly moved his arm. His face twisted with pain, but his range of motion was good.

Grimhildr patted Äke on the shoulder—causing Äke to wince—as she stood up. "Thank him," she said to Äke. She seemed almost pleased that Halldor had—literally—taken matters into his own hands.

"Thank you," Äke ground out as he let his arm flop in his lap.

Halldor produced a small clay bottle from a pouch on his belt. Peeling away the wax seal with his thumbnail, he poured some of the contents in a small, shallow soapstone bowl. "This is *Uis Gë*," he said as he handed the bowl to Äke. "The druids swear that an open wound washed with it will not become infected."

Äke looked at him suspiciously as he held the bowl gingerly. "I don't have an open wound."

"It has other uses," Grimhildr said dryly. "Don't sit there and sip it like a virginal maid. Drink it down all at once."

Äke glared at her next, and his nose wrinkled as he sniffed the liquid in the bowl. With a final glance at Halldor, he raised the bowl to his lips and drank the contents in one gulp. A moment later he was gasping as he tried to catch his breath, tears streaming from his eyes. "Blood of our Fathers," he gasped, "it burns all the way down. Is this to help with the pain?"

"After a fashion. A couple of those and you'll still hurt," Halldor said as he poured another measure into the bowl. "You just won't care."

Äke took a deep breath to steel himself and drank it. "It's a little better the second time," he wheezed.

Halldor took the bowl and refilled it again, extending it to Grimhildr. "Once the seal is broken, it doesn't last if it isn't used," he said in reply to her questioning look.

She took the bowl and drank her measure quickly. Her grin was wide and fierce, her teeth clenched together as the *Uis Gë* burned its way into her belly. "*Ah*," she sighed. "It has been a long time since I've partaken of the Waters." Halldor poured a little more into the bowl, and as Grimhildr raised it to her lips, he brought the bottle up to his mouth and upended it, taking the last measure for himself.

It did indeed burn all the way down. He choked lightly, feeling as if he had just inhaled burning ash, and he pressed a knuckle against the edge of his right eye as tears started to form.

"So, Äke," Grimhildr said once they had all recovered, "why don't you tell us what possessed you to think that it was a good idea to surprise a warrior who had just felled a dozen men in battle as casually as she might step on so many bugs?"

Äke moved his tongue around his mouth, as if he were trying to clear any remaining drop of the *Uis Gë*. "You know how some of the young ones get after their first battle. She was showing all the signs. I just wanted to get some sort of reaction from her. Some sense that she wasn't trying to bury all that she knew."

"You're an idiot," Grimhildr said. "How can she forget what she doesn't really know she knows?" She looked at Halldor. "Truth is: she was an easy student. It was never difficult to teach her how to fight. She came to it all as if she was just remembering how to hold a langsaex. How to move. How to fight. I've been a warrior my life long, and never have I seen the likes of what I saw yesterday."

"I have," Halldor said.

"Aye," Grimhildr replied. "I thought you might."

Äke looked between them, a blank expression on his face, not understanding what they were talking about. There was a glimmer of something in his eyes. Halldor wasn't entirely certain, but it made him uneasy.

"Are you going to tell her father, or shall I?" Grimhildr asked. She gestured at Äke. "She can't keep breaking the Jarl's men every time she is surprised or out of sorts."

EIGHT

◆

Sigrid sat in a corner of the yard, hard at work removing a nick in the blade of her hewing spear with a stone. Nicks in blade edges needed to be carefully removed lest they turn into cracks, and she focused on the work, trying to shut out everything around her. Even when Malusha came and sat by her, spreading out some embroidery on her lap, Sigrid made no effort to interact with her cousin.

More than ever, she wanted to be left alone.

She didn't blame Äke. He was too full of bluster; being First among the Sworn Men and surviving the battle with the Danes only aggravated his sense of self-worth. He had thought he was doing her a favor, and perhaps he had done so, but the way he had gone about it had been so completely...*wrong*.

She could feel it—down in her belly, tingling in her fingertips—that unknowing knowing that had come over her as soon as he had spun back toward her, his lang ax raised. She couldn't drum up the memory of what she had done—all that was in her head was the image of the aftermath—but she would do it again. Without thinking.

"Here comes your giant," Malusha said quietly.

Sigrid focused on the edge of her spear, working the stone intently against the metal. Pretending not to hear her cousin. Pretending to be unaware of Halldor's approach. Malusha made a tiny noise in her throat and aped Sigrid's intensity with her own needlework.

Halldor nodded briefly at Malusha as he reached the pair. "I hope I am not intruding on some private talk," he said. He was carrying a pair of blunted training swords.

"No," Sigrid said, trying not to stare at the wooden weapons in his large hands. "We were just—"

"Enjoying the fine weather," Malusha finished for her. She grinned up at Halldor, pleasure at seeing the tall man clear on her face.

"It is a fine day," Halldor agreed.

"What do you want?" Sigrid asked, more bluntly than she meant.

Halldor took no offense at her tone. Without asking, he settled down next to her, leaning the pair of blunted swords against the rough-hewn wall of the palisade behind him. "Yesterday was your first battle," he said, talking as casually as if he were still discussing the weather. "Nearly all of your father's Sworn Men died, and many Holmgard would have too if you hadn't saved the day like a hero out of the Sagas. I saw little of it, as I was busy on the other side of the berm, but I have heard the stories."

Sigrid growled deep in her throat, wanting to tell him to go away, but was caught by a desire to hear him out.

"This morning you were caught flat-footed, surprised and scared out of your wits by Äke, your father's best man who is half again your size and has been a warrior since you were a babe in arms. You disarmed him and screwed his arm so far out that I wasn't sure I could get it back in."

Malusha made a disagreeable noise in her throat upon hearing the news, and Sigrid reached over and rested her hand on her cousin's back.

"Yet you did…?" Sigrid asked.

"Aye," Halldor said. "I did. He'll be sore for some time, though his pride may suffer a bit longer."

"I did not mean to hurt him," Sigrid said.

"You could have done much worse," Halldor said.

"Aye," Sigrid whispered, looking inside her breast at what lay in there. "I could have."

"That is what sickens you, isn't it?" Halldor asked. "You are confused, scared, and don't know what is happening to you. You don't know what to do, so you sit in the corner and mope like a little girl. Hoping that it will go away. That everyone will forget that you exist."

Sigrid's hands tightened in her lap as a hard knot formed in her breast. Her fingers started to burn. "Who are you to judge me?" she spit. "You don't understand. You can't understand."

"No?" Halldor said, raising an eyebrow. "Tell me then?"

"Why should I?" she retorted, her voice shaking.

"So that I can *understand*. So that I can help."

✦ ✦ ✦

"On the one hand, my heart is bursting with pride for what she did for us," Pettir said as he paced the length of his private chamber. "On the other," he continued, "I do not know her anymore. Have I done something to offend the gods? That they have taken my daughter from me?"

"She is still your daughter," Fenja said. The Jarl's wife reclined on the sleeping platform, her face still pale with exhaustion from the vision that had come over her the previous night.

Kjallak shifted his weight awkwardly, trying to stay off his stiff leg. Halldor had reminded him that if the Jarl's wife was, indeed, a Seer, then it was possible that the Virgin's Grace might manifest in the daughter as a natural *Vor* talent. Privately, he had a great deal of sympathy with the Jarl, but he had to keep that opinion to himself. It was not his place to intrude upon the family.

"Aye," Grimhildr said, agreeing with Fenja. "I've told you she had an uncanny ability. I told you she had the talent to be the best fighter you or I or anyone has ever seen. That was why you agreed to let her take her vows and become a *skjölmdo*. It wasn't just to please me."

A nervous chuckle bubbled out of the Jarl.

"We have some experience with this," Kjallak said. "At Týrshammar. I could speak to my elders and see if they would be willing to put her through a trial—"

"She is not a criminal," the Jarl snapped.

Kjallak spread his hands. "A poor choice of words, perhaps. Merely, that she be tested."

"And if she passes?" Fenja asked from the sleeping platform.

Kjallak shrugged. "I cannot make any promises beyond what I have already offered."

"So I could send her to Týrshammar, where she would be subjected to whatever trial you desire, and then she could be sent back *here*?" The Jarl glared at Kjallak. "How would that help her? She would be just as dangerous as when she left. More so, perhaps, having been *rejected* by you and yours."

"There will be no rejection," Kjallak countered.

Grimhildr snorted, and the Jarl continued to glare at him. "All she has ever wanted was to be a fighter. If I send her to Týrshammar, what chance is there that such a journey will end up crushing her spirit?" His voice rose. "What sort of father would I be?"

Fenja tried to shush the Jarl, but he cut her off with a hard stroke of his hand. "No, this stops now. It is too dangerous for her to continue to hold arms. I have few Sworn Men, and I cannot risk her injuring more of them. What if the Danes return? How will I defend my hold and my subjects? Do I send her first and hope that this…this *berserking* of hers will be enough? Do you suggest I sacrifice my daughter?"

"No," Kjallak said quietly when the Jarl ran out of breath. "That is not my suggestion. Not at all."

He was interrupted from saying any more by the Jarl's hauscarl, who opened the door and, somewhat apologetically, poked his head into the room. "My Jarl," he said, bobbing his head, "there is something you must see." He glanced at Kjallak and Grimhildr. "All of you," he said.

◆ ◆ ◆

Halldor waited patiently for Sigrid to speak of her experience on the battlefield, though he already knew she would not tell him. It did not matter overmuch to him, in any regard. He knew fairly well what she had experienced.

He sat quietly beside her, watching the folk come and go across the yard, listening to the sound of her breathing. Listening to the sound of Malusha's needle poking its way through the heavy fabric of the dress she was embroidering. He was thinking about his initiation at Týrshammar: the unease in his guts, the way his legs hadn't stopped shaking, the dryness of his mouth. His ears had become stopped up, and everything had become hollow sounding as if he were listening through a shell at the world. His sword had felt awkward in his hand, like it was something he had never held before, even though he had slept with it the night prior, his hand never leaving the hilt.

And then, when the master of the Rock had called upon him to strike with his sword, all of that had fallen away. As he had raised the weapon and struck, he had seen everything perfectly.

With a sigh, he heaved himself to his feet. He leaned over and picked up one of the two training swords. "Malusha," he said quietly, "perhaps it is time for you to take your needlework elsewhere."

Sigrid raised her head—her eyes bright, her face frozen in an angry mask.

He swung the wooden sword at her head, meaning to slap her with the flat of the blade, but she was already moving, shoving her cousin aside. Halldor backed up quickly, sensing how she was going to try to grab his blade, and he was slightly surprised when she went for the other training sword instead. She came at him in a rush, her sword coming at him even faster. He blocked it, the sound of the wooden blades ringing through the morning air. *Gods, she was fast.*

He attacked her with a fighting style he thought she would not know—one of the more advanced techniques taught at the Rock—and he was impressed at her intuitive grasp of the defenses. When he shifted into a more common set of attacks and defenses, she was almost too quick for him, moving into the counter of his counter almost before he did. She was reading his footwork before he finished; sensing the turn of his body before he started to move; and knowing where his blade would go before it even turned in that direction.

Her face was fixed in an expressionless mask, her eyes staring. He knew she was not seeing him. Her breath moved easily in her throat, and her body acted in complete concert with her sword.

She knew she was going to beat him and, for a moment, he thought she might.

And then the stillness that had been lurking in his belly rose up, filling his arms and legs. He let the *Vor* come over him, and he stopped worrying about her sword.

He sped up, without thinking, and she kept pace. She found ways to turn his attacks into opportunities for her own attack, but he always knew the counter and how he might regain the advantage. He was deep in the *Vor*, lost within its pure beauty. They were no longer fighting; rather they danced, they flirted, he courted her and she rebuffed him only to turn about and be rebuffed by him in turn.

Finally, knowing without realizing, she went to disarm him and he let her. As his sword flew out of his hand, she let go of hers too. In an instant, they were both weaponless, and as he stepped back, he felt the *Vor* leave him.

His body shook with an intense sorrow, but he pushed it down, deep within his belly, where it belonged.

◆ ◆ ◆

As the wooden sword left her hand, Sigrid staggered back, falling to her knees. She had no memory of what had happened since Halldor had warned Malusha, other than a long series of flickering images that were fading even as she tried to hold on to them. Gradually, she remembered where she was, and when she looked around the yard, she found her family and Kjallak standing nearby. As well as many other folk of the hold.

They were all staring—some looked stunned, some looked horrified—and her father wore a thoughtful expression. Only Halldor was smiling. She wanted to scream at them, to tell them nothing had changed, she was still their Sigrid, still the woman they had grown up with, had known all their lives. But she knew it was too late: the battle yesterday, her encounter with Äke, and now this bout with Halldor in the yard. She had become some new thing in their eyes. The Sigrid that they had all grown up with was gone, and this new person was...

She realized she did not know.

Still smiling, Halldor turned his head to the assembled watchers. "She's incredible," he said. "I've never fought so hard in my life."

"You shouldn't have been fighting at all," Kjallak snapped. "What did you think you were doing?"

"Showing us what we already knew," Halldor said. He wandered over to where his sword had fallen and picked it up.

"This wasn't your decision," Kjallak said.

"Nor is it yours," Halldor replied. "Nor theirs." He raised his sword in salute to Sigrid, and then turned and saluted the Jarl as well. "You should be proud of her," he said.

The Jarl flushed and nodded curtly at Halldor's words.

Halldor collected the other wooden sword, which meant his body was turned away from the group for a moment. He glanced at Sigrid. "Thank you," he said quietly.

He turned around and spoke once more to the group. "I am going to inquire of our horses," he said. "We should be leaving on the morrow. Eight of us, I suspect."

It was Kjallak's turn to bristle at the young man's words, but he said nothing as his second walked off, leaving Sigrid to face her family alone.

"Sigrid," her father began. His hands moved awkwardly, and he could not look directly at her. She had difficulty catching her breath, and all she wanted was to see his eyes. To know what he was feeling.

"Sigrid," he started again, finding his nerve. "You are hero to us all, equal to any…" His voice trailed off, and she realized he was only repeating what he had said the previous night at the feast. "I do not know what to do," he said instead, glancing at his wife and Grimhildr. "I have a responsibility to my folk, to the security of this hold, and yet she is my blood. She is…"

"Father," she started, but he stopped her with a terse shake of his head.

"Sigrid Pettirsdottir," he said, his voice clear and strong, "I release you from your oath as my Sworn Man, and you will set aside the practice of the warrior's arts. I command this for the safety of your fellows and the folk. We cannot afford more accidents as we had earlier."

"No," she whispered, feeling her legs stiffen.

"It is possible that you may take up arms and your oath again," he continued, fighting to hold back a strong emotion that threatened to overwhelm him. Beside him, tears were already starting to roll down her mother's cheeks, though Fenja's head was held high. "Kjallak tells me that the elders of Týrshammar may have some insight as to your…they may have an understanding that can help you overcome this affliction."

Sigrid's head swam with his words. An affliction? He thought she was cursed? His own daughter? Taught by his sister? She couldn't understand his decision, nor could she comprehend what he was saying. That she might not take up arms again, that all her life might revert to the model of a woman's in this man's world. She shrugged to calm her mind, to slow her breathing. To find something to cling to in this tumultuous wave of sensation and emotion that was roaring over her.

In her mind, she saw Halldor's face—both the calm and thoughtful expression that had composed his features during their duel and the resolute determination in his eyes as he had thanked her for the opportunity to fight. She felt a sensation very much like the *Vor* settle over her, and she took a deep breath, filling her lungs and frame.

"No," she said again, letting the air out of her lungs. Letting the word ring out more loudly.

She almost laughed at the panoply of expressions that crossed their faces. Her father was so shocked by her single word—her flat denial—that he could only manage, "Sigrid! What…?"

"I said no, Father." Her voice was stronger, flush with her resolve. "While you can release me from the oath I swore to you as you see fit, that does not mean that I have to become your little girl again. I am a woman grown. If you release me, then you release me as any other man. I am a free person. I will do as I see fit, and I will not abandon my arms or my arts. Had I any inclination to

allow a bunch of old men to decide my fate, I would not have chosen the warrior's path. But I did choose that path, and you can't
undo that decision."

"I do not know what you have become," her father said thickly.

"Then let me find out," she said. "Let it be *my* choice to find
out. That the elders of Týrshammar may know best how to deal
with this situation I grant; this is wisdom. If they must be con-
sulted, then I shall go and speak with them myself."

"Sigrid," her father tried again.

"No," she said, her voice harder than his had ever been to her.
"I have stood in a field of blood, fighting for you. I have put myself
in your shield wall to protect your hold and your lands. I have
killed men for you, and I will not meekly submit to your judgment
when it commands me to act against my honor, my training, and
my very nature."

She ran out of words and fell silent, staring at them. Waiting
for them to say something. To do something other than stand
there with their mouths hanging open like beached fish.

Finally, it was Kjallak who broke the silence. "My Jarl," he said,
and Sigrid caught his choice of words. "It has come to my attention that many of your Sworn Men gave their lives in order to
protect both your lands and me and my men. That is a debt I cannot easily pay, but perhaps I can alleviate some of that burden by
offering my services to you."

Pettir glanced blankly at Kjallak. "I do not understand," he
finally managed.

Kjallak rested his hand on his left hip. "I will be in no shape
to ride a horse for some time," he explained. "And several of my
men are in similar straits. We would throw ourselves upon your
merciful hospitality in the hope that our experience and training could be of benefit to you and your Holmgard. Many of your
Sworn Men have fallen and you just lost one more." He nodded at
Sigrid. "Allow us to make up the lack."

Grimhildr nudged Pettir. "He accepts your generous offer, Shield-Brethren," she said, fighting to keep from smiling. She nodded toward Sigrid. "If there were any doubt, brother of mine, that she was of your blood, there can be none now. All of my life I have never known anyone as stubborn and bull-headed as you. Until now." She made a small, ironic bow of respect to Sigrid.

Pettir sputtered for another minute or so, casting more than one sour glance at both Kjallak and Grimhildr. "She can't simply leave for Týrshammar on her own," he said, attempting to regain control of the conversation. "There are arrangements that must be made. Provisions, a letter of introduction, an escort..."

"Father," Sigrid interrupted him. "I'm not your little girl anymore," she said as she walked over to him and took his hands in hers. "I'm *skjölmdo*. I can take care of myself."

"And Halldor," Kjallak said. "Someone needs to watch over him on the road to Týrshammar." He glanced at Grimhildr. "Though I suspect that the two of you will strike terror in any Danes foolish enough to stand in your way."

"Aye," said Grimhildr. "And wouldn't that be a sight to see."

THE BEAST OF CALATRAVA
A TALE OF FOREWORLD

MARK TEPPO

ONE

"I am not a mountain goat, Brother Lazare," the rounder of the two priests complained as they skirted a wash of loose rock, detritus left in the wake of the ice and stone that had once flowed down the mountains into the valley behind them.

"Yes, Brother Crespin," the first priest replied. "Much like last week when you informed me you were not a badger." He paused, glancing back at his companion.

Crespin stopped several steps behind Lazare and leaned forward, one elbow on a knee, trying to catch his breath. They had been climbing for more than an hour now, and the camp below was small enough that it could be obscured with an outstretched hand. The bowl of the cirque was filled with a lush forest, and on their left, a silver cascade of water tumbled down. It flowed through the trees, emerging at the edge of the bowl—not far from where the Templars had set up their camp the previous night— and proceeded in a winding course down into Gascogne. On the other side of these mountains lay Aragon and Iberia.

"Is it not a magnificent view?" Lazare asked, his hands on his hips. "Were you indeed a mountain goat, you might be inured to the beauty of such an expanse, but how fortunate is it that you are not?"

Crespin turned slowly, placing his feet with care so that he didn't step on a piece of shale that might slip beneath his weight. "My heart trembles to be the recipient of such fortune," he said breathlessly.

Lazare skipped down the slope and clapped Crespin on the shoulders, startling the stouter man. "We congratulate ourselves with our ability to build churches, but what are they but hovels of mud and stick compared to the majesty of these mountains and the valley below us?"

"An observation you could have made an hour ago before we had started this climb," Crespin said, glaring at Lazare.

"Yes, but you would have accepted my words on faith, Brother Crespin," Lazare said. "Are they not imbued with much more gravitas now that you have seen God's majesty for yourself?"

"'Tis a lesson I would not have minded skipping," Crespin replied.

"And missed the opportunity to see what lies at the top?" Lazare shook his head. "Come now, Brother Crespin, we are almost there." He clapped Crespin on the shoulder once more and resumed his climb.

From the valley below, the upper rim of the mountains was an unbroken ring of stone cliffs, impassable to a company that included horses and wagons. Nor had their guides suggested they try to cross the Pyrenees here. The valley—with its bouncing spring of glacial runoff, open fields, and verdant forests—was simply a good location for a camp, and the Templar commander, Helyssent de Verdelay, had meant to stay for several days to replenish stores. While the senior religious official accompanying the army was the archbishop of Toledo, the task of providing sermons fell to Abbot Arnaud Amairic, the master of the small group of Cistercians, and the abbot was a priest who took his role as orator very seriously. Lazare and Crespin had dutifully offered their services to the knights, but as the company had seen no combat, nor had it ridden hard, there was little for the small company of Cistercian priests to do.

During his morning prayer, Lazare had noticed the notch in the cliff, and when he had inquired of the local guides about it, he had learned that it was known as Roland's Breach. From the valley floor, it did look like a cleft caused by a blade striking a stone. And, of course, learning this, he had to climb up and take a closer look. Crespin hadn't even tried to talk Lazare out of going; he knew that was a fool's effort.

The first part of the climb was the most strenuous, and for the last hour, the route had been no steeper than walking from the outer wall to the abbey at Clairvaux. The mountain air was crisp, and Lazare enjoyed the feel of it in his mouth and throat as he breathed deeply during the hike. Much like the water from the stream that ran by the camp, the air seemed purer as if indicative of its proximity to Heaven.

Unlike he and Crespin. Their white habits were streaked with dust from the rocky climb. Filthy creatures scrambling up the aged bones of God's creation.

As he reached the cleft, Lazare marveled at the precision of the cut through the rocky spur of the peak. While he waited for Crespin to catch up, Lazare paced off the width of the gap—just over twenty-six paces—and inspected the marbled wall of the cleft, running his hands over the rough stone.

Crespin reached the cleft and stood in the shade of the left-hand wall, looking at the mountain range the company of knights still had to cross before they reached Aragon. "Well," he said after he had caught his breath. "Here we are. Is it as marvelous as you hoped?"

There were loose stones at the bottom of the cleft, shards that had fallen from the walls; on the left-hand side, a knob of stone protruded from the cleft-face like a pustule waiting to burst; at the top, the edges were straight and there was no overhanging stone lip. Lazare left his hand on the rock, feeling its texture under his calloused hands.

"The guide told me the story of this breach," he said. "It was supposedly made by Roland when he tried to break his sword to keep it from falling into Moorish hands."

Crespin glanced up at the walls of the cleft. "You have heard a different version than I," he said. "I don't recall Roland being a giant."

"Of course, he wasn't," Lazare replied. "Looking at the stones of battlements and walls, haven't you seen cuts like this and wondered what happens when steel meets stone?"

"I haven't for I know that—in most instances—stone wins. Even if notches like this are made," Crespin admitted, his mouth turning down as if he had sampled something sour. He looked up at the knob of rock above his head. "Is this why we came up here? For you to fondle the stone?"

"No one knows where his sword went," Lazare said. "When the Saracens overran Charlemagne's rear guard, Roland rallied the Christians with Oliphant and Durendal."

"He had an elephant?"

"No," Lazare laughed. "He had a hunting horn."

"And he called it *Oliphant?*" Crespin frowned. "I suppose *Durendal* was the name of his sword."

"Yes, it was. Supposedly its hilt contained relics that gave its wielder great powers."

"But the Saracens killed him," Crespin pointed out.

"It took a great number of Saracens," Lazare responded. "Thousands."

"Thousands," Crespin repeated. His gaze roamed around the loose rock in the cleft between Gascogne and Aragon. "I don't see it," he said. "I fear the magic sword with a name isn't here."

"No," Lazare said wistfully, "it isn't. Nor did I find it in Rocamadour where the monks think it landed after Roland threw it."

"Rocamadour," Crespin said. "That's quite far from here. Even for a giant, which he wasn't." He sighed and levered himself to his feet and approached the other priest. It was his turn to rest his hands on Lazare's shoulders. "It's just a sword, Brother Lazare, and one that was, most likely, of much lesser quality than the blades you have made. You shouldn't trouble yourself so much with this obsession with magic swords. Magic isn't what makes a sword strong. Faith is. Let your faith reside with God. God will guide your arm. God shows you how to make strong steel just as he directs my hand when I place the stones and raise my arches. We are His instruments."

"You are right, Brother Crespin," Lazare said, sighing. "It is just a sword."

"Come then," Crespin said, squeezing Lazare's shoulder. "Let us make the much less arduous journey back to the camp. Perhaps the Templar commander has discovered a spot of rust on his blade and he will need you to clean it."

"I am but a mere instrument of God's," Lazare said wryly. "It is my duty to serve."

"Precisely." Crespin idly knocked some of the dust from his robe as he started back down the trail. Behind him, he heard Brother Lazare mutter quietly, "Though, to name a sword..." Crespin shook his head as he kept walking.

TWO

⟶

Ramiro Ibáñez de Tolosa followed the dry river bed along the base of the hill. The ground was rocky enough that he kicked up little dust as he moved, and with his dun-colored clothing, he could be mistaken for a large stone should he stop and raise the cowl of his robes. The only sound he made as he walked was a light tapping of the butt of his oak staff against the rocks.

His torso was thick and short, out of proportion with his long arms and legs, and his head was a sturdy block atop his broad shoulders. His dingy gray hair was long and untamed, unlike his beard, which was neatly trimmed along the edge of his jaw. Unlikely allies, the beard and hair conspired to hide the long scar that pulled the left corner of his mouth down, but little could be done to hide the missing tip of his nose.

Scar tissue notwithstanding, his sense of smell was not diminished, and it was the odor of cooking meat that he was following. The river bed wound around the base of the plump oak-covered hill, and he knew it turned to the west just past an outcropping of splintered rocks that served as a dependable windbreak against the storms that drifted up from the south. He could have approached the lee of the rocky break from above, but the oaks were not dense enough on that side of the hill to conceal his approach. The rocks obscured the course of the dry river bed, and unless they had posted a lookout, he would be able to sneak up on the camp without anyone noticing him.

He saw no watcher in the obvious position atop the rock, and as he came up on the edge of the ragged edge of the splintered stone, he heard voices and the crackling of a fire. The smell of roasting goat was much stronger. Even before he came around the rock, he had decided there would be at least three men sitting around the fire.

There were four—one was lying on his back a little distance from the fire, and judging from the bloodstained rags clutched to his stomach, he had a reason to be less talkative than the others. The other three wore stained tunics that militia typically wore under maille hauberks, though Ramiro saw no evidence of chain shirts in their scattered baggage. They wore no colors, showed no insignias or seals, and their swords were plain and worn. *Deserters,* Ramiro decided as he cleared his throat and tapped his staff lightly against the nearby rock.

"Pleasant day to roast a goat," he said, nodding toward the smoking carcass hanging over the recently made fire. He spoke slowly and carefully, making sure that his lips closed when they should with each word so that the men would be able to understand him.

Two of the four scrambled to their feet, their hands falling on their worn sword hilts. The dying man flinched, reacting more to the sudden movement from the others than from Ramiro's words. The other man remained seated beside the fire, though his hand drifted toward a long knife stuck through his belt. The two standing were nervous, their eyes bouncing back and forth between the seated man and Ramiro, waiting for some signal.

"It is," the seated man said. "Did you—" He swallowed his words, and his eyes slid off and then returned to staring at Ramiro's angular nose.

"Yes," Ramiro said, nodding politely. "You can smell it for quite some distance. If there are scavengers in these hills, I suspect they're already watching you."

"Is that what you are?" the man asked. "A *scavenger?*"

"Diego!" one of the standing men hissed.

"He's not a priest," the seated one—the one named Diego—said. "Not with that face. And—"

"Why not?" Ramiro interrupted. The man stared at him, and he gestured at his scarred visage. "Why couldn't a man like me be a servant to God? Does God care what I look like?"

The one who had hissed at Diego tried to smile as he stepped toward Ramiro. "My friend means no disrespect," he said. "He—we—have been traveling for some time. We have not eaten a decent meal in days. It makes us forget our manners."

"Yes, I can see that," Ramiro said. "That goat, for instance, was not yours to slaughter."

The halfhearted smile on the man's face faltered and he hesitated, licking his lips as he glanced over his shoulder at Diego. Looking for a signal. Diego inclined his head a fraction and the man's hand tightened on the hilt of his sword.

As the ruffian began to draw his sword, Ramiro stepped forward and rapped him smartly on the knuckles with the tip of his staff. The tip then caught the man in the chin, knocking him back into the arms of his friend. Ramiro took another step, letting go of the staff with one hand and whirling it around his head. Diego, half rising, leaped back to avoid getting struck in the head by the fast-moving end of the oak staff, and he ended up on his ass beside the dying man. Far enough away to not be any concern for a moment or two.

Ramiro swept his staff around, keeping the pair of swordsmen at bay, and then he brought the staff back into a two-handed grip. The one who had spoken managed to pull his sword free of its scabbard on his second attempt, and he came at Ramiro with a clumsy thrust. Ramiro stepped to the side, using his staff to knock the man's sword blade away from his chest. He snapped the staff back with his hands, catching the man on the side of the head, just below the ear, with a vicious hit. The man's teeth clicked as they snapped together, and he collapsed instantly, his limbs flopping like those of a child's rag doll.

The second man had to step over his fallen friend and his attention dropped to his feet as he came, his sword raised high. Ramiro closed the distance between them, catching the man under the arm with his staff. He shoved the staff up, forcing the man to raise his arm over his head. Ramiro flicked the end of his staff not once but twice, smacking the man in the face with each strike. After the second hit, the man staggered back, his sword hanging loosely in one hand.

Ramiro scooped up the first man's discarded sword and turned to assess the situation. Diego had gotten to his feet and drawn his knife, but when he was confronted with both sword and staff, his grip loosened and the knife fell to the ground. "My sincerest apologies to the owner of this goat," Diego said, bowing his head. "Would that I could return what has been lost, but alas the beast is dead and burned."

"Who is your master?" Ramiro asked, ignoring the other's efforts to ingratiate himself.

Diego flushed, and he gazed down at his discarded knife for a second as if he were considering picking it up again. "We're not slaves," he said. "We're free Castilians."

"We're not in Castile," Ramiro pointed out.

The two men on the ground had both recovered from their ignominious treatment at Ramiro's hands and had carefully crept out of range of both sword and staff. The one who had been struck beneath the ear tried to glare at Ramiro, but his eyes kept wandering. The other one had tried to wipe away the blood from his nose, leaving a red smear across his left cheek.

"Don Enrique Rodríguez de Marañón," Diego said.

"He's dead," the one with the bloody face blurted out.

"Not by our hand," Diego said quickly, forestalling a conclusion that he feared Ramiro might be leaping to. "When the Moors took the citadel at Puertollano."

"When?" Ramiro asked, his heart quickening. Puertollano lay to the north and west; while that land was claimed by both the Almohad caliphate and kings of Castile and Aragon, there had been few skirmishes between Christian and Moor in the last few years.

"A week ago," Diego said. "They overwhelmed us. We only had a dozen knights and"—he gestured at his companions—"not enough men. They captured Don Enrique and two other caballeros. The rest of us were not worth ransoming, and they would have killed us had we not fled."

Ramiro let his gaze wander across the supine member of their group, taking in the bloodstained bandages, the pale skin, the thick sheen of sweat. The man had sustained his wound more recently than a week ago. "And where are you going?" he asked, his gaze returning to Diego.

"North," Diego said, lifting a hand and pointing along the verge of the forest behind Ramiro, as if such motion might make up for the lack of specifics in his reply.

It was the wrong direction, but it was away from Ramiro's villa and orchards. Ramiro nodded. "Then you should continue on your way," he said.

"Now?" Diego asked.

Ramiro nodded.

"But what about the goat?" one of the two men complained.

"It's not your goat," Ramiro reminded him.

"But—" the man continued, and Diego cut him off with a hiss. He gestured for the others to gather their gear as he strode around the fire toward their scattered baggage. The pair followed his lead and began gathering up their meager belongings.

Ramiro walked around the other side of the fire to inspect the wounded man more closely. He was bleeding from the belly, and his breaths were shallow and slow. His eyes remained closed as Ramiro knelt and touched his forehead, feeling the heat of his fever.

"What of your friend?" he asked. "He certainly won't last *another* week."

The man beside him, as if summoned from the depths of his fever by Ramiro's voice, slowly opened his eyes. They grew even larger as he saw Ramiro's disfigured face, and his chest rose and fell with increasing desperation. He opened his mouth, and if it was to speak or scream, none of them would ever know as his life ended before he could draw enough breath.

The sight of Ramiro frightening a man to death spooked one of the two men, who left off gathering his belongings and ran, sprinting for the forest along the hillside. The second man followed suit, and only Diego lingered for a second, sneering at Ramiro in a fit of false bravado. "Monster." He spat into the fire before he followed the others.

Unmoved by the reaction of the men, Ramiro calmly closed the corpse's eyes and mouth before turning his attention to the goat roasting on the fire. It was one of six he kept; earlier in the day he had noticed it missing. The mystery was now solved, but the reason for its disappearance was troubling.

The Almohads were moving north. War was coming to Iberia again.

THREE

Upon hearing the commotion at the rear of the cathedral, Brother Lazare raised his head from his silent prayer and looked over his shoulder. A messenger was in earnest conversation with the archbishop's steward, and both kept glancing toward the choir of the cathedral where Rodrigo Jiménez de Rada, the archbishop of Toledo, continued to pray. Kneeling behind the archbishop, Helyssent de Verdelay, the Templar commander, stirred slightly but he did not succumb to the same curiosity that had overtaken Lazare. On the archbishop's left, Abbot Amairic was intent on matching the archbishop's focus in prayer.

Lazare sensed that Crespin was trying to get his attention with a wide-eyed glance and a surreptitious head shake, but Lazare ignored him. He was done with his vigil; he didn't have the same need to impress the archbishop with his religious fervor. Levering himself to his feet, he walked stiffly toward the nave. *How long had they been praying?* he wondered. *Two hours?* He was out of practice with such demonstrations of piety, though he felt that God would forgive him. Some of His servants were meant for duties other than personal sacrifice and rigorous abasement. As he reached the wooden gate that separated the choir from the nave, he waved at the pair.

The messenger scurried over, his head bobbing up and down as he attempted to bow and walk at the same time. "His Majesty, King Sancho the Strong, has received word of your arrival in Pamplona," the messenger said hurriedly. "While he regrets he cannot receive the archbishop immediately, he hopes that you will join him at his estate for a late supper."

Lazare's stomach sounded noisily at the idea of dining at the king's table, and he quietly lamented that he hadn't anticipated the archbishop's tenacity. Somewhat sourly, he glared at the archbishop's steward, Bartholo, a thin man with sunken cheeks, who now appeared beside them. "Did you press upon this gentleman the earnestness of the archbishop's desire to wait right here for the arrival of the king?"

Bartholo nodded, one eyebrow raised. When he spoke, he moved his lips as little as possible. "I did."

Lazare knew better than to wait for the archbishop's steward to elaborate. The man was incredibly sparing with his words. During more than a few of the abbot's endless sermons, Lazare wished that the abbot could take his cues from Bartholo's reticence. But, in fact, perhaps he had; the last few hours had been the quietest period Lazare had ever spent in the abbot and archbishop's presence.

The messenger scratched the side of his neck and shuffled his feet, nervous gestures that Lazare immediately read as signifiers of guilty knowledge. "Is there a response you would like me to take back to His Majesty?" the messenger asked.

"No," Bartholo said, and Lazare raised his hand to forestall the messenger's departure.

"A moment," he asked, considering how to resolve this impasse between church and king. He didn't know the details of any history between the archbishop and King Sancho, but there was clearly some unresolved enmity that was driving each man to pressure the other. The archbishop was going to remain in the cathedral, praying and fasting, until the king of Navarre deigned to present himself; Sancho was pretending to be too busy to see the archbishop, making the Church wait upon his leisure. Lazare had seen this sort of nonsensical behavior compound difficulties between rulers and churchmen. The simplest disagreement could turn into armed conflict over these sorts of slights. Was attempting to mediate this dispute within the bounds of his role as a monk of the Cistercian order, or would doing so reveal his own interests in a way that would draw unwanted attention?

The archbishop needs the support of Navarre, he thought, trying to figure out the priest's motivation. The army of northern knights the archbishop had assembled wasn't enough; the kingdoms of Iberia needed to work together. *How was this impasse helping the crusade against the Moors?*

"What's going on?"

Lazare turned to greet the Templar commander who had finally succumbed to temptation. Helyssent de Verdelay thought he was taller than he was, and he carried himself with his head back so that he could look down his nose at those with whom he spoke. And when he did speak, his large teeth were prominently displayed.

"A messenger from King Sancho," Lazare said.

"Where is he?" Helyssent demanded, as if the king of Navarre were nothing more than a truculent manservant.

"Perhaps it might be best if I were to accompany you," Lazare said to the messenger, ignoring the Templar's query. Answering it might provoke Helyssent into a diatribe about the arrogance of provincial rulers—a rant Lazare had no desire to suffer through. "I would be more than happy to offer my apologies to the king in person," he continued. "There is no reason for you to be burdened any further by this delicate conversation."

The messenger nodded vigorously. "Yes, Father," he said. "I think that would be best."

"Please," Lazare corrected him. "I am a just a lay brother of the Cistercian order. *Brother* Lazare is fine."

"You still haven't told me what is going on," Helyssent demanded.

Bartholo raised an eyebrow as he glanced at Lazare.

"Very little," Lazare said with a sigh. "The archbishop is praying, the king is not here, and I wonder if the possibility of a visitor, such as myself, might help bring all of this to a much more expedient resolution."

Helyssent stared at him for a moment and then looked back at the archbishop and the abbot. "Very well," he said. "My men and I will be continuing on to Toledo in the morning, with or without the priests. I am not interested in local politics. They have no bearing on our crusade."

Meaning there are no spoils to be won, Lazare thought, biting his tongue to keep the words from coming out of his mouth. Helyssent narrowed his eyes as if he suspected what was on Lazare's mind, and his nostrils flared in an imperious sniff. "I am going to the inn," he announced to Bartholo. "God knows of my love for Him. I do not need to continue prostrating myself."

Bartholo inclined his head, and Lazare stepped quickly out of the way as the Templar commander shoved open the gate between the choir and the nave. With a final sniff of derision, Helyssent departed.

Lazare was somewhat taken with the idea that the Templars might go on without the rest of the archbishop's party. He tried not to let his enthusiasm show.

✦ ✦ ✦

The messenger apologized for not having more suitable transportation from the cathedral, but Lazare dismissed the other man's concerns with a wave of his hand. It felt good to walk, and the messenger's pace made him stretch his legs to keep up. Pamplona was not unlike Paris or Carcassonne—a burgeoning city that was not so far from its ramshackle youth that the accretions of growth weren't readily visible. Around the Cathedral of Saint Mary, the buildings were made from stone and sunbaked brick, and the streets were straight and wide; as Lazare and the messenger moved north, their route traced a path through a maze of crooked alleys and haphazard lanes that made no sense to Lazare. The buildings that crowded the street were newer than the aged stone structures near the cathedral, but they weren't built as robustly. Some of them leaned slightly, as if they were looming over the street.

And then the architecture changed again. The streets became wide boulevards, lined with walls that marked the edges of villas owned by landowners and Navarrese nobility. Ahead, the street opened into a round plaza; in the center were three fountains surrounded by low hedges. Beyond, Lazare spotted the towers of the castle keep, the residence of the king of Navarre. Soldiers patrolled the plaza, wearing the king's colors.

The messenger led Lazare toward the castle, and when they neared the main gate, he gestured that Lazare should wait while he spoke with the guard. Lazare idled out of earshot, quietly examining the swords carried by the guards. French blacksmiths were much less inclined to fanciful cross guards and pommels on their swords.

"Come with me," one of the guards said, waving Lazare over. Lazare nodded and let the man lead him through the gates and into the castle proper. There was the usual bustle about the grounds of the castle yard, and Lazare found his attention straying toward the smithy when he heard the sound of the smith's hammer ringing against a piece of unfinished steel. Lazare lost track of his escort momentarily and looked about for the man, somewhat confused that he wasn't being taken to the main keep. When he spied the man once more, he hurried after him.

They went around the main keep, slipping between a barracks and the stables, until they reached a secluded yard, set off by a low wooden wall. The arena had a floor of hard-packed dirt, and it was large enough to exercise several horses or perform martial drills with dozens of men. Four men stood in the center of the arena, and a dozen or so more were arranged along the nearest fence; they were all watching the single horse and rider who were galloping around the circuit of the yard. The rider was the tallest man Lazare had ever seen, made taller by the height of his proud mount. The horse was as gray as a winter sky, and its mane and tail were long and luxurious, combed more often than Lazare attended to his own hair.

"King Sancho," his escort pointed out in case Lazare was oblivious to the identity of the rider.

Lazare nodded absently as he wandered close to the railing, where he became aware of a swell of noise from the watchers. He couldn't make out any individual words; they were like the wind moving through trees in the forest. The men in the center of the arena were calling out individual words of praise at least, though Lazare could not fathom what activity of the king's was eliciting such boisterous approval.

The third time the horse and rider passed, Lazare noted that the king was looking at him. King Sancho had a broad face with wide-spaced eyes and a flat nose. He didn't appear to be enjoying his ride all that much, and Lazare thought he saw a flicker of curiosity in the king's gaze as he galloped by. On the fourth pass, the horse came to a complete stop directly in front of Lazare with no sign that the king had given the horse any direction.

Lazare took such mystery as a sign that he should abase himself, and he did so, touching his forehead to the rough wood of the railing. His Castilian wasn't nearly as good as his *langue d'oc*, but he stuttered out a few honorifics, focusing his efforts on praising the beautiful horse.

"I wasn't aware the Cistercians knew much about horses," Sancho said in *langue d'oc*.

Lazare kept his head down. "Not as much as the king of Navarre knows of the land beyond the northern mountains," he said.

"Bah," Sancho said. "It was my sister's husband. He couldn't even bother to learn his own tongue, much less his bride's native language." He shook his head. "You have an eye for horses. Are you one of the knights of Calatrava?" he asked.

Lazare looked down at his once-white but now rather dingy robe, momentarily wondering if the king saw something that no one else in the last few years had discerned. "I'm sorry, Your Majesty," he said. "I am merely a priest. I pray for God's mercy; I don't go to battle in his name. Not like the Order of Calatrava."

"Why not?" Sancho asked. "They were monks once and then they became knights. The Templars are priests, are they not?"

"They are," Lazare said. "But they study the arts of war and not the arts of piety and devotion."

"Can a man not be devoted to God through feats of battle?" Sancho inquired.

"Yes," Lazare said. "Well, no. It is not...proper devotion to God..." He trailed off as he realized he was not presenting himself very well.

Sancho laughed at his discomfort, and several of the nearby courtiers tittered in kind, echoing the king's mirth with a vapid hollowness. "Is this how the archbishop means to sway me? By sending a dottering fool of a priest?"

Lazare flushed and raised his head. "I am not the archbishop's fool," he snapped, denying the king's accusation even though the very thought was making his cheeks sting with embarrassment.

"No?" Sancho raised his right eyebrow. "Then who are you, and why have you interrupted my morning ride?"

It was a very good question, and Lazare realized he had mere moments before his efforts pushed the archbishop and the king farther apart. The delay in arranging an audience with the king had nothing to do with the monarch's busy schedule. Lazare did not know who had offended whom, but it was clear there was an unresolved dispute between the two—one that was probably more about an imagined slight than any real injury. Each man wanted the other to show contrition first. "Your horse is truly magnificent," he said quickly, focusing his attention on the mount more than the rider. "As is your city and its people. They reflect the love you have for them."

Sancho's horse tossed its head and pawed the ground, eager to return to running. The king said nothing, though his gaze remained on Lazare.

"Archbishop Rodrigo is on his knees at the Cathedral of Saint Mary," Lazare continued, "and gives every sign that he will be there for some time. The abbot of my abbey, Arnaud Amairic of the Cistercian order, prays next to him. It is regrettable, Your Majesty, that neither can step outside that house of God and see the same things that I have seen. Your city. Your people." Lazare raised his hand gingerly toward the horse who extended its head and blew air on his knuckles. "Your horse."

Sancho laughed and nodded curtly at the guard standing behind Lazare. "You will join me for a meal when I am finished," he said, "and we can discuss my city and my people. And whether or not you are a fool." Without waiting to hear Lazare's reply—not that any reply was necessary—he tapped his heels lightly against his steed's sides. The animal tossed its head and trotted off, gathering speed as it returned to its run.

◆ ◆ ◆

Lazare managed to extract some of the story from the king's steward while he waited for the king to finish exercising his horse. There was a complicated history between the kingdoms of Navarre, Aragon, Leon, and Castile that went back more than ten years.

A treaty with the Almohad caliphate had allowed the kings of Spain to quarrel amongst themselves, and there were some lands that both Castile and Navarre claimed as theirs.

Almost as an afterthought, Lazare mentioned the king's sister and was rewarded with a name: Berengaria. He mentally chastised himself for not recalling this detail earlier. Berenegaria had been married to the king of England, Richard the Lionheart, and he recalled the tension that had swept the Frankish lands during the English king's unexpected stay at the court of the Holy Roman Emperor. The French king, Philip, had taken it upon himself during Richard's incarceration to annex some of the lands that had belonged to Berengaria, and by extension, Sancho's family.

Some time later, Lazare mulled over what he had learned as he waited in an audience room. This sort of internal conflict among Christian rulers was not uncommon, but he sensed there was something more complex about the disputes between the Iberian kings. The steward had intimated that, on occasion, the various kings had allied with the Moors against other Christian rulers. He was starting to wonder how safe it was to insert an army of French crusaders into this complicated history when the door to the chamber was thrown open and King Sancho entered, ducking to clear the doorway. Sancho held a goblet in his hand, and several servants scurried in behind him, bearing trays of food and pitchers of wine. Sancho swaggered over to the balcony and stood beside Lazare, slurping noisily from his goblet. "Has my steward explained everything to your satisfaction?" he asked.

Lazare flushed. He had felt quite clever in how he thought he had managed to get the steward to tell him of recent events. "He has, Your Majesty."

"Why are you participating in this charade? Not because you hope to save men on the field of battle." He said the latter matter of factly, and Lazare appreciated his outspoken brusqueness.

"No, Your Majesty," he admitted. "My Cistercian brothers and I hope to be of assistance to the Order of Calatrava—they are our brothers, after all." He left off mentioning Amairic's role in the procession from France to Toledo, deciding that since Sancho had not asked specifically, he would not volunteer any information. "But we are not knights like they," he said, keeping the conversation focused. "Brother Crespin is a stone mason, for example, and I am knowledgeable in the artifice of steel."

"Stone and steel, eh?" Sancho drank from his goblet. At Lazare's elbow, a servant tried to give him a goblet of wine as well, and Lazare hesitated for a second before accepting. The wine was warm and red; it wasn't sour at all, and he found himself gulping it all too readily. "So they mean to retake Calatrava?" Sancho asked.

"The Templars do," Lazare said. Which was true.

Sancho nodded, his lips pursed in a grim line. "What was once theirs must be theirs again," he said.

Lazare nodded. He knew the history of the Order of Calatrava. The citadel at Calatrava had been a Templar stronghold, but they had relinquished it many years ago when they could no longer muster the knights to keep it secure. The king of Castile had offered it to anyone who could defend it and two Cistercian priests—Father Raymond, abbot of the monastery in Fitero, and Father Diego Veláquez—put aside their previous duties and had taken up the sword. Naming their order after the citadel, they had stood fast against Moorish invaders until 1195 when the Almohad army swept across the plain of Alarcos. The Templars had been gone long enough from Iberia that their claim to Calatrava was fairly specious, but who was to deny the Templars what they wanted? Especially when getting what they wanted meant driving the Moorish threat out of Iberia?

"Do you know that the Pope sides with the king of Castile in this crusade?" Sancho asked. "His offer of holy redemption for those who fight in God's name comes with the decree that no

Christian may take up arms against another Christian during this conflict."

"I think that is not an unwise decree regardless of any crusade, Your Majesty," Lazare said.

"And yet, the lands that Alfonso has taken from me remain his, and the lands that the archbishop and these Templars seek to conquer will become Castilian. What benefit is there for Navarre in this crusade?"

"Before I met Your Majesty, I would have said that the security of all Christians is benefit enough, but I fear I do not know enough of the history between Navarre and Castile and the Moors to make such a claim," Lazare admitted. "The Pope, in Rome, sees the Almohad caliphate as an enemy that must be destroyed, but Rome is very far away, isn't it?"

"It is," Sancho said. "Rome knows little of the history of the peninsula. His proclamations of crusade, along with his threats of interdiction and excommunication, can be as readily abused as they can benefit the kingdoms of Iberia."

Lazare nodded, thinking of the ongoing struggle between the people of England and King John. At the Cistercian abbey in France, there was little awareness of the complex issues that separated king and subject. How could anyone—especially a spiritual ruler hundreds of miles removed—issue broad proclamations against a perceived enemy and not fail to misread the nuances of the conflict?

"I remember stories, from when I was a child, about Richard the Lionheart and the treaty he made with Saladin," Lazare said. "He was pilloried for failing to conquer the Holy Land, but he managed to secure assurances that Christians could make the pilgrimage to Jerusalem safely. He thought that was a satisfactory victory."

"Aye," Sancho said. "It was." He gazed at Lazare intently as he drank from his cup. "The archbishop of Toledo went to France to gather an army to aid the king of Castile and, on his return, he deigns to stop in my kingdom to speak to me about setting aside my differences with Castile against the Moors. Why did he not seek this audience with me *before* he went to France?"

Lazare swallowed another sip of wine before answering. "Because he didn't have an army with him before he went to France," he said carefully. Without an army, any conversation between Sancho and the archbishop would have been between Navarre and the Church in an attempt to set aside differences between Navarre and Castile; now, it was not a conversation, but a veiled command to join the crusade against Castile's enemies.

"The archbishop can come to me if he seeks my assistance," Sancho said. "Otherwise, he and his army of marauders should march on to Castile as swiftly as possible. And you"—he pointed a finger at Lazare—"I hope you are a better smith than you are a diplomat."

"The last is undoubtedly true, Your Majesty," he said before he gulped the rest of his wine. "As to the former, I will deliver your words to the archbishop, and I am certain the Templars are already inclined to move farther south expeditiously." He bowed to the king, and turned to depart.

"Priest," Sancho called, bringing him up short. "What you have said about aiding the knights of Calatrava, does that extend to other people of Iberia as well?"

"Why wouldn't it?" Lazare asked, though he wondered if he fully understood Sancho's question.

FOUR

Rain water sluiced off the narrow overhang of the porch, spattering the muddy ground around the villa. The clouds were portentous and gray, and they hung low in the sky, trapping the chilly air close to the ground. It had been raining since the previous night, the skies weeping a continuous stream of water as if hidden dams that had been frozen shut since winter began were now open.

Ramiro sat on a wooden stool, a wool blanket wrapped around his aching shoulders. He always felt the seasonal change coming, a dull throb in his jaw and left shoulder. It had been a week since he had run off the deserters and buried the dead man in the hills; two nights ago, the dreams had come back. Nightmare memories of the battle at Alarcos. The last defense of the old citadel. The waves of armed Moors scampering up the siege ladders. The lines of archers sending volley after volley of arrows over the walls. The screams of the dying Christian soldiers to whom no succor could be given.

And then the dreams would change. The Moors would grow furry legs and their helmets would turn into glowing eyes. Their curved swords would become wicked fangs, and they would scramble across the stone bulwarks of the citadel with a nimbleness that defied rational thought. The dead would reanimate, and the shambling ranks of rotting soldiers were a solid wall behind him, constantly pressing forward against the few living knights. They couldn't fall back, not with the ranks of the moaning dead behind them. They could only stand their ground against a monstrous enemy that boiled over the walls.

In the dream, he already had his scars and the dead flocked to him because he was the least disfigured of them all. He was their radiant king, and they all rallied at the sound of his beautiful voice. He always woke just after he gave the command to push the eight-legged invaders back, the throaty sound of his shout echoing in his ears.

Several of the goats called out to him from the pen, and he shifted his weight on the stool, shivering slightly beneath the blanket. He knew he should go back inside the villa; he should crawl back into bed with Louisa and wrap his arms around her swollen frame and hold her tight. She was unlikely to suffer the constraint—especially in sleep—and for a little while the dreams wouldn't come back.

The child was due sometime in the next month. He had hoped to give it a lifetime of solitude and peace, a simple life free of the conflict that had left its mark on him, but what he had learned from Diego the deserter continued to gnaw at him—a persistent poison that infected his dreams. A reminder that the war would never stop.

◆ ◆ ◆

"You didn't sleep," Louisa said as she waddled across the main room of the villa. She was a fine-boned woman and her distended belly seemed to constantly endanger her balance.

Ramiro shook his head as he inspected the heavy pot suspended over the fire in the hearth. "I had the dream again," he said.

When she reached his side, she ran her long fingers through his hair and he closed his eyes as she stroked his head. She was half his age; in the beginning he had questioned her desire to be with him. What could a woman like her see in an old crippled soldier like him? Was he a convenient shield against the suitors in her village who had persistently taken an interest in her late father's farm? Was he like the wounded lamb that could no longer care for itself? Worthy of love because he was so clearly an outcast and pariah? He had resisted her affection for so long that, when he finally allowed her to touch his face, he wept for having denied himself the simple pleasure of another's touch for so many years.

"You are awake now," she said soothingly. "It cannot hurt you."

He nodded slightly, leaning into her ministrations. She stroked harder, running her nails across his scalp. Like she did with the goats when she fed them scraps of carrots and beets from their garden. "The Almohads are back," he murmured, finally telling her what he had learned a week ago. "There is an army on the plain. They mean to march on Toledo."

"They won't come here," she said.

He didn't share her conviction. The ache in his shoulder told him otherwise. He glanced down at the wooden spoon in his hand. He was holding it loosely, fingers wrapped around the shaft, thumb resting on the wood. The same way he held a sword.

It was buried out past the orchard, wrapped in the white tabard of the order with its red cross and fleur-de-lis. Along with his maille. He half hoped the roots of the oak would have claimed the oilskin bundle, but he knew the tree would give back its secret cache readily enough.

The thaw had come. The ground would be soft.

FIVE

For the first few days after the army reached Toledo, Brothers Lazare and Crespin remained with the army, assisting in the menial work of establishing camp. Helyssent was eager to press on and cross the mountains that lay to the south, but the archbishop reminded him that the Templars and the rest of the crusaders from the north were here to assist the king of Castile. They would wait for the other allies that Alfonso VIII had convinced to join him in his war against the Almohad caliphate.

While the army waited outside the city, the archbishop and Abbot Amairic retired to the archbishop's estate within Toledo. Several of the other lay brothers accompanied Amairic, but Lazare opted to remain with the army, as did Brother Crespin. The pair had become friends during the travel from Toulouse, and while Crespin was not as intellectually curious as Lazare, his stolid belief in the Scripture and his dedication to God provided an engaging counterpoint.

It was with some shame then that, one morning, Lazare crept soundlessly out of the narrow tent he shared with Brother Crespin an hour before sunrise. The sky was clear, brightening in the east, and he set off toward the city at a brisk pace. It was a chilly morning, and his breath steamed around his face as he walked. It would take him until shortly after dawn to reach Toledo; by that time, the cold grip of night would be loosened from his bones.

In time, he hoped he might be able to bring Crespin into his confidence; but for now, he had to keep secrets from his fellow Cistercians.

◆ ◆ ◆

Lazare had seen the sigil scratched into the soft sunbaked brick of the alley several days ago when he and Crespin had come to the city's markets. The farmers and merchants were still setting up their wares when he reached the marketplace, and none of them paid any attention to the sight of a priest wandering through the near-empty square. He turned down the alley without hesitation, his eyes flicking up to the wall as he passed, noting once again the lines scratched in the brick. As he walked down the alley, he kept watch for another sign like the first and he spotted it scratched into the upper corner of a dark wooden door after the first turn. He paused, glancing back over his shoulder to make sure no one was following him, and then he stopped at the door and rapped lightly.

There was no immediate answer, and he waited, a tiny spark of fear blooming in his heart. Had he misunderstood the signs? Was no one here? And then he heard muffled sounds behind the door and it slowly opened, revealing nothing but dim shadows and the dim light of a banked hearth.

"I am a good servant," Lazare said quietly, "who seeks a good master."

"A good master is he who accepts no students," came the muffled reply after a moment.

The door did not move, but Lazare stepped up to the portal and pushed it slightly. It swung inward and he stepped into the dark house. The door shut behind him, and he stood still, letting his eyes adjust to the lack of light inside. He heard and felt more than he saw the presence of the other person. Several twigs and a log were added to the slumbering blaze in the hearth and it slowly woke, orange tendrils of flame curling around the thick slab of wood. As the growing fire illuminated the room, Lazare got his first look at the man who had answered the door.

He was entirely nondescript: robes neither too threadbare, nor too refined; hair and beard kept in the prevailing style of the day; neither too fat nor too thin. Dark blotches of ink stained the fingers of his right hand.

The room, while sparse, contained a tall cabinet filled with books and a lectern and bench, along with a table covered with sheets of paper and various writing implements and ink pots. A heavy tapestry hung on the wall opposite the cabinet, and it depicted a fantastic scene of woodland creatures in a forest of tall trees with slender branches and silver leaves.

The man, having fed the fire, returned to Lazare, squinting at him as if the light was still not strong enough to bring the Cistercian's features into complete focus. "I am Marcos," he said, linking his fingers together as he examined the Cistercian priest.

"Lazare. I come to you from Paris, by way of Clairvaux. I have read some of your work."

Marcos grinned at him, tilting his head to the side. "My work?" he echoed. "I have written nothing and created even less."

Lazare raised his hands, showing his palms. "I, too, create nothing."

Marcos grabbed Lazare's right hand and felt the calluses at the base of his fingers and along the edge of his thumb. "A smith," he divined. "And a philosopher." He let go of Lazare's hand, nodding. "Wine?" he asked, wandering toward the table.

"It is too early for me," Lazare begged off, his stomach rebelling at the idea of sour Iberian wine.

Marcos shrugged, taking no offense at Lazare's refusal of his hospitality, and he poured a measure for himself from a jug on the table. "You are not the normal courier," he said.

"I am not here to carry books back to Paris," Lazare explained. "I am with the crusaders."

Marcos shook his head. "Rodrigo returned with an army, did he?" he sighed. "How can he have failed us so?"

Lazare wandered over to the table and glanced at the scattered pages. They were covered with a fine flowing script he knew was Arabic. "How has the archbishop failed?" he asked.

"How much of the history of Iberia do you know?" Marcos said.

"I know the story of Roland," Lazare admitted. "And I have learned that the king of Navarre is not on the best of terms with the king of Castile and the archbishop of Toledo."

Marcos offered a short laugh as he raised his cup. "You know so little," he said. "Who killed Roland?"

"Saracens," Lazare said.

"Saracens," Marcos repeated, shaking his head. "It was the Basques." He sat down on the bench, idly looking at the cup in his hands. "The Basques are neither Christian nor Moor. They're *Basques*. They've been here for hundreds of years; they remember the Visigoth kings. The Muslims tried to rule them and failed. The Christians tried, and their hero, Roland, was butchered along with hundreds of knights—all of whom were slain as Charlemagne's army was retreating, having failed to conquer Iberia for the Frankish kings. The Muslims came from the south and they, too, have tried to subjugate the Basques and failed."

"But the crusade is not fighting the Basques; it is to drive the Almohad caliphate out of Iberia."

"And replace it with what?"

"A Christian nation," Lazare said.

"And the Basques?"

Lazare said nothing, for he knew—as well as Marcos did—what would eventually happen. The Church would be unsettled by the presence of non-Christians and would make an effort to bring them under the rule of Rome.

"This land—from the Pyrenees to Gibraltar—is neither Christian nor Islamic," Marcos explained. "The Basques are a distinct people, but they are a part of the peninsula. Do you see? This land has its share of Jews and pagans in addition to those who believe both the Bible and the Qur'an. Some call this land *Iberia*; some call it *Al-Andalus*. Most call it *home*. A Christian crusade isn't going to save Iberia. Putting this land under the sway of Rome is going to destroy what has been carefully cultivated for the last four hundred years." He raised his cup, hesitated, and lowered it again. "Roland was an invader," he explained. "He was driven out by those who belong here."

"But there are songs about Roland. Stories of his virtuous stand against the infidel," Lazare protested.

"There are songs about El Cid too," Marcos replied. "And most disregard the fact that he fought for both Muslim and Christian coin."

"Who?"

"Rodrigo Díaz de Vivar," Marcos said. "A Castilian who fought many campaigns against either side until, in the end, he fought for himself."

"A mercenary," Lazare said. "But why did they write songs about him?"

"He conquered Valencia and made it his home, and said he would be beholden to neither king nor caliph. His people would live freely, coexisting with each other. That is Iberia."

"And you think the crusade will destroy this Iberia?"

"Toledo has been a center of learning for more than a hundred years because Christian, Jew, and Muslim can all live in harmony. We have an understanding with the archbishop. Tolerance provides us with access to the literature and sciences of the Muslims." He gestured at the pages on the table. "If I want to read Plato and Aristotle, I don't learn Greek, I learn Arabic. There are many translations and commentaries written by Arabic scholars— easy to find. The original Greek?" He shook his head. "Lost to Christendom."

"That is where you are finding the material you send to Paris," Lazare realized.

"Aye, we have the library collected by Gerardo da Cremona, but it will take years to finish translating it all to Latin." He stood up and shuffled through the pages on the desk, showing Lazare a sheet covered in Arabic that looked much like any of the other pages on the desk. "This is part of the *Almohad Creed*. It argues for the existence of the Islamic God in a cogent and reasoned manner; to disagree with the author's conclusions is to disagree with the methods of rational inquiry as laid out by Aristotle in his *Metaphysics*. Translating it is...both illuminating and terrifying." Marcos sighed and put the page down. "I am committing heresy every time I translate a passage into Latin," he said, his words spoken proudly but his voice was soft.

After a moment, the translator raised his head and stared at Lazare. "Why are you here?" he asked, finally realizing the import of something Lazare had said earlier.

"I am looking for a sword," Lazare said.

Marcos's brows pulled together. "Durendal?" he asked, recalling the mention of Charlemagne's champion, Roland. When Lazare offered a tiny nod, Marcos shook his head. "It is a myth," he said. "Such a sword doesn't exist. You would have better luck looking for Tizona."

"Tizona?"

"El Cid's sword."

Lazare raised his shoulders. "Perhaps I will seek that blade as well."

"Why?"

Lazare looked down at the page of Arabic script. "How much news do you hear from Christendom?" he asked, considering how much to tell Marcos. "Regarding France? And England?" Marcos shook his head slightly. "Our queen is English, named after her mother—Eleanor of Aquitaine. Leonor, as she is known here in Castile, is the sister of both the Lionheart and John, who is king of England now. I know that John is concerned about Philip, the king of France, and he seeks allies to forestall an invasion by the French."

"Yes," Lazare said. "They used to be friends, but that friendship has been strained of late. King John's subjects are ill at ease too. There is talk of a revolt."

"There is always talk of revolt," Marcos said. "Countered only by the cost of such an uprising."

"Some happen without much bloodshed. Provided the people have a clear symbol to rally behind."

"Ah," Marcos said. "Like a sword, perhaps. Like that one in England, once upon a time."

"Excalibur," Lazare said.

"Yes, Excalibur. Why aren't you looking for that one?"

"I have been," Lazare said. "I'm looking for any of the swords of legend."

"Why don't you make one instead?" Marcos asked.

"If it were that easy," Lazare pointed out, "I wouldn't be here now."

SIX

L ouisa kissed him lightly on the right cheek, and as he walked away from the villa, along the path that ran between the gardens and the apple orchard, she remained outside, watching him go. Just before the land dipped and the house disappeared from view, he turned and raised his hand. She was a tiny figure, swollen around the middle. She rested one hand on her large belly and was shielding her eyes with the other. Spotting his wave, she returned it in kind before turning and disappearing back into the villa.

He didn't like leaving her but he had to go to the nearby town. He had to inquire after a midwife and see if he could hire workers from the other farms. In the last few years, he had hired young men to help in the fields at harvest time—their land was becoming too bountiful for one man to tend alone. Harvest was many months off yet, but he only needed one or two men. Just in case.

The dreams continued, and he had seen signs of other men traveling through the hills. Abandoned fires. Slaughtered deer (though no more of his goats disappeared). Horse tracks near the river crossing. The rest of the world was encroaching on his hidden sanctuary. He couldn't ignore the signs any longer.

His villa and tiny farm were a day-and-a-half's walk from the tiny village of Almuradiel, out of the mountains and onto the high plain of La Mancha, that autonomous region conquered and lost by both Muslim and Christian. The mountains at his back were the tall peaks that separated the plateau and the farm lands that lay along the Guadalquivir River.

It had been almost twenty years since the battle at the fortress of Alarcos, since he had been left for dead with the other knights of the Order of Calatrava. The following five years were a blur; even now, he had little desire to fill in the holes in his memory. He remembered enough to know that what was said of him was probably true. *Monster*, the deserter, Diego, had named him. It had been a long time since he had been spoken of thusly.

He walked, ate, slept, and walked again when the dawn came. When he spotted the first herd of cattle roaming the sere plain, he dug out the leather mask from his satchel and fitted it over his head. It covered most of his face and neck, and to lessen the attention given to his mask, he raised the hood of his mantle as well.

Faceless and nameless was the manner in which he would enter the village of Almuradiel.

◆ ◆ ◆

"Is she in distress?" the midwife wanted to know. Maria was a frail-looking woman with sun-darkened skin and a dancing light in her eyes. "Is she bleeding?"

Ramiro shook his head. "Louisa is fine," he said.

Maria put her tiny hands on her hips and stared at him. He was sitting on a worn bench in the corner of the common house, which was cheerless in its emptiness—a sure sign Almuradiel was under Muslim control again. When he sat, she was taller than he, but not by much. "She's not due for another moon," she said.

"She might be early," Ramiro said, "and it is a long walk to the villa. It would be best for you to come soon and stay with her until the child is born."

Maria wriggled her nose and then used her fingers to scratch it. "There are other expectant mothers in the village," she said.

"Who?" Ramiro asked, and when the midwife said nothing but played further with her nose, he offered to pay extra. "I suspect your husband can manage the tavern by himself for several weeks," he said, nodding toward the man who leaned against the short bar on the far side of the room. "And this coin will more than make up for any business he might lose."

"It might be longer than a month," she said. "Firstborns are never in a rush."

Ramiro shrugged, indicating that the length of her stay was of no consequence to him. Only that he wanted her to tend to Louisa sooner than later.

Maria grunted. "I'll have to talk to Fernando," she said. Ramiro nodded, and she gestured at his empty lap. "You hungry? There isn't much, and there's no wine."

"A little bread and oil will be fine," he said. He reached into his satchel and fumbled for his purse of coin. Withdrawing a handful, he pressed them into her hand. "For the food," he said. "And your time today. And some more so that you know of my earnestness."

Keeping her hand partially closed, Maria touched the coins discretely. Her mouth tightened, and after she counted them a second time, her lips relaxed, almost stretching into a smile. "It has been a dry winter," she said. "I'll get you that bread."

As she left him, the door of the common house opened and three men entered. They were wearing long linen tunics that had been dyed blue and brown and red. Silk scarves adorned their heads and shoulders. They carried short-handled, curved swords. They stood near the door for a moment, letting their eyes adjust to the dimness of the common room, and two of the three stared at Ramiro.

He examined them briefly and then turned his attention to the fire in the hearth. They were Almohad riders, and their appearance confirmed his suspicion. The last time he had come to Almuradiel, there had been militia wearing the colors of a noble family in Toledo. He wondered briefly if those men had been allowed to return to the city.

Fernando—the barkeep—approached the trio, bowing and babbling in Arabic, offering hospitality to the riders. The leader nodded absently as Fernando rattled on, and then dismissed him with a curt word and a flick of his hand. He and one of the other two walked over to the table near the fire and sat; the remaining man was still looking at Ramiro.

Ramiro heard him approach, and the man stood in front of him, blocking his view of the fire. He didn't move his head. The man was carrying his sheathed sword and Ramiro stared at his knuckles. He only looked up when the man repeated his words and let his other hand fall on the hilt of his sword. The pommel cap was a plain orb, scratched with use.

The rider jerked his chin at Ramiro, and Ramiro reached up and pushed back his hood. The man's hand tightened on his sword and his voice was hard, his words chopped and quick. Ramiro looked at the Muslim, noting the wideness of his eyes and the taut muscles in his neck. Slowly, so as to not alarm the man, he reached up and took off his mask. The Muslim recoiled, his hand pulling his sword a hand's width from its sheath. Recovering, the Muslim slammed his sword back into its sheath and spat at him, backing away and jabbering at him in Arabic.

Ramiro said nothing. He sat still, staring at the man, the leather mask held loosely in his lap.

The other two Muslims were looking at him now, and as the third continued to gesture at him, Maria rushed across the room.

She pressed part of a loaf of hard bread into Ramiro's hands. "You have to leave," she said. "Please."

Ramiro raised his hood and stood. Maria pushed him toward the door, while Fernando tried to engage the Muslims, entreating them to ignore the ugly one who was leaving. Ramiro left without saying a word, listening carefully to every word that was hurled after him.

It had been a long time since he had heard Arabic, and a long-quiescent part of his mind was being stirred awake. As he stepped out of the common house, his lips began to move, repeating the words he had heard. Remembering their meaning.

The village square was empty. A pair of oak trees leaned together, consoling one another for being the only trees within the village limits. Nearby, the three horses belonging to the riders nibbled at the sparse clumps of dry grass that grew near the wall of the common house. In the distance, he spotted a pair of villagers walking away from the square. Their pace was not hurried; they were simply unaware of his presence behind them.

Lacking any other destination, Ramiro wandered toward the pair of desultory trees, but he had only taken a few steps before he heard the door of the common house bang open. The Muslim he had spooked was yelling at him again, and Ramiro heard the rasp of steel as the man drew his sword.

He understood the man's words, the memories of those years following the defeat at Alarcos filling his head again. *Abomination. Blasphemy. Monster.* Ramiro turned and, seeing the man striding toward him, sword in hand, he tightened his grip on the piece of hard bread. As the Muslim raised his sword, Ramiro threw the bread.

It bounced off the Muslim's chest, startling him, and then his eyes widened as he realized Ramiro was nearly upon him. He tried to swing his sword, but he only got as far as raising it higher before Ramiro slammed into him. Ramiro pinned the Muslim's hands, and snarling, leaned forward and bit down hard on the end of the

Muslim's nose. Blood flowed into his mouth, a hot sap as familiar as the words he had once forgotten, and he shook his head savagely from side to side.

The Muslim screamed and jerked his head back, and Ramiro's teeth clicked shut as flesh separated. Ramiro snapped his head forward, breaking the Muslim's already injured nose, and as the man wobbled and fell down, Ramiro stripped his sword free. When the man struggled to sit up, Ramiro kicked him in the face and then plunged the curved sword into his chest. He leaned on the hilt until the man stopped squirming.

Only then did he spit out the piece of bloody gristle in his mouth.

One of the horses blew air heavily out of his nose and Ramiro blinked, suddenly aware of what he had just done. He stared dumbly at the ruined face of the dead man—it was even more deformed and monstrous than his own. Ramiro wiped at the tears streaming down his face—dimly he knew the source of the sorrow that produced them, but it felt like it belonged to someone else— and staggered away from the body. The sword remained mostly upright in the man's chest, swaying back and forth.

He exhaled, letting his breath shudder out of his frame. Pressing the heels of his hands into his eyes, he dashed away the stinging tears. There was blood in his mouth. His tongue flicked out, touching the ragged scar tissue of his lower lip. There was more blood there.

He lowered his hands and looked at the swaying sword. With a sigh, he grabbed the hilt, pulling the weapon free of the corpse. There were two more men inside; he was going to have to kill them too.

Fleetingly, he lamented ever going to look for the missing goat.

The sword felt good in his hand. His tongue touched the scarred ridge of his lower lip again.

SEVEN

⸺

Lazare had been pounding a piece of steel since dawn, and he had lost himself in the rhythm of his work. It took many hours to turn an ingot of steel into a blade, and many more hours to shape that blade into a real weapon. He liked the process—the concentration required, the endless ringing repetition of his hammer against the blade, the gradual change that came over the piece of metal. He had not been entirely truthful with Marcos: while he did not create the steel of the sword, he certainly shaped it. He gave it form. Much like Marcos did with his translations of the Arabic philosophers and alchemists.

And in Lazare's head, tantalizingly out of reach, was an idea. But no matter how he pulled at it, how he tried to extricate it from the dark morass of his thoughts, he could not bring it into shape.

He let the hammer bounce along the blade one more time and then as he turned to thrust the steel back in the forge of hot charcoal, he noticed Brother Crespin standing beside the bellows that blew air into the charcoal-filled forge.

"Brother Crespin," he said, somewhat startled by his lay brother's appearance. "I did not see you there."

"I have been watching you work," Crespin admitted. "You seemed to be happy." He offered Lazare a tiny smile. "I have felt the same when I am shaping a block of stone. I can feel God's hand on mine, guiding my chisel and hammer."

"We are mere instruments," Lazare murmured, moving the blade back and forth in the hot charcoal.

"Did you acquire that piece of steel the other day, when you went to the city?" Crespin asked.

"Yes," Lazare said, feeling only momentarily guilty for not saying more about his trip into Toledo.

"I would have liked to have gone with you," Crespin said. "I have been told there is some intricate stonework in some of the mosques. I would like to see it. Not today, though, it is too hot."

Lazare looked out of the open tent that kept the sun off his makeshift smithy. The light was bright and made him squint. His forge was hot and he wore a leather apron over his robes, which made him sweat more heavily. Still, the day itself was warm. May, in France, was still damp and wet; the weather in Iberia was much drier and hotter.

"Perhaps, we could walk to the city in the morning," Crespin added. "Before the sun gets too high in the sky."

"Perhaps," Lazare said.

Crespin watched him work for awhile. "You have been quiet as of late," he said finally.

Lazare considered making an excuse, offering some mention of the heat or the dust, but it only took a quick glance at Crespin's earnest face to feel the dull burn of shame creep up his cheeks. "I have been thinking about the purpose of our crusade"—he shook his head and corrected himself—"Rome's crusade."

Crespin gave him an odd look. "It is the same as any other crusade against unbelievers," he said. "Abbot Amairic speaks often of our duty to serve God and the Church—of the necessity of taking up arms against those who would destroy our God. Haven't you been listening to his sermons?"

Lazare shook his head. "I have heard Abbot Amairic speak as often as you," he said. "I have heard him quote from Scripture and offer homilies to the men. I have studied the Bible myself. I am not unaware of these things that Abbot Amairic preaches. But..."

"Your heart is conflicted," Crespin said when Lazare trailed off.

"Aye," Lazare agreed. "Do you remember when I dragged you up the mountain to see Roland's Breach?"

Crespin nodded. "I do. The walk was quite vigorous."

"Are the stories of men such as Roland not a variation of the homilies offered by Abbot Amairic during his sermons? The spirits of the soldiers who may very well give their lives in service of their lords or Church are bolstered by these tales of other men who have fought selflessly. But what if these stories are fabrications?"

Crespin frowned. "Are you suggesting there was no such man as Roland?"

Lazare shook his head. "No, I believe there was, but what if the story we know is a romanticized one? A tale that has been rewritten to make his sacrifice more than it was."

"That is true of any story told by a troubadour," Crespin pointed out. "That is part of their charm."

"Here, in Iberia, I have heard a version of Roland's story where he is the villain. Charlemagne was the invader, and the local peoples—the Basques—had driven him out. The Frankish army was running away, and Roland was commanding the rear guard. It was only because he refused to go, only because he stood and fought—*on land that was not his*—that he was slain. If this is true, then why do we glorify his sacrifice?"

"Because his actions saved Christian lives," Crespin said.

"Is that all that matters?"

Crespin shrugged. "Isn't it enough?"

"But if Charlemagne had remained within his own borders, if his army had not come to Iberia, would not more Christian lives have been saved?" Lazare lifted the glowing sword out of the forge and inspected its length.

"I suspect that neither I nor anyone will have a satisfactory answer to that question," Crespin said.

Lazare dropped the sword blade on the anvil and started pounding it again. "Should I not ask the question then?" he asked between blows of his hammer.

Crespin waited until Lazare's pace slowed—each hammer blow less noisy than the one prior. "If it cannot be answered, then perhaps the posing of the question itself is that which you mean to consider," he said. "Which is to consider how best to save the largest number of Christian lives."

Lazare let the hammer skip off the blade. "At what point is violence not the path for peace?" he asked.

"Every time it happens," Crespin said. "That is the difference between the two. You cannot have peace with violence, and violence does not necessarily beget peace. It typically leads to more violence." He gestured at Lazare's work. "Why are you asking this? Is that not the sole purpose of a sword: to create more violence? It is not used to plow a field for God. Or raise a church wall for God."

"It is used to kill, in the name of God," Lazare shouted at him, his hand tight around the shaft of his hammer. "Or Muhammad. Or some other pagan deity. The sword is a tool with one purpose." He was breathing heavily, his body slick with sweat, and his heart pounded in his chest. He wanted to bend the piece of steel around the edge of his anvil, pound it into a twisted shape that would have no use for anyone.

Crespin stared at him, blinking solemnly. "I build churches," he said softly, "so that men may commune with God. Is that why you make your swords?"

"No," Lazare said quietly. "I make swords so that men can be free."

"You do God's work then," Crespin said.

◆ ◆ ◆

Lazare continued to work on the sword until he could no longer lift his arms. He could coax it into the shape of a blade because he had that skill, but he could not divine the answer to the questions that hounded him. He left the blade on his anvil and collapsed on the ground near the forge, letting sleep claim him. He was exhausted, both in body and spirit.

He was dragged out of his dreamless slumber by Brother Crespin, who stood over him, shaking him roughly.

"What…what is it?" he asked. His mouth was caked with dust and his tongue stuck to his teeth.

"The Templars," Crespin said breathlessly. "They've gone to Toledo."

Lazare did not understand Crespin's consternation. The Templars were free to ride into the city, much like any other Christian. Why would such news be so alarming that Crespin would wake him?

"They've been restless," Crespin said. "Late this afternoon, after I spoke with you, I saw Abbot Amairic visit the Templar compound."

"And?" Lazare said, sitting up.

"I do not know if he offered them a sermon or he spoke to Helyssent, but they rode out a little while ago. In full armor." Crespin shook his head. "I could not help but reflect on our conversation this afternoon, and in doing so, I became concerned about some of Abbot Amairic's rhetoric. The crusaders have been given a dispensation to fight Rome's enemies, but who are those enemies?"

Ostensibly, Lazare knew the answer to that question. The enemy was the Almohad caliphate, the army of Miramamolin that was slowly creeping northward from Seville. The crusaders had been in Toledo nearly a month and they were still waiting for Alfonso VIII, the king of Castile, to decide his army was large enough. The Aragonese army had arrived last week, and a force sent from Portugal by Pedro II was due any day. Combined with the thousands of men who had marched south from Toulouse and regions north, the Christian army would number nearly two hundred thousand strong.

An army that size would get, as Crespin put it, *restless*. Over the last few weeks, he and Crespin had watched their master, Arnaud Amairic, preach on the glory of fighting the enemies of Christendom. The priest's rhetoric was noisy and inflammatory, prone to hyperbolic rhapsody; more than once, Lazare had found himself politely excusing himself from such sermons, citing distemper of his bowels.

He felt a loose tremor pass through his body now as he accepted Crespin's hand and got to his feet. "Do you think the Templars mean to harm the residents of Toledo?" he asked, though he feared he already knew the answer to his question. His visit with Marcos of Toledo had opened his eyes to the broad civility of the disparate cultures living in Iberia—Muslim, Jew, and Christian coexisted. It was as if the region thought itself to be autonomous, immune to the greater conflicts that ebbed and flowed across the Holy Land and Christendom. But such equality and peaceful coexistence could easily be overlooked by zealous crusaders. Men who had marched far from their homes and who were easily inflamed by fiery oratory.

Crespin nodded solemnly. "I do, Brother Lazare. I truly do."

◆ ◆ ◆

They could see a muted glow in the north as they walked hurriedly along the dry track. Wisps of black clouds floated low in the sky. Lazare walked quickly, Crespin huffing a step or two behind him, and within a half hour, they were able to see that the light and smoke were coming from fires burning within the city.

In the foreground, dark shapes moved, and Lazare pulled Crespin off the beaten road as the horsemen galloped past them. The white tabards of the Templars were dirty and stained, and Lazare held Crespin back as the other man shouted and raged at the Templars as they rode back to their compound. In a few moments, the company was gone, and the only sound was the echo of the hooves against the hard ground and a sobbing wail from Crespin.

Lazare tried to get Crespin's attention, but the portly Cistercian had fallen to his knees and refused to budge. Lazare left him there and kept walking, anger propelling his steps.

By the time he reached the outskirts of the city, the fires had been contained. A swath of burned timbers and soot-blackened stone cut through the Jewish quarter like a ragged ax wound. The surrounding buildings had been soaked—over and again— with water in the efforts to keep the fire at bay in much the same way that a wound is smothered with poultices and ointments to stop the spread of infection. All such ministrations were after the fact. The Templars had come, and their passage was savage and bloody.

Lazare helped as best he could: hauling buckets of water, attempting to console the grief-stricken, finding cloth that could be used for bandages, distributing food and drink to the exhausted survivors, and assisting families in finding each other among the chaotic aftermath of the Templar assault.

Shortly before dawn, he recognized one of the soot-stained men staggering through the streets, lugging a pair of heavy buckets. He approached Marcos and took one of the two water-filled buckets from the translator. Marcos stirred, rising out of his exhausted daze, as Lazare reduced his load, and he stared at the Cistercian brother, his tongue slowly wetting his blackened lips.

Lazare nodded, indicating there was no need for speech, and he fell in beside Marcos, silently hauling water for the wounded. Carrying the heavy weight of Marcos's unspoken recrimination.

EIGHT

A half-day's ride from Almuradiel, when the grasses gave way to shrubs and stands of trees, Ramiro took the pair of horses off the narrow track and began to look for a suitable place to dispose of the three dead Moors. There were several washes, narrow tracks between nascent hillocks where winter runoff carved transitory streams. Some were deeper than others, but he didn't think he would find one deep enough that scavengers wouldn't get to the bodies. In fact, he needed one deep enough that *only* the scavengers would find them.

As the shadows of the mountains started to darken the terrain, he found a suitable place. Two of the corpses were slung across one horse, and he pulled those two off first, rolling them into the rocky stream bed. The third had been slung across the rump of the horse he had been riding, and the animal kicked lightly as he undid the ties holding the body in place. After dragging the third body into the gully, he spent some time hauling rocks in place, obscuring the corpses.

He hadn't bothered striping them naked. He kept their swords and what other trinkets about their persons that might have value, but otherwise he left them alone. It was monstrous enough that he wasn't burying them, but he hoped that anyone who might find them would think they had been waylaid by bandits.

Unencumbered, he led the horses back to the path, and when he looked to the north, he spotted a horse approaching. It was carrying two riders, and as it got closer, he recognized the pair. He stood, letting his horses crop the isolated clumps of grass.

Fernando slowed his horse as it reached Ramiro. Maria spoke first. "Your wife needs someone to care for her," she said.

"Aye." Ramiro nodded, not trusting himself to say any more than simple acknowledgement. He had let his temper get the better of him, and the death of the riders had not only put the lives of Fernando and Maria in danger but Louisa as well. He had failed to secure the services of the midwife; in order to find another one, he would have to travel over the mountains—a journey of several days. He would do it, if that is what it took, but it meant leaving Louisa alone for nearly a week. In her condition, he feared what might happen.

This fear made him angry, which only fueled his self-recrimination for what had happened in Almuradiel. He knew this never-ending cycle—it was what had sustained him for years after Alarcos—but it would not help Louisa. That which had kept him alive was only going to kill the one thing that he cared about.

Which only increased his fear.

"You will do anything I ask of you," Maria continued. "Including staying away from her."

"Aye," Ramiro agreed.

"I will stay until I am confident that she and the child are strong enough, and you will provide food and shelter for me and my husband during that time."

"Aye," Ramiro said. "You and Fernando may stay in the villa; I will sleep in the stables with the horses."

Maria nodded, finding this acceptable. "You will pay us well when we leave so that we might have enough to start a new life," she said.

Ramiro hesitated for a moment before agreeing.

Maria nodded, and turned her head to say something quietly to Fernando. He slid off the horse and she nudged it into a walk. She did not look at Ramiro as her horse ambled past, leaving Fernando and Ramiro and the two remaining horses in her wake.

Ramiro and Fernando stood awkwardly, unsure of what to say to one another. The horses noisily cropped grass nearby. Finally, Fernando cleared his throat. "We couldn't stay in Almuradiel," he said. "Other riders would come. They'd ask questions. The bag of silver you left would not have done away with all the questions, and then…" He shrugged. "My father was a farmer; I never cared for the back-breaking work, and so I sold it when he died and bought the tavern. This land has been both Christian and Muslim for many years, and no one ever cared much. Just as long as we knew who to give tribute to." He glanced down at his boots, seemingly embarrassed by these words. "If the caliph comes north and means to make these lands his, I fear Maria and I would not be safe. We need to make a new life somewhere."

Ramiro struggled to find the right words. He knew he was responsible for their decision to leave Almuradiel, and while it would benefit Louisa, it was not the way he had meant to engage Maria's services. "I am as rough and broken as I appear," he said. "I do not know how to apologize for what I did and more silver cannot undo the grief I have brought to you and Maria, but know that I am grateful nonetheless for the decision you have made to aid me and mine." It was the longest speech he had made in a long time.

Fernando tried to smile, but his mouth kept drooping down. "Where else would we have gone?" he asked.

◆ ◆ ◆

Louisa was waiting for them outside the house. The day was over-cast and cool, and she stood mutely, one of the heavy wool blan-kets wrapped around her slight frame. Ramiro did not know how long she had been standing outside, waiting for them, but it had been long enough that she was over any surprise at seeing three people and three horses instead of just Ramiro.

Fernando helped Maria down from her horse, and the mid-wife went to Louisa and began asking questions about her health. Louisa offered terse replies, her eyes not leaving Ramiro. When Maria started to lift the blanket to peer at Louisa's belly, she finally looked down at the inquisitive midwife and caught the older woman's hands with her own. "In a moment," she said, politely but firmly.

Maria frowned, and then glancing back and forth between Louisa and Ramiro, waved Fernando over. "I will go prepare some water," she said curtly. Louisa nodded absently, and Maria marched into the villa as if she owned the place—Fernando fol-lowing behind her.

"What happened?" Louisa asked when she and Ramiro were alone with the horses.

"I brought the midwife," Ramiro said. "And her man. They'll stay with us until the baby comes."

Louisa touched a horse lightly above its nose and then let her hands trail along the bridle and the neck of the animal until she could finger the fringe on the saddle. "This is Moorish tack," she said.

"It is," Ramiro nodded, aware of the three swords wrapped in an oilskin bundle across the back of the horse. They, too, were Moorish blades.

Louisa looked at him, staring at his face. In the past, he had disliked her attention, and he had, on more than one occasion, shouted at her to stop looking at him. His scars would never go away. He would never be anything other than the wrecked man standing in front of her—no matter how hard and long she looked at his face. But, over time, he had come to realize that such a reaction sprung from his own guilt and fear. For too many years, his face had frightened people—much like that dying mercenary weeks ago—and he had come to believe that was the only way he would ever be seen.

Louisa wasn't afraid of him, which only made her inquisitive stare so difficult to bear. She saw past the scars and the anger and the rest of the armor that he had carefully built over the years; she saw *him*, and what she saw sometimes saddened her.

"Go inside," he snarled.

She lifted her hand from the saddle and reached out to him, but he took a step back, turning his ruined face away.

"Ramiro…" she trailed off into a sigh, and then with a slight shake of her head, she turned away from him and began her slow walk back to the villa.

He watched her go. He knew that she would get the story from Maria and Fernando, and he knew he should have offered her his version. But what would that be? One of the riders took offense to his face and so he killed the man? And he killed the other two simply because…well, why? What reason could he give to Louisa that she would understand?

The fire in his chest had not gone out, not even after his speech to Fernando. It had died down, but it was still there, deep in his chest. Fueled by a tiny refrain, the thing he told himself over and over: *I did it to protect you, Louisa.*

NINE

~

Alfonso VIII, the king of Castile, stalked about the choir of the cathedral, his dark cloak trailing behind him like a shadow struggling to keep up. When Lazare had arrived with the other Cistercians, including Abbot Amairic, Alfonso had been sitting in a cedar chair that had been brought out to the main altar, but the king had not remained in his seat very long. The gathered council—the Cistercians, a pair of men representing Pedro II, the archbishop Rodrigo Jiménez de Rada, a few rabbis from the Jewish community, elders and scholars from the city, and the other commanders of the force camped outside Toledo—had quietly listened to the king's heated condemnation of the Templar action. The king paused after a few minutes of railing at the group when he realized the target of his invective was not present.

His face purpling with rage, Alfonso shouted for someone to fetch the *impudent* and *insubordinate* Templar, Helyssent de Verdelay.

As the king stormed about the cavernous space, those in attendance did their best to avoid his ire. Lazare tried to eavesdrop on the terse conversation between the archbishop and Abbot Amairic, but the pair separated themselves enough from the rest of the group that Lazare's efforts would be readily obvious. Instead, Lazare wandered around the cathedral, feigning interest in the stained-glass panels as he listened to other conversations that were not so carefully conducted.

The Jews were conversing in Hebrew, and while he did not understand what they were saying, he had seen enough of the aftermath of the Templar attack to know what they were talking about. One synagogue had been completely destroyed by fire, and nearly a dozen surrounding homes had been lost as well. Nearly three dozen had died, and double that had sustained injuries from sword and smoke. He had heard stories that the Templars had looted as well, but the amount of goods and silver taken varied widely in the stories. Crespin and the three other Cistercians who had accompanied Amairic moved among the commanders, offering conciliatory comments and nodding a great deal in response to expressions of outrage and disbelief. The scholars kept to themselves, a clump of bearded men who muttered quietly to one another while they looked on like nervous sheep regarding a pack of circling wolves.

Lazare caught sight of Marcos, and indicated with his head that the translator should join him at a shrine to the Virgin Mary. Lazare lit a candle and placed it in the rack of melted stumps, offering a quick prayer to the Virgin to guide those who had suffered greatly the previous night. He heard Marcos step up beside him, and he waited for the translator to offer his own candle and prayer.

"He is much calmer today," Marcos said, nodding toward the distant figure of the pacing king. "I heard he had to be restrained from donning his armor and riding out to the Templar camp."

Lazare shivered briefly at the idea. "Was there any provocation?" he asked.

Marcos peered at him. "You were there last night," he said. "The Templars didn't discriminate between men and women. The Jews do not have a militia. What provocation could there have been?" His manner was terse and his words clipped, revealing his frustration at Lazare's question.

Lazare flushed and shook his head.

"Do you know of the crusade led by Boniface of Montferrat?" Marcos asked. "They were bound for the Holy Land, and the doge of Venice offered them ships to sail across the Mediterranean. The crusaders accepted but were diverted to Constantinople. Do you know what happened next?"

"Aye," Lazare said. "I have heard the stories. The crusaders attacked and sacked Constantinople instead."

"Rome threatened to excommunicate the doge and Boniface, but they offered to pledge allegiance to Rome once they took the throne. Constantinople was the seat of the Eastern Church—they were still Christian, but they were not subjects of Rome. The Pope withdrew his threat of excommunication and the crusade never made it to the Holy Land. There was more than enough plunder in Constantinople to satisfy the venal desires of these knights. Nor did they care. They were far from home, fighting in the name of God. Their salvation was assured. It did not matter whom they were killing."

"The attack last night is similar," Lazare said, "But…"

"What? Is it less of a crime because they were Jews and not other Christians? Their god is not so different from the Christian God, not like the pagans in the north or those marauding tribes of Vikings."

"You could argue that the Muslim God is not dissimilar to the Christian God too."

"I have made that argument," Marcos said. "I have translated too many of their treatises not to see that we are more similar than not. We are all descendents of Abraham." He grabbed Lazare's arm. "The archbishop understands. That is why he has been tolerant of the others in Toledo. That is why the king of Castile is so angry. Toledo is a center of great knowledge because we strive to live in harmony with other cultures and beliefs. We want to learn from them. And your Templars—"

"They're not *my* Templars," Lazare interrupted.

"These *Frankish* Templars," Marcos corrected. "They're like the barbarian tribes in the north. They kill indiscriminately. They only see the *other* and think the other must be subjugated and conquered. They think of their kings like Charlemagne—and his hero, Roland—and want to finish what their forefathers could not."

"But Alfonso called upon Rome for aid. These crusaders want to strike against the enemies of Christendom. Is that not what your king wanted?" Lazare asked.

Marcos stared at the flickering light of the newly lit candles. "It's Toledo," he said, and when that didn't seem to be enough, he clarified. "It's complicated."

Lazare recalled his conversation with Crespin when he had been working on the sword. "Aye," he agreed. "But I fear the Templars—and Rome—care little for these *complications*. They have a more simplistic view. The victor can always lay claim to righteousness."

"Aye," Marcos said. "And therein lies our greatest fear. If the Moors are defeated, who among the Christian leaders will claim this victory? And what will be the cost?"

◆ ◆ ◆

Eventually the heavy doors of the cathedral opened, and all conversation within the cathedral stopped. A single figure trotted slowly up the nave, and while it was clear almost immediately that the individual was not the Templar commander, everyone waited expectantly for the message he would deliver. As soon as the sweating man reached the choir, he dropped to his knees, and without waiting for the king to recognize him, he blurted out his news. "They're gone."

Alfonso, remaining implacably calm in the face of this announcement, approached the kneeling messenger and asked him to clarify. "Who are gone?"

"The Templars," the messenger said, and the cathedral was filled with an eruption of noisy voices. Alfonso raised his hand, and the voices trailed off like lines of swallows vanishing into a darkening sky.

"All of them?" Alfonso asked.

The messenger nodded.

"They're marching for Salvatierra," a burly man with a long black beard said. Lazare didn't recall his name, but he knew he was one of the field commanders who had met Miramamolin's troops last fall when the first Moorish sorties had taken place in the plain south of Toledo.

Alfonso slapped his hand against the hilt of his sword, his rings striking the pommel with a clash of metal. "Let the messenger speak," he thundered.

The burly man inclined his head, but the motion was perfunctory and lacking in real humility.

"Yes, yes," the messenger stuttered, "the Templars mean to march south, along the road to Calatrava and Salvatierra." He glanced around at the gathered assembly. "Others mean to follow him, Your Highness."

"Master Ruy," Alfonso said, and the burly man stepped forward. "How many knights march under the Templar banner?"

"Nearly a thousand, Your Majesty," Ruy replied. "And ten times that number in men-at-arms."

"And what is our latest estimate of al-Nasir's strength?"

"More than two hundred thousand men," Ruy Díaz said.

Al-Nasir, Lazare thought, finding it interesting that the king of Castile referred to the Almohad caliph by his Muslim name and not the Christianized version—Miramamolin.

"Such odds, even for the Templars," Marcos whispered to him. "They would be fools to face al-Nasir directly."

"Aye," Lazare said. He, like everyone present, had heard stories about the Templars. Each knight was worth more than ten men on the battlefield. Only the famed Shield-Brethren had a stronger reputation for their value in battle. "They must mean to harry the Moors," he said. "But such tactics cannot be sustained for a long period of time. The main force will surround them eventually."

The crusaders needed to be unified in their attack against the Moors. The Templar decision to march ahead would only diminish the chances of a Christian victory against the Almohad army.

Alfonso dismissed the messenger with a wave of his hand. "How soon can your knights march, Master Ruy?" the king asked.

"Immediately, Your Majesty," Ruy replied. Whether this was true or not, Lazare sensed it was the only response the man would have given.

"What knights does that man command?" he asked Marcos.

"Ruy?" Marcos said. "That is Ruy Díaz de Yanguas. He is the master of the Order of Calatrava. It was their citadel that fell last year—their second citadel. They lost Calatrava nearly twenty years ago. At the battle of Alarcos."

"What of Sancho?" Alfonso was asking of the archbishop, and Lazare found his attention being drawn back to the king. "Will he join us?"

The archbishop shook his head. "I have received no word of his intentions, Your Majesty."

"We need his forces," Alfonso said.

Abbot Amairic leaned over and whispered something in the archbishop's ear, and the archbishop's eyes flicked toward Lazare. "I understand, Your Majesty," the archbishop said smoothly. "I will endeavor to discover what is delaying the king of Navarre."

Alfonso nodded curtly and then let his gaze rove over the remaining assembly. "Ready your troops as soon as possible. We must not let the Templars engage al-Nasir's forces without us. "

✦ ✦ ✦

Lazare was not surprised when Archbishop Rodrigo motioned that he should stay as the others departed from the cathedral. Making a polite excuse to Marcos, he wandered toward the altar and stood, hands behind his back, staring up at the crucifixion until the babble of voices and the sound of feet against stone faded. The cathedral doors swung shut, the echo rumbling through the empty cathedral with a sonorous thunder of finality.

The archbishop sighed noisily as he walked up beside Lazare. Clasping the heavy cross that hung on a silver chain about his neck, the archbishop gazed up at the immense portrait of the suffering Christ and offered a short prayer to God. Lazare ducked his head as the archbishop prayed, echoing the other man's final words as the archbishop finished.

"What do you think of my city?" Archbishop Rodrigo asked after he had completed the requisite attention to God. "I understand you have met some of the local scholars."

Lazare nodded. "I have, Your Grace. I am given to understand that Toledo is… *complicated.*"

The archbishop snorted. "Philosophers see everything as being overly complex. Suffused with multiple layers of meaning and inference, even."

Lazare did not know the work—or inquiry—that the archbishop was referring to, and so he only nodded sagely as if he understood the distinction being made. As he glanced around, he noticed Abbot Amairic wandering around in the nave, strolling between the pillars in the back of the cathedral.

Archbishop Rodrigo noticed his gaze. "Ah, the abbot," he said. "Your superior." When Lazare did not immediately agree, the archbishop pursed his lips thoughtfully. "When we traveled through Pamplona, we were not able to reach an accord with King Sancho. Hmmm?"

Lazare nodded. "Yes, I recall that being the case. Though—"

"Yes?" the archbishop prompted. "You may speak plainly, Brother Lazare."

"The lack of an accord may have more to do with a failure to actually *meet* than any other reason," Lazare said.

"Was it necessary for me to meet with the king?"

Lazare thought back on his conversation with the kin of Navarre. "That might have depended on how you approached such a meeting," he said.

"And if I had failed to properly measure the king's mood?" the archbishop said.

"I suspect his response would have been unfortunate."

"Instead of…?"

"No response at all."

"Did I fail then?"

"You certainly didn't succeed," Lazare pointed out.

"That is not the same as failure," the archbishop explained. He spread his arms to encompass the empty cathedral. "That is Toledo."

"That sounds like philosophical wordplay," Lazare said.

"All negotiations are," the archbishop said. "Every agreement made between kings and caliphs, popes and princes, is a matter of inference and wordplay. Each decides how he will interpret the words of the treaty or agreement. It is not like the word of God, which is immutable. Our words are imperfect. Do you know the theories of Plato and Aristotle?"

"I do, Your Grace," Lazare said.

Archbishop Rodrigo waved a hand at Lazare's expression. "Don't look so surprised. I can read Latin as well as any man in this city. I am not like that overzealous abbot of yours. I can read the commentaries written by the Moorish philosophers without screaming heresy and calling for an inquisition. I can read a treatise supposedly written by Muhammad al-Nasir that calls for the death of all Christians and the destruction of Rome and see that it is nothing more than a mere forgery. Unlike your friend over there."

"What...what treatise?"

The archbishop regarded him shrewdly, one hand idly tapping his cross. "I have heard that King John of England has been excommunicated, that his country is under interdict. He fears a French invasion, and cut off from the rest of Christendom, he has made overtures to others who might come to his aid...in return for certain concessions. Have you heard this story?"

It was Lazare's turn to hesitate. "It does not surprise me that King John seeks to make an alliance with one of the kings of Iberia."

"Not one of the kings," the archbishop corrected. "A caliph."

Lazare stared. "That's impossible."

"Why? Because Muhammad al-Nasir is Muslim? It wouldn't be the first time a Muslim and a Christian have made an agreement against a greater enemy. It happens more often than you might think in Iberia."

"No, John would never convert to Islam. His subjects would never convert."

"I suspect al-Nasir thought the same thing, which is why he turned the English envoys away," the archbishop said. "It was a decided failure for King John."

"Aye," Lazare said, clearing his throat. "It sounds like it was."

"You seem relieved," the archbishop noted. "And you seem to be well-informed as to the mood of the English people. Odd for a *French Cistercian,* don't you think?"

"It is," Lazare agreed, his breath catching in his throat. His thoughts raced, wondering how he had let himself be trapped by the archbishop. Had he said too much to Marcos? Had the translator passed along the details of their conversation to the archbishop?

The archbishop, though, appeared unconcerned. "Do you think King Sancho would receive you again?" he asked.

"Excuse me?"

"If I were to order your abbot to allow you to return to Pamplona, would he let you go? As an emissary from both myself and King Alfonso. Do you think the abbot would acquiesce to my request?"

"He wouldn't refuse," Lazare said.

A tiny smile creased the archbishop's lips. "But that isn't the same as saying *yes,*" he noted.

Lazare nodded in agreement. "I profess I know little of Abbot Amairic's moods," he said.

"You credit the abbot with too much subterfuge," Rodrigo said. "He has the ear of the Templar commander. I suspect it is his voice that Helyssent de Verdelay listens to. The abbot is much too narrow-minded in his rhetoric, and it may be the undoing of all of us."

"Aye," Lazare said, eyeing the distant shape of the abbot.

The archbishop nodded. "Someone must bring Sancho and his army, and someone else must temper the abbot's words," he said. "I cannot be in two places at the same time. Which do you think I will have more success at accomplishing?"

"Short of stripping the abbot of his office and imprisoning him, I don't think you can stop him," Lazare said.

"Should I have him killed?"

When Lazare said nothing, Rodrigo stroked his chin.

"That is an interesting silence you offer me, Brother Lazare."

"Your question was one that only God can answer for you," Lazare said.

The archbishop laughed. "Well said." He sobered. "Where were you born, Brother Lazare?"

"Rievaulx," Lazare sighed, deciding to tell the archbishop the truth. "Not far from Yorkshire."

"An orphan, taken in by the local abbey?"

"Aye."

"Were you simply brought up by the Cistercians, or did you take the vows there as well?"

"The brothers at Rievaulx took a great deal of interest in my education," Lazare said.

The archbishop waited a few moments for Lazare to offer more and, as the cathedral fell into a solemn silence, he raised his cross to his lips.

"Very well," the archbishop said eventually. "I will worry about Sancho and the Navarrese army. Go with the abbot. Try to minimize the impact his sermons have on the soldiers. Don Ruy is a friend. He can help you. There are too many foreign soldiers in this army. I fear that King Alfonso will not have the authority to command them should they be swayed to a different course."

Lazare nodded, relieved and a little surprised that the archbishop was placing such trust in him. "Why?" The word slipped out.

The archbishop raised an eyebrow. "Why am I trusting you?" he asked. "Because all I want is to ensure the safety of the people of Toledo—of all of Castile—regardless of their faith or origin. You understand that, don't you?"

"I do," Lazare said.

"See?" the archbishop said, smiling. "It isn't that complicated after all."

TEN

On horseback, Ramiro could ride much farther and still return by nightfall. As Louisa became more comfortable with Fernando and Maria's presence, he spent more time away from the villa. He roamed throughout the hills and along the verge of the great plain, seeking sign of the Almohad army. After a week of scouting, he was confident no army was lurking in the mountains or creeping along the pass carved through the Sierra Morena by the Despeñaperros River. Al-Andalus, on the southern side of the mountains, had belonged to the various Moorish caliphs for many generations; it was the high plain on the northern side, La Mancha and the territories surrounding Toledo, that were contested again and again.

If the Almohads were moving north, they would harry the isolated castles and cities of the high plain before taking the road to Toledo. Ramiro hoped that any army that Castile and the other Christian kingdoms could field would be enough to turn back the Almohad decisively. If the armies spent the spring and summer warring on the plain, the chances of one side or the other spilling into the foothills of the Sierra Morena would increase dramatically.

He couldn't move Louisa now. Maybe in a few months, after the child was born. Until then, he had to be patient. He had to stay hidden.

In the distance, Ramiro spied a small citadel, its man-made outline clear among the rocky outcroppings that poked out like naked fingers from the verdant, tree-covered hills. Castillo del Ferral had once been a fortress of the Order of Calatrava, but it had fallen into Moorish hands after the battle of Alarcos. The defeat at Alarcos had been tantamount to cutting out the heart of the order, and afterward, the rest of the body—the outlying citadels of Malagón, Benavente, Caracuel, Castillo del Ferral, and Calatrava itself—had sickened and died.

He had removed most of the markings on the saddle that would clearly identify it as Moorish, though there was little he could do about the shape of the saddle or the swords that hung off his right side. His robe and hood were plain and uncolored by dyes. If he were spotted, his mere presence would incite some curiosity, but he had no intention of being seen.

The wind shifted as he approached the base of the hill, and it carried the scent of cooking fires and the faint echo of voices, speaking Arabic. A Muslim garrison. There was no way to determine how many were quartered there without approaching the walls of the citadel, and Ramiro did not plan to get that close.

He found a small glade where his horse could graze, and he found a comfortable position beneath a sprawling oak which afforded him a view of the peak of the hill. The Castillo del Ferral was about a half-day's ride from his villa; if he returned immediately, he could make it back before nightfall. But he settled in to watch the citadel.

Diego and the other deserters had said they had been fleeing the Moorish capture of Puertollano, which lay twenty miles or more to the north and west. There was no reason for those men to have gone south—toward Al-Andalus and the Moorish caliphate—unless they had been diverted by the presence of a sizeable Moorish army. It was possible they had been making for Valencia, but fleeing along the southern edge of La Mancha was not the most direct route. And then to stumble into the hills and run afoul of the garrison at Castillo del Ferral seemed like ill luck indeed, but Ramiro could not fathom any other way the men could have ended up near his lands, roasting one of his goats. The wounds suffered by the one who died had been fresh—a day or two old at most, which was in keeping with what Ramiro knew of stomach wounds. In all likelihood, Diego and the others had gotten lost, their sense of direction woefully incorrect, and they must have mistakenly thought the citadel housed Christian soldiers.

It had been built by Christians, but to believe that Christians still held it was a dangerous mistake in these times and in these lands.

Ramiro leaned back against the tree. The wind blew lightly against his cheeks and forehead, and he inhaled deeply, smelling the faint wetness of a distant storm. The voices of the Moors were a distant buzz, like the sound of grasshoppers during the hot summer months. He blinked slowly—once, twice—his mind wandering through memories of other citadels. Eventually, his eyes closed and he was swallowed by the past.

◆ ◆ ◆

There was only one sentry pacing slowly back and forth atop the southern wall. A brazier at the eastern end of the wall provided a beacon in the moonless night that the sentry returned to time and again. Ramiro crouched behind the bole of an oak near the edge of the tree line, watching the sentry. The man took twenty paces in one direction before pausing and turning back. After a few iterations, Ramiro turned his attention to the rough stone of the wall, gauging the route he would take up its surface. The wall was not that tall—he estimated it wasn't more than three times his height. Provided he could find purchase on its surface, he thought he could climb it before the sentry completed one circuit of his watch.

When the man reached the farthest point from the flickering beacon of the brazier, Ramiro scuttled out from the cover. He darted to the wall and leaped up to grab the first handhold he had been eyeing. The knob held his weight, and he hoisted himself up to a pair of protruding edges where he could rest his feet. He reached up, straining to his left, and found his second handhold. He moved his legs up and continued his rapid ascent. Just below the top of the wall, he stopped, clinging tightly to the surface. He heard the faint scrape of the Moor's boots as he walked past, and he quickly hauled himself up to the top of the wall. He padded up behind the sentry, and when the man turned, he stood upright and shoved his knife into the man's throat.

The Moor's eyes grew large, and he opened his mouth to scream, but he couldn't get any air. His eyes got bigger and his hands scrabbled at Ramiro's arms, but his grip was already weakening. As the man's legs gave out, Ramiro knelt too, twisting the knife up and to the left to make sure the Moor's throat was cut.

As the man gurgled into death, Ramiro surveyed the interior of the citadel. There were a handful of tents scattered around the interior, and from the tumbledown keep came the glow of a weak fire. There were no sentries posted inside the walls. Apparently, the Moors felt the walls and a single sentry to patrol them were protection enough.

Ramiro dropped into the main courtyard of the citadel. A half dozen horses milled about in a roped-off arena, and several exhaled noisily at the scent of fresh blood on his robes and knife. Ramiro ignored them and moved stealthily toward the first tent. There were two men inside, and the first died from Ramiro's knife without ever waking up. The second man caught sight of his face and had to be held down as he thrashed in fear. The man's panic only made him bleed out faster.

Ramiro moved from tent to tent, repeating his silent assassinations, ten men in all. Once he had finished with the tents, he moved on to the keep. It took him longer to find the residents as they were scattered throughout the building. The four sleeping in the great hall before the fire were his final challenge, and he squatted on his heels for some time, watching them sleep, deciding on the best way to kill them all. Three of the four had thrown off their sleeping furs, and he decided that the one farthest from the hearth—huddled beneath a woven blanket—would be the one he let live.

He always let one live so that the Moors would know what had happened. They would know who had come among them and slaughtered them all.

The first died noisily, coughing and gagging on his own blood, which woke one of the others. He managed an abrupt shout, cut short by Ramiro's sword, but it was enough to rouse the third, who reached for his weapon. Ramiro beat it aside, stepping on the man's arm to keep the weapon at bay, and drove his sword into the man's chest.

The fourth man moved under his blanket, sitting up, and Ramiro raised his sword. The blanket slipped down and the light of the dim fire revealed long black hair that fell down over an oval face. As the figure recoiled from him, the blanket slipped farther and revealed a vast belly, hard and swollen.

Louisa…?

Ramiro started awake, gasping for air. His heart hammered in his chest, and his skin was slick with sweat. Nearby, his horse whuffed air noisily; in the distance, he heard the mournful cry of a night bird. The moon was high in a sky that was beginning to fill with clouds. Atop the hill nearby, a glow of firelight limned the walls of Castillo del Ferral.

He had been dreaming. Except for Louisa, it was always the same. He had killed so many men in nameless citadels throughout the years that his mark was known. He always left a survivor to tell the tale of the Beast of Calatrava.

ELEVEN

⤙

The castle at Calatrava perched on the eastern end of a mound that was longer than it was tall. The Guadiana River lay across the plain like a discarded line of blue thread, and its banks were lined with pale dirt. The river's course protected the northern flank of the citadel, and the rest of the hill was protected by sections of wall built from interlocked stone and masonry. A moat had been dug years ago, diverting the Guadiana around the entire hill.

The Templars crossed the moat near the western end, where the wall was nothing more than a contour of loose stones, and surged up the slope to secure the flat top of the hill. The Moors in the citadel had several trebuchets, but only a few were pointed back across the hill. They hurled rocks halfheartedly for a while and stopped when the Templars quickly figured out their range.

A line of crossbowmen protected the first wave of infantry who reached the wall. While some attacked the gate, the rest tried to get ropes and hooks in place so that they could scale the outer wall. The Moorish resistance was sparse. It seemed that every arrow shot from the wall was answered by two or three crossbow bolts. In less than an hour, the Templar soldiers gained control of the outer wall, pulling down the Moorish standard that had been fluttering from the top of one of the square towers.

The second wall was more stoutly defended and the Moors threw down rocks and burning pitch to keep the attackers from reaching the base. The assault took several hours, during which the heat from the sun started to take its toll on the attackers. As many collapsed from exhaustion as died from arrows, but still more came.

The gate fell eventually, and now that the path into the citadel was open, the knights could attack. They came, a river of white and silver that flowed across the hill, through the gates and into the main yard of the citadel. Templar knights on horseback roared into the castle like a torrential flash flood, foaming and overwhelming the Moorish defenders, leaving nothing in their wake but a blood-slicked field of corpses.

Calatrava, which had been lost to the Christians for nearly twenty years, was retaken in less than a day. It was a victory that should have boosted the morale of the Christian army.

✦ ✦ ✦

Lazare and Crespin were among the group that followed the Templar commander and the abbot as the pair hurried through the camp toward the Castilian compound.

The Christian army sprawled along the banks of the Guadiana River, and given the somber mood brought about by the oppressive heat, it would have been easy to think that this army had been savagely defeated. The camp felt deserted, filled with supine bodies that shifted only to chase what meager shade their tents could provide. Only the Castilian camp showed much life, as the men of Castile were accustomed to the heat of the high plain.

The standards hung limply above King Alfonso's tent, the walls of which were rolled up in an effort to take advantage of any breeze that might find its way through the dust-choked camp. The king was quietly standing beside a table, examining a large map, when Helyssent and Abbot Amairic arrived.

"Where is he?" Helyssent raged without any preamble as he stormed into the king's tent. "Where is Miramamolin? The force protecting Calatrava was nothing but a rabble."

Helyssent was wearing a pale linen robe, loose leggings, and his riding boots—concessions to the heat, as he normally paraded about in a padded tunic and heavy tabard. There were sweat stains on his chest and under his arms. His hair hung lank and damp about his face.

The king raised his gaze from the map and regarded the sweating Templar. Lazare was impressed by the king's poise. He was, like the abbot and Brother Crespin, sweating profusely in his Cistercian robes, and he fought the urge to pant when he breathed. The king gave no indication that he was perturbed in any way by the suffocating weather.

"I have word that he and his army have left Seville," King Alfonso said.

"Why was he not here?" Helyssent snarled.

"It will take him more than a week to reach and cross the Sierra Morena," Alfonso explained patiently. Lazare marveled at the king's restraint. The Templars' departure from Toledo had thrown Alfonso's plans into utter disarray, and while the Order of Calatrava and the bulk of the Castilian army had managed to catch up with the Templars shortly after the assault on Calatrava had begun, the rest of the army was still arriving. "We will be fortunate if we can manage to arrange our armies properly before al-Nasir crosses the mountains," he said. "Now is not the time to hurry ourselves into battle."

Helyssent's sunburned face darkened. "We are here to destroy the Moorish threat," he said. "The longer we stand around in this heat, the more sapped our strength will be. We must march and fight. We are stronger than the Moors."

"Al-Nasir has twice as many men," Alfonso said.

"He doesn't have God and the Templars," Helyssent replied. "And the other military orders," he added hastily, noticing Don Ruy in the group that had gathered.

"You do not know the terrain," Alfonso said. "You have never fought al-Nasir. Your arrogance will cost us the battle."

Helyssent bristled. "I took Calatrava without losing a single Templar," he said. "There are other citadels scattered about this plain that my knights can take as readily. The Moors cannot stand up to our swords and lances."

"That is your opinion," Alfonso said, his voice hardening. "But this is my kingdom. My command."

"This is a crusade ordered by the Pope in Rome," Helyssent said. "We are the sword of God. We are under no command but His."

"You are marauders," Alfonso snapped. "Murderers—"

"You call yourself a Christian ruler," Helyssent shouted, interrupting the king. "And yet you make treaties with the Muslims. You let Jews live openly in your cities. They plot—"

"Your oaths to God are meaningless," Alfonso shouted. "You are nothing more than wild dogs—"

"You welcome them into your house. You lie with them, and they will slit your throat—"

Alfonso gave up trying to shout over the Templar leader and he strode over to one of his guards and pulled the man's sword out of its scabbard. Helyssent faltered for a moment as the king turned on him with the naked sword, but he stood his ground, his indignation straightening his back. Alfonso raised the sword and may have struck at Helyssent had Don Ruy not forced his way through the crowd and interposed himself between the two men.

Alfonso stopped, his eyes bright with rage. His grip on the sword was firm. "Stand aside, Don Ruy," he growled.

"I cannot, Your Majesty," the master of the Order of Calatrava said.

Helyssent tapped Don Ruy smartly on the shoulder. "What sort of king—what sort of man!—would strike another Christian?" he sneered.

Alfonso raised the sword slightly.

Abbot Amairic stepped forward, clutching his cross tightly in his raised hands. "This is not what God wants," he pleaded. "This is nonsense. We are not here to fight each other. Set aside your sword, good king. Master Helyssent, calm your spirit."

Lazare followed Amairic, slipping through the hole created by the abbot. The archbishop's words echoed in his head. *The safety of all people in Toledo*...Having watched the crowd's reaction as the two leaders had shouted at one another, he realized how many of those assembled were from the north. *Too many foreign soldiers...*

The abbot reached Helyssent's side and laid a hand on the Templar's arm while still holding his cross aloft with his other hand. "We have journeyed far from our homes to aid the king of Castile in his war against the Moors," he said, "and so removed, we have only our faith to sustain us—the unfaltering knowledge that we do God's work in this land. Miramamolin—the infidel—will not march on Rome. He will not be allowed to continue to subjugate good Christian peoples. We must remain steadfast in our crusade."

Everyone seemed to relax as the abbot spoke. Alfonso lowered his sword. Helyssent nodded gruffly, stepping back from Don Ruy. The tension in the sweltering tent lessened.

But then the abbot kept talking. "We are surrounded by heretics," he said. "And our crusade will cleanse—"

Without thinking about the ramifications of his actions, Lazare jumped forward and reached around the abbot's shoulder to clap his hand over the Cistercian leader's mouth. Amairic spat and shook his head, startled by Lazare's grip, and

Helyssent shouted in surprise. A noisy chatter rose in the crowd behind them.

"My apologies," Lazare said loudly and forcefully, making himself heard. "The abbot has had too much sun."

The abbot struggled in his grip. With a growl, Helyssent turned and grabbed Lazare's shoulder. Don Ruy, in turn, grabbed Helyssent. The noise of the rabble increased.

"Enough," Alfonso said. He did not raise his voice, but his tone was that of a man used to issuing a command and having it carried out. The strident voices of the crowd petered out and Lazare, the abbot, Don Ruy, and Helyssent all stood motionless, caught in a bizarre contortion of grabbing and being grabbed.

"We have all had too much sun," the king said. He turned and dropped the sword noisily on the table. "Go," he said, his back to the crowd. "There will be no more discussion of these matters today. We shall meet in the morning, after daybreak, and continue this discussion as reasoned, *rational* men."

Helyssent opened his mouth, but Don Ruy shook the Templar's sleeve and wagged his head. Helyssent glowered for a moment at Don Ruy's grip, and when the master of the Order of Calatrava did not move, Helyssent released his grip on Lazare. Don Ruy followed suit, and only then did Lazare remove his hand from the abbot's mouth.

The abbot jerked himself away from Lazare, sputtering in anger. "How dare you—" he started.

"No," the king interrupted. Alfonso turned back toward the group. "There will be no accusations. We should all reflect on our own words, our own actions, in this meeting. We should abase ourselves before God and ask if we have served Him well in the last few minutes."

The abbot made to say something but Alfonso cut him off with a curt shake of his head. "Go," the king said. "Leave me. Until the morning."

The abbot whirled on Lazare, raising a finger and waggling it in front of Lazare's face. Lazare was more concerned about the Templar commander, who he felt was still staring at him.

The crowd started to disperse, and Lazare heard more than a few muttering discontentedly at the king's command. The abbot glanced at Helyssent and nodded slightly, and Lazare wondered what sort of signal had just passed between the two men. The abbot shouldered his way past Lazare, and with a loud exhalation, Helyssent withdrew as well.

Don Ruy was appraising Lazare openly, a tight smile on his lips as if he approved of what Lazare had done. Lazare shrugged slightly, knowing that he would be summoned to the abbot's tent as soon as he left the king's camp.

"Not you," the king said as Lazare started to turn away. Lazare sighed, and when he looked at Don Ruy, the master of the order's smile tightened.

◆ ◆ ◆

"Rodrigo, the archbishop, mentioned that I might find you useful," the king of Castile said as the pair of servants finished setting out a small meal of bread, olive oil, and wine. He was seated in a high-backed chair behind the table on which the map was still spread; Lazare sat on his left, perched on a narrow wooden stool. The plates of food were arranged along the edge of the table. The king leaned forward, picking up a thick piece of bread and tearing off a large chunk. He pressed it into the dish of oil and swirled it around.

"I am but a mere instrument," Lazare said quietly, and when Alfonso glanced at him with a curious expression, he shook his head gently. "The archbishop is overly kind in his praise," he said more loudly. "I am but a mere lay brother of a minor order of monks."

"A Cistercian, yes?" When Lazare nodded, Alfonso raised the dripping piece of bread to his mouth and took a large bite.

"I understand a number of your order traveled south with your abbot. Abbot Amairic's interest in the crusade is readily apparent in every bombastic utterance, but what of the rest of your company? Are you as zealous in your devotion to the mission of Rome, or were you hoping to accomplish other deeds?"

"My order has ties to the Order of Calatrava," Lazare said, reaching for a piece of bread himself. "Your original call for aid mentioned the loss of one of their citadels late last year. We thought we might be useful to the order if they managed to retake that land."

"By fighting alongside them?"

Lazare shook his head. "We are monks. We can help the sick and wounded. Some of us have other skills. Brother Crespin, for example, is a stone mason. I have some experience with smithing."

"Stone and sword, eh?"

Lazare inclined his head fractionally as he dipped his bread in the oil.

"But you do more than make horseshoes, nails, and the occasional sword, don't you?"

"What do you mean, Your Majesty?"

"You know something of the old philosophers."

"A great deal of knowledge comes through our abbey," Lazare said, dismissing the notion of his education. "I know very little of its substance."

The king picked up his cup of wine. "Don't take me for a fool," he said.

"I beg your pardon, Your Majesty?"

"Your actions today are going to put you at odds with your abbot. Depending on his mood, he may take a great deal of offense at being handled so roughly—in front of witnesses— by one of his laity. You do not seem terribly concerned that the head of your abbey might declare you unfit to remain a Cistercian."

"I...it had not occurred to me," Lazare said truthfully.

"Precisely," Alfonso said, sitting back in his chair.

"I am not sure what you are implying, Your Majesty," Lazare said.

"I don't believe you are truly a Cistercian monk," Alfonso said.

"That is a curious supposition," Lazare said.

Alfonso raised his cup. "You aren't denying it," he said.

"I had an interesting conversation with the archbishop before we left Toledo," Lazare said. "He and I talked about the subtleties of saying yes and no, and how one might have a conversation wherein nothing that could be construed as a rational demonstration of facts would be said, but both parties would still feel they expressed their thoughts quite plainly. Do you have conversations like that, Your Majesty?"

"I believe I may be having one right now," the king said with a laugh.

"Previously, the archbishop spent time at the cathedral in Pamplona, not taking an audience with the king of Navarre—which is not the same thing as avoiding the king, mind you. I went in his stead, as Abbot Amairic was not willing to act contrary to the archbishop's desires."

"And you had no problem acting contrary to the archbishop's desires?"

"The king of Navarre wished to meet a representative from the northern coalition that was traveling through his land. Would it not have been tantamount to an invasion if we had not paid our respects?"

"Did you know that the archbishop and Sancho were out of sorts?"

"I did not, at the time. I did, however, hear of Sancho's disagreement with both the archbishop and Your Majesty."

"And...?"

"And I am a Cistercian monk from France, Your Majesty. My opinion matters little."

"Or it might matter a great deal, depending on who you might be if you were *not* a Cistercian monk."

Lazare weighed his next words carefully. "The king of Navarre expressed a hope that I might be a better smith than I am a diplomat," he said.

"Are you?"

"A better smith?"

"A smith. A diplomat," Alfonso shrugged. "Maybe even a spy. I know you have a different master than you lead me to believe, but do we have common goals?"

Lazare dipped his piece of bread in the oil again, debating what to tell the king. Would the king of Castile believe his story? What would happen if Alfonso scoffed and dismissed his tale as pure fancy? It was true that he was not concerned about the abbot's reaction to being manhandled, but if the abbot insisted that he leave the camp—and if he told the Templars to make sure that the disgraced brother was driven off—then his mission could be compromised. And what of his mission? Was he really searching for a sword of legend, or was that merely a physical relic of what he truly sought? A sword was a tool, but it was only as useful as the hand that wielded it.

Lazare wondered if he had been searching for the wrong thing. At the same time, he kept sensing that his quest had not been abandoned; that what he *truly* sought was within reach.

Old Ox—the enigmatic companion of the lady of the woods—spoke of a knowledge known as *Vor*. The art of knowing without learning. The art of seeing what was not there, but knowing what was true nonetheless. Lazare had scoffed at such a pagan notion, but the more embroiled he had become in the politics of the Iberian kingdoms, the less foolish such a notion seemed.

That was the idea that had been tickling the base of his brain as he had tried to navigate the complicated mores of the local peoples. The strict rule of Rome did not apply, any more than the hard creed of the Muslim faith. There was mutability in the Iberians, and nowhere else had he seen such flexibility on the part of each individual in regard to the differences of his immediate neighbor.

It was something more than trust and something less than divine inspiration.

"I only seek to ensure the freedom of all people," Lazare said. "In this case, the people of your kingdom. Of Navarre." He gestured out past the open walls of the tent. "Of those who dwell in Al-Andalus, even."

"It is an admirable desire—foolish even—but still quite worthy of effort. But how do you hope to accomplish this lofty goal?" the king asked. "By conquering all those who threaten them? If you mean to protect the Moors in Al-Andalus, then you are in the wrong camp."

"Am I?" Lazare asked.

Alfonso grimaced and took a long drink from his cup. He picked up the jug and poured more, leaning over to refill the scant amount that Lazare had drunk so far. "I have emptied my coffers to pay for these…these *peregrini*. And the coffers of my priests as well. The Templars—for all their vaunted claims otherwise—would not be here if there were no coin in it for them. They attacked the Jews not out of any desire to save good Christians, but simply to plunder the wealth they assumed was there. Had we not arrived when we did, they would have done the same here at Calatrava. They're not interested in bringing Christ to Iberia and Al-Andalus. They only want the gold and silver and riches that can be taken from those they conquer."

"Are you going to let them?" Lazare asked.

"Of course not," Alfonso said with a snort.

"What will they do?"

"If I don't pay them? I don't know. What does any army do when the money runs out?"

TWELVE

As he crested the wooded hill that hid the valley where the orchard and villa lay, he spotted Louisa wandering through the field of wild flowers along the northern edge of the pasture. He let his horse find its own way down the slope as he rested his forearms on the horn of his saddle and watched her. She was wearing a blue linen dress beneath a gray cloak, and her hair was loose, streaming down her back in a glossy black wave. Her rotund belly made it difficult for her to bend over and pick flowers, but every once in a while, she would make the effort to add another long stalk of purple flowers to the basket she carried under one arm.

As he neared the bottom of the hill, she heard the sound of his horse's hooves against the stony ground and she looked up, shading her eyes against the glare of the midmorning sun. She recognized him and waved, and he felt a huge desire to wave in return while part of him shivered with shame for having stayed away over night. She was glad to see him; nothing else mattered.

Thus it had always been with Louisa: nothing else mattered. He wondered if he would ever truly be able to accept that truth about her. His scars did not frighten her. His past did not alarm her. She did not see any sign of the blood that had stained his hands for many years. She did not know—or even need to know—about the anger that lurked inside him. She looked at him and saw what she saw, and it was enough. Anything less was his own failure to acknowledge the innocent simplicity with which she chose to live.

Such earnestness—such purity—made him weep. Even he, who had lived for five years as an animal—constantly hunted by both Moor and Christian alike—and whose resolve was tested time and again, was not that strong.

"Ramiro," she called, moving through the field of flowers.

He dismounted before she reached his horse, so that she would not have to look up at him. She spread her arms, embracing him awkwardly, both her belly and her basket getting in the way. He held her tightly, though, inhaling the scent of her hair and skin. "I missed you," she whispered in his ear. It was true, and it did not matter if he had been gone an hour or a day. Her face lit up the same way.

"Hello Louisa," he said gruffly.

"Did you go to the village?" she asked.

"Almuradiel?" He shook his head. "There were other things I had to see."

"Like what?" she asked.

"Did Fernando tell you what happened in the village?" he asked.

She frowned slightly, her free hand dropping to her belly. Absently, she rubbed her bulge through the linen robe. "He said there was an altercation."

"An *altercation*?" Ramiro raised an eyebrow.

"He said it was all a misunderstanding."

"I apologized afterward."

"Good," she said simply, loosening some of the knotted lines on her forehead.

"How are Maria and Fernando?"

She considered the question briefly. "Good. She likes to tell me what to do—in my own house!—but I think she means well.

Her resting hand patted her stomach. "He is strong and healthy, she says."

"He?"

Louisa beamed. "We're going to have a boy."

"We are?" Ramiro could not believe what he was hearing. He reached out and grabbed the edge of his horse's saddle to steady himself. A boy! He did not know what to think. Up until this moment, he realized he had not fully recognized what was about to happen in a few weeks. He was about to become a father, to a child who would not be able to protect itself for many years. To a small boy child, who would look up to him and emulate everything he did.

"Why are you crying?" Louisa asked.

"It's nothing," he said, dashing away the water leaking from his left eye.

A boy!

Then the crippling doubt swept over him, a quaking terror about the world into which his child was being born.

✦ ✦ ✦

Fernando found him as he was brushing down the horse at the stable. Without a word, Fernando hung up the tack, fussed with the saddle where it hung across the rail of the stall, and shook out the blanket that usually lay between the saddle and the horse's bare back. He set the saddlebags near the stable door, leaving only the sword and scabbard propped up against the wall of the stall. Only when the horse was contentedly munching on grain and Ramiro had put away the brushes and closed the stall door, did Fernando ask about Ramiro's ride.

"How far did you go?"

"To the Despeñaperros," Ramiro said. "There is a citadel there that watches over the road. Castillo del Ferral."

"Christian?"

Ramiro shook his head. "Not for some time."

"How many?"

"Enough," Ramiro said. His lower lip curled awkwardly as he tried to smile. "But not too many."

"Maria says the baby will come in the next few weeks."

"Let us hope nothing happens during that time," Ramiro said.

"If the Muslims come?" Fernando shook his head. "I am not a soldier."

"We will not fight them," Ramiro said, the words coming out with difficulty. "Not here. Not with…"

Fernando took a step back. His expression was a familiar one—not unlike the one worn by the Moor in Almuradiel shortly before the man died. Ramiro was not hiding his anger well. It was distorting his already-monstrous face.

The last time he had fled from battle had been Alarcos, and the retreat should have killed him.

It was not lost on him that had he died there, he would not have been a father.

Nor was he one now. Not yet.

◆ ◆ ◆

That night, as he lay on his makeshift bed, listening to the sounds of the horses breathing and quietly moving about their stalls, he heard the stable door creak. A shadow flitted up the aisle, and one of the horses nickered softly—recognizing the mysterious visitor. He recognized her too from her distended shadow that crossed the wall at the foot of his bed. He moved his blanket back, inviting her to join him, and Louisa sat down slowly and then lay back against his chest. He flipped the blanket over her and then wrapped his arms around her ample stomach.

Beneath his hands, he felt a distant ripple of movement. Louisa laid her hands over his, guiding him down and back. Her hands settled, holding his to her belly, and he waited. It didn't take long. He felt movement again, like a fish swimming, and then a very pronounced and distinct kick against his spread palm.

"He's restless," she whispered. "When the moon comes up, he turns and kicks."

Ramiro pressed his face against the back of her head, inhaling the scent of her hair and sweat. Beneath his hand, his son kicked again. "He's strong," he said.

"And big," Louisa said. "Maria tells me not to worry. She knows how to coax a boy out, but it will hurt. She doesn't say so, but I know it will."

Ramiro thought of the Muslim saber that had taken the tip of his nose and laid open his face. For weeks, he had lain in constant, unbearable agony. The memory burned less now, worn by time and the memory of other injuries that had been sustained more recently, but he could remember how excruciating the pain had been. How much he had wished for it all to go away. To feel nothing, ever again. "It will pass," he whispered. "And when it is gone, you will have a son."

"I know," she whispered back, snuggling against his chest. "All the suffering will be worth it for this gift."

Their son kicked again, as if in happy agreement.

THIRTEEN

S omeone kicked him awake. Lazare groaned, dragging one eye
open and peering into the half-light of dawn. The flaps of
his tent were pulled back, and he could make out several shapes,
obscured by recalcitrant shadows. As he stirred, a booted foot
launched itself into his tent again and cracked him on the hip.

He shoved away from the aggressive boot, and as it—and the
shadowy figures retreated—he clawed his way out of his tent to
stand, shivering, in the pre-dawn. He wore only a long linen shirt
that fell nearly to his knees. His legs and feet were cold. The night
air was in stark contrast to the sweltering heat of the day.

Abbot Amairic stood nearby, his face obscured by his hood.
Lazare recognized the heavy cross about the man's neck. He was
accompanied by a trio of mailled men who wore sheathed swords
at their hips and ugly helmets jammed down low on their heads.
They wore no surcoats, but Lazare knew they were Templars.

"What is it?" he snapped. His hip ached and his teeth chat-
tered. He was in no mood for skullduggery.

"You laid your hands on the head of your abbey," the abbot
said, his voice pitched lower as if such subterfuge would be enough
to disguise his identity.

Lazare clenched his fists and raised his right hand. "I can do it again," he said. "Right now. If there is any doubt as to my previous actions."

One of the Templars stepped forward, hand on his sword hilt. Lazare relaxed his hands, opening them and letting the Templar see his palms.

"You are not fit to be Cistercian," the abbot said. "You have desecrated the order, you have violated your vows, and you have abandoned your covenant with God."

"I have?" Lazare wondered. "Simply by touching you? Which part of our code—specifically—did I violate?"

The abbot shifted from foot to foot. "You act unbecoming of a Cistercian," he snapped.

"As compared to you?" Lazare said. "As compared to the Templars who murdered innocent people in Toledo?" He shook his head. "I fear I am not the one whom God will punish."

"God is going to punish all the unbelievers," the abbot said. "We are the fire with which Iberia will be cleansed. Our inquisition will stamp out heresy and—"

"I know what it will do," Lazare interrupted. He glanced at the Templars and sighed. "Would it be easier if I volunteered to abandon my vows?" he asked. He put up his hands again. "Okay, I forswear my brothers and the vows of the Cistercian order. I am vile. I am unclean. I am…I am…tired, and I would like to go back to sleep. Can I do that now?"

The hooded figure of the abbot nodded once, and the three Templars stepped forward. The one in the lead started to draw his sword.

"Brother Lazare!" Brother Crespin emerged from the gloom, stumbling into the tense tableau before Lazare's tent. "Oh," the round priest said, coming to a sudden halt as he spotted the Templars.

"Brother Crespin," Lazare said happily. "Are you here to collect me for our morning prayers?"

"Our what?" Crespin asked. "Oh, oh! Yes, of course." He beamed at the Templars as if he knew exactly what Lazare was talking about.

The Templar slammed his sword back into its scabbard, and with a curt nod to the other pair, he backed away from Lazare and Crespin. The abbot waited for a second; while his hood obscured his face, Lazare was fairly certain the abbot was glaring at Crespin's beaming face. The abbot raised his hand and pointed at Lazare. "You are no longer one of us," he intoned. "You are no longer my responsibility."

"I can't say I'm saddened by this turn of events," Lazare said, nodding politely as the abbot withdrew as well.

As the quartet disappeared, Lazare clapped Crespin on the shoulder. "That was judicious timing," he said.

"For what?" Crespin wanted to know. "Was that the abbot? Did he just throw you out of the order?"

"He did, Brother Crespin."

"Can he do that?"

"He just did." Lazare slapped Crespin lightly again. "Or maybe I quit. Maybe the weight of all these vows is too immense for me. I cannot bear the strain."

"What are you talking about?" Crespin wanted to know.

"I'm not really a Cistercian," Lazare said. "I have been carrying this lie for so long, and I am so glad to be rid of it."

"What lie? Wait, what just happened?"

"Shall we go for that stroll now?" Lazare asked.

◆ ◆ ◆

As they strode through the sprawling camp along the Guadiana, Crespin doggedly trying to extract an explanation from Lazare, they noticed an unexpected level of activity in the various camps.

The men were not rushing to put on their maille and gather their weapons; instead, they were taking down their tents and packing their wagons and mules. By the time the pair reached the Castilian camp, Lazare had counted a half dozen companies that were readying to march, including the Templars.

The walls of King Alfonso's tent were rolled down, and a quartet of stern-faced soldiers guarded the entrance. Light spilled out through the drawn flaps, and a crowd gathered just beyond the entrance, people pushing and shoving in an effort to peer inside the tent.

Lazare walked up to the entrance as if he were expected, and the two guards extended their arms so that their spears crossed over the lit entrance. One of the other two put a hand on Lazare's chest and gently stopped his forward movement. "Not you," the guard said gruffly.

"He's with me," a voice said, and Don Ruy walked past Lazare and pushed the guards' spears aside. The guard holding Lazare back removed his hand, and Lazare and Crespin followed Don Ruy and his two companions into the tent.

A pair of torches were mounted on low poles in each of the four corners of the tent. The table and map were still in the center of the tent, and the king, his gray hair mussed from sleep, slumped in the wooden chair he had sat in the day prior. The rest of the tent was filled with the various commanders of the armies and other stewards, and they were all talking noisily. A pair of men in hooded robes flanked the king's chair, hands in the folds of their sleeves.

The only man who was not engaged in the discussions was Helyssent de Verdelay, who was dressed as if he were about to ride out to battle. He stood off on the left, watching the crowd squabble, a satisfied smile on his lips.

The abbot, his hood now pushed down, caught sight of Lazare and Crespin and stormed over, pointing at Lazare. "This man is a criminal," he yelled. "He is a disgrace to our order, and a dangerous insurrectionist."

The abbot's voice carried and his words cut through the other arguments like a sword through cloth. When Don Ruy replied to the abbot, he did not have to raise his voice for the room had fallen silent. "Is he not a Cistercian?" Don Ruy asked. "Is not his disgrace reflected upon the head of the order?"

"He is a Cistercian no more," the abbot said, his face darkening. "He is a heretic."

"I used to be a Cistercian," Don Ruy said, glancing at Lazare. "But not anymore. Not since I took up the sword. Does that make me a heretic too?"

The abbot sneered at Don Ruy. "You think your order protects you."

"My order is recognized by the king of Castile and the Pope in Rome," Don Ruy said. "If that is protection, then yes, I am protected." When he slid his sword out of his sheath, Helyssent and his Templar companions—the same three who, Lazare noticed, had accosted him earlier—half drew their swords as well. Don Ruy held up one hand, inverting his sword in his other hand so that he held it loosely by the pommel stone. He offered it to Lazare who, somewhat cautiously, accepted it.

"Now he has a sword," Don Ruy said. "If he would swear to wield it in the service of the Order of Calatrava, then he would come under that same protection." He glanced over at Helyssent. "Templar," he called. "Is that not how it is done in your ranks?"

Helyssent bristled, but said nothing. He let go of his sword and indicated to his men that they should relent as well. "This foolishness is no concern of mine," the Templar commander said. "You may play these games as much as you like after we have departed."

His words sparked the arguments again, and the room was once again filled with agitated voices. The king leaned his head back and stared up at the ceiling.

Lazare handed Don Ruy's sword back, ignoring the abbot's heated gaze. Instead, he tried to make sense of the arguments billowing around him. There was talk of abandoning the crusade, of spoils of war, of fighting Miramamolin's army, and a lack of leadership. He glanced at Helyssent out of the corner of his eye and realized why the Templar commander appeared in control of the room.

The Templars were leaving, and a not-insignificant portion of the northern armies were going with them.

Finally, the king lowered his head, looking no less weary than he had a few minutes before. He banged the flat of his hand against the arm of his chair until the hammering sound broke through the impassioned discussion. Once the room was quiet, he cleared his throat and addressed the Templar commander.

"Your mind is set?" King Alfonso asked. "You will return to France?"

"Aye, Your Majesty," Helyssent said with false dignity. "Your command constrains us too greatly. We cannot hope to uphold our commandment to God and Rome under your leadership."

"And for you to stay?"

"Your Majesty knows what must be done."

The king shook his head. "I will not condone the murder of innocents. Nor will I allow you to wantonly pillage my kingdom or the lands of the caliph."

Helyssent nodded curtly. "Then we have nothing else to discuss." Without another word, he strode for the entrance of the tent, his men and a number of other commanders falling in behind him. Lazare, Crespin, and the men of the Order of Calatrava got out of the way. Those who remained stood silently, watching, as the strongest part of the assembled army abandoned the crusade. As the last man exited the tent, the abbot stirred and scuttled after them.

After the abbot's departure, no one spoke, and the only sound was the crackling pop of the torches. Finally, a timorous voice rose up from the few remaining commanders. "What...what are we going to do?"

The king looked at the men standing beside his chair. The one on the left lowered his hood, drawing a collective gasp from the group as his face was revealed.

"We fight," King Sancho the Strong of Navarre said. "We fight—not for Rome, but for our homes and families."

FOURTEEN

She came out to the stables every few nights, and he said little when she crept into his bed, and he spoke of her nocturnal company even less during the day. It was as if she were a dream that visited him, and if he spoke of the phantom that filled his arms, she would never visit him again. He would never feel the tiny life dancing and jumping under her skin. As the sky turned black and the stars scattered across the sky, he would lie on his bed, unwilling to sleep. Waiting for her to come.

The nights she didn't, he slept poorly. Restlessly. Waking every few hours when one of the horses stirred, making noises that never became familiar to him. Dreams, much like the one that had come to him the afternoon and evening he had spent watching the Castillo del Ferral, began to visit again. He would wake, sweating and gasping—screaming occasionally. In the morning, his body would ache as if he had spent the night running. Or fighting. Or dying.

The nights she came, he slept soundly. Deeply. Repairing the nervous damage he suffered on the other nights. For a time, he thought her visits would be enough to keep the demons at bay. Each night with her in his arms, with his unborn child close, would offset the two or three nights in which the past haunted him.

And the night when he started awake and found himself curled up beneath the old oak behind the orchard, he knew her visits weren't going to be enough. He knew the past was too close. He knew the Moors were too close. He had to become what he had been once before. One last time.

He knew where to dig. The moon hovered over his shoulder, shining ghostly white light on the roots of the tree so that he could see what his hands were doing. He dug, scraping at the hard ground with his bare hands. When his fingers started to bleed, he found a stick and scratched at the ground with that. It took hours, but much later, when the moon was teetering on the tip of the mountains, he crept into the stable and fell onto his bed, utterly exhausted.

In his arms, he clutched the dirty scabbard of a longsword.

It remained cold, and he could not feel any heartbeat in the steel. Nor did it kick and twitch in his arms. But it was familiar, more familiar than anything else, and he slept soundlessly for the rest of the night, free of the dreams.

◆ ◆ ◆

In the morning, Ramiro studiously ignored the dirt-caked scabbard lying on his bed as he went about his other chores. After feeding and watering the horses, he walked the perimeter of the farm. The goats called to him from their pen, and he let them out so they could roam around the orchard. They bounced happily past him, eager to explore the fragrant, budding apple trees. The pasture was covered with a fine sheen of dew, and there was deer sign among a few of the rows in his garden. He would have to set up a blind in the next few days and see if he could bring one of them down. The leather and meat would be welcome in the main house.

The ground around the old oak was disturbed, mounds of dirt piled around a gaping hole. Half buried in the loose dirt near the hole was a tattered piece of clothing that had been white once, before years in the ground had permanently discolored it. The surcoat was falling apart, and it tore as he tried to pull it free of the dirt. He brushed some of the clinging dirt off the piece in his hands, revealing a portion of the elaborate sigil of the Order of Calatrava.

He dropped the scrap of cloth in the hole, and as he shoved dirt back into the hole with his foot, he made sure to rebury the torn surcoat as well.

He heard his name being called and he turned toward the house, spotting Fernando, who waved. Ramiro kicked the dirt around the oak a final time and walked away from the tree.

"We need herbs, cloth, and some other supplies," Fernando said. "I have to go north, perhaps as far as Valdepeñas, where there is a good market."

"I will come with you," Ramiro said.

"Is that wise?" Fernando asked, ducking his head so he wouldn't have to look upon Ramiro's face.

"I need to hear the gossip. I need to know who is traveling on the *campo*. I will not make trouble," he promised.

Fernando nodded, though his expression suggested he was not entirely convinced. "Very well," he sighed. "I will tell Maria. We should depart soon. We have a long day ahead of us."

They separated—Fernando returning to the main house, Ramiro, to the stables where he began to prepare two of the horses for the ride. Almost as an afterthought, he picked up the dirty scabbard and tried to brush most of the grime and dirt off, and then he covered it with his sleeping blanket. He would not need it in Valdepeñas; not if he was going to hold to his word.

Fernando arrived shortly after he had finished hiding the sword, and they finished readying the horses. They led them outside and mounted. Ramiro looked toward the villa as they rode down the lane, but he did not see Louisa. He wondered, briefly, if he should go back and say good-bye, but he set that worry aside. He would see her again, tomorrow morning at the latest. There was no reason to fear otherwise.

◆ ◆ ◆

They reached Valdepeñas in the early afternoon, and despite the heat, the market was busy. While Fernando sought to buy the supplies Maria needed, Ramiro sought out a tavern and found one that was filled with boisterous customers. He managed to drag a stool into a corner where he would not be jostled or disturbed overmuch by the noisy patrons. With his face obscured by a heavy hood, he sat and listened to the raucous stories.

There was an army on the plain—crusaders and Castilians—and it was slowly moving south. The Moorish garrisons in a number of citadels had been defeated. Calatrava had been retaken. A lesser topic, but one that cast a pall on any celebratory oration, was the caliph's army, marching up from Seville. The naysayers in the audience—who were shouted down more often that not—said the Moorish army was three times the size of the Castilian army. Others said that Miramamolin meant to march all the way to Rome, and that he was allowing all the Christian victories in the last few days so that the northern forces would become arrogant and careless with these minor conquests. They had not faced a real threat, and when Miramamolin managed to cross the Sierra Morena, the armies of the north would run in terror.

Ramiro nursed his cup of wine, his heart pounding in his chest. Calatrava had been retaken! What of the other citadels along the road to Castile? Were they in Christian hands again? Malagón. Benavente. Torre de Guadalferza.

Alarcos.

Would they even remember who had been left behind at Alarcos? After the Lord of Vizcaya had negotiated the terms of his surrender, assuring the safety of the women and children who had been trapped by the Moors at Alarcos, some of the knights of Calatrava had been held as an assurance of the ransom being paid. After a month, it was clear to the Moorish commander that Vizcaya had no intention of paying the ransom. He had left the knights to die.

A pair of dusty travelers came into the tavern, and after they quenched their thirsts, they told new stories. Rumors that the northern armies were splitting up. The Templars, having been disgraced in some dispute with the king of Castile, were leaving. They were taking most of the northerners with them too, and Ramiro listened intently to the speculative bedlam that filled the room in the wake of these rumors.

Fifty thousand fighters were leaving the field. Miramamolin's army now outnumbered the Christians, four to one. There were no knights left. Without the Templars, the king of Castile only had the military orders of Iberia to call upon, and everyone agreed that these orders were not suitable replacements for the fabled Templars. Someone tried to start a rumor that the Templars had left because the Shield-Brethren were coming, and everyone knew the Shield-Brethren and the Templars would not fight on the same field, but this story was quickly shouted down as utter nonsense.

After awhile, the tenor of the room slid from chaotic celebration to somber rumination. If the stories were true—and the dust-stained travelers stood by their news—then the plain of La Mancha was going to be a bloody battlefield again, and many recalled the last time the Almohad caliph and the kings of Iberia hurled themselves at one another. Ramiro finished his wine and pushed his way through the crowd toward the door.

"The Beast," someone shouted. "We need the Beast of Calatrava!"

He froze, fearing someone had seen his face in the shadows of his hood, but no one was paying any attention to him. The room was focused on a drunken man near the hearth who was too fair-haired to have been born in Iberia. He waited, swaying slightly, until he had everyone's attention, and then he launched into a wild tale, filled with the sort of poetic nonsense that only a troubadour could find possible, and Ramiro pushed his way through the crowd.

It hadn't been like that, he thought as he shoved the door open and left the tavern and the troubadour's tale of the battle at Alarcos. *It hadn't been like that at all.*

The name wasn't even used until four years later, after two garrisons around Calatrava had been killed by the scarred madman who always left one survivor so that the Moors would know who was killing them.

FIFTEEN

⸺

"**T**hat is a beautiful blade."

Lazare faltered, struggling to steady himself as his rhythm with the grindstones was interrupted. The sword blade on the anvil was nearly finished, less than a hand's breadth near the tang remained unpolished. He had been working on it extensively over the last few days, since the Templars had abandoned the crusade. Since he had been cast out of the Cistercian order by the abbot. There had been little else to occupy his time. Like everyone else, he was waiting for the kings of Castile and Navarre to reach a decision.

"Thank you, Your Grace," Lazare said as he looked up and recognized the three men who were gathered at his makeshift smithy.

His visitors this morning were the archbishop, Don Ruy, and Brother Crespin. The archbishop had been the other mysterious figure in the tent when Helyssent had refused to aid the king of Castile. He and the king of Navarre had arrived during the night, and they had secretly waited to see the outcome of the dispute between Castile and the crusaders before revealing themselves.

"Toledo steel?" Don Ruy asked as he stepped closer and inspected the shaped blade.

"Aye," Lazare said, lightly brushing off some of the dust clinging to the sword. He squinted at Brother Crespin, who was standing a little separate from the other two. He and Crespin had not spoken in several days, and the few times he had seen the other man in the camp, Crespin had avoided his gaze. Crespin smiled weakly as Lazare looked at him, but said nothing.

"The king has received word from Al-Andalus," the archbishop said as casually as he had spoken of Lazare's smithing. "Al-Nasir's army numbers nearly two hundred thousand men. More than four times our number. The king has been consulting with King Sancho day and night in an effort to assemble a successful battle plan, but..."

Lazare nodded. The loss of the Templars was devastating, not just in pure numbers—each knight was invaluable on the battlefield—but in morale as well. Campaigns had been won with worse odds, but to willingly engage in battle at such a deficit was the sign of an ill-prepared commander. Miramamolin might show mercy on the field, but the other kings of Iberia would be less forgiving.

"But he needs an edge," Lazare finished for the archbishop. "He needs an advantage that is not simply numbers."

"Yes," the archbishop said. "An edge." He flicked his thumb against the tip of Lazare's sword. "Something that will give his men a reason to fight. A reason to believe they will win."

Lazare thought about what King Sancho had said in the meeting. "For hearth and home isn't enough?" he asked.

"If it were, would you be here?" the archbishop asked. "Marcos of Toledo told me you spoke of seeking symbols that would rally men's hearts." He flicked his thumb against the sword again.

"Durendal," Lazare explained to Don Ruy who was following the conversation with a raised eyebrow. "Tizona."

"Ah," Don Ruy said, his face brightening. "Now I understand."

"Good," the archbishop nodded. He held out his hand to Lazare, who took it without fully understanding why. The archbishop clasped his other hand over Lazare's. "Good luck," he said,

THE BEAST OF CALATRAVA ✦ 243

staring intently at Lazare, and then he let go of Lazare's hand. As he turned away, he laid his hand on Brother Crespin's shoulder and whispered a blessing to the Cistercian, who nodded sagely.

Lazare watched the archbishop walk away. "I don't understand," he said to Don Ruy.

Don Ruy cast about for something to sit on, and finding a stool, he pulled it close and leaned toward Lazare. "We need a symbol," he said. "It could be a sword such as this one. Or it could be a man. Or it could be both."

"Me?" Lazare said, trying to figure out what Don Ruy was suggesting.

Don Ruy shook his head. "You are not Castilian," he said. "The archbishop trusts you. He says you understand what it is to be an Iberian, even though you are from... where? England?"

"France," Lazare corrected, stealing a guilty glance at Brother Crespin, who gave no indication he had heard or cared about Don Ruy's slip.

"It is okay to be English," Don Ruy said, mistaking Lazare's correction. "King Alfonso's wife is English. Sister of the Lionheart, in fact."

"So I have heard," Lazare said, licking his suddenly dry lips.

"Have you heard the local legend of Calatrava?" Don Ruy asked. "The monster that is neither man nor beast, but who haunts this plain, slaughtering Moors in their sleep?"

"I have not," Lazare admitted.

"Nearly twenty years ago, the Moors drove my order out of Calatrava. After the battle at Alarcos. Those of us who survived became knights without a castle. We even changed our name for a while, but such a decision diminished the sacrifice of our fallen brothers, more so when stories started to circulate about the Beast of Calatrava. Whoever he was, he didn't accept the loss—he would never accept the loss—of our namesake. How could we call ourselves the Order of Calatrava if we did not fight for what was ours?

Calatrava was abandoned by the Templars long ago, because they were not Castilian. They did not belong here. This is our home, and our name reflects who we are and who we protect. For many years, we have been less than we should have been."

"You want me to masquerade as this man?" Lazare asked.

"No, no," Don Ruy said with a chuckle. "I want you to help me find him."

"Me? Why me?"

"Because you believe in the stories, and because you believe in the truth that lies behind the stories." Don Ruy fumbled with his hands in his lap. "And because you are not from Iberia. Sometimes we listen to a stranger more readily than we do our own countrymen."

"This man is a legend," Lazare said. "A twenty-year-old legend. How is this not a fool's errand?"

"Because he has been seen. Less than a month ago. In a tiny village named Almuradiel, near the Sierra Morena."

◆ ◆ ◆

They all wore plain garb, though Brother Crespin was loath to set aside his Cistercian robes. Lazare wondered aloud why the Cistercian brother was even joining their mad quest, and Crespin's simple response had been *Better a mad quest than a mad priest.* Lazare had embraced him for that, and after an awkward pause, Crespin had returned the show of affection.

On horseback, with an escort of three other knights of the order—equally attired, though outfitted with maille hauberks and helms—they headed west across the wide campo of Calatrava and the plain of La Mancha, chasing the story of the Beast of Calatrava.

Two days later, in Valdepeñas, they heard of a drunken troubadour who told a stirring version of the legend of the Beast, and Lazare heard for himself the story of what had happened in Almuradiel. Though, later, Don Ruy told him that it was only four Moors that the Beast had slain, and not six.

A day later, in a squalid tavern in Cózar, they met a man named Diego who, for a price, told them a story about a stolen goat.

The next morning, they turned south, heading for the Sierra Morena. They were looking for the Despeñaperros River and the valley it had carved through the mountains.

SIXTEEN

Ramiro heard the goats bleating, calling out to foreign beasts that were approaching. They didn't sound alarmed, which meant horses—which they had become accustomed to—and not predators. Ramiro retrieved his sword from the stable and ducked into the orchard to investigate who was approaching the villa. From the edge of the orchard, he spotted the six riders approaching. They were making no effort to hide themselves, and in their plain tunics and robes, they did not seem to be Moors. He saw longswords, and three carried crossbows slung across the backs of their saddles.

Christian soldiers.

Unlike the deserters from months ago, these men did not appear to be lost.

He met them at the oak, carefully putting the bulk of the tree between himself and most of the party. He made no effort to hide his face, and he noticed two of the men seemed pleased to look upon his scarred visage.

"God be with you," one of them said, nudging his horse forward of the rest of the group. His skin was as dark as the rest, but his hair was lighter. He had been in Iberia for some time, but he was a foreigner, and he spoke with an accent that reminded

Ramiro of the Latin spoken by the priests in the churches in Toledo.

"And with you as well," Ramiro said, not unaware that they had just exchanged a variation of the Islamic greeting. "Are you lost?"

"That would imply we had a destination in mind," the man said with a laugh. "Is there a place ahead where we might have a drink and water our horses?"

"No," Ramiro said.

The man glanced at his companions, his gaze lingering on the stout man who sat in front of the armed escort. The stout man lifted his shoulders slightly and the foreigner slid off his horse. Ramiro let his hand fall on the hilt of his sword as he watched the man fumble with one of his saddlebags and extract a wineskin.

The man walked toward him, pulling the stopper out of the skin. He paused, a respectful distance from Ramiro, and drank from the skin. "It is good I have my own wine then," he said, offering the skin to Ramiro.

Ramiro stared at the man, noting that while he did not have a sword, he stood in a loose stance that spoke of some experience wielding a sword. "I do not drink before noon," he said, offering a reasonable excuse that would not be offensive.

The man squinted up at the sun. "Is it still morning?" he asked. "It feels later. This sun…" He left the sentence unfinished and took another pull at his wineskin.

"Why are you here?" Ramiro asked, not liking the easy insouciance of these strangers.

"My name is Lazare," the one with the wineskin said. "That is Crespin and Ruy." He pointed to the pair behind him in turn. "Hernando, Lope, and Miguel are our escorts back there."

"That does not answer my question," Ramiro said.

"Do you know the story of El Cid?" Lazare asked, ignoring Ramiro's comment. "Prior to coming to Castile, I did not, and

I have found it the most fascinating tale. He fought for Castile against the Moors, and then he fought for the Moors against… other Moors, I think. Maybe even against Leon. It gets confusing. And then he founded his own fiefdom, in Valencia."

"Everyone knows the story of El Cid," Ramiro said.

"He had a sword too," Lazare continued, his face brightening. "It was called Tizona. No one knows what happened to it after he died. A beautiful sword, from what I hear. A most distinctive guard and hilt. Very ornate."

"I know of no such sword," Ramiro said. "It is nothing more than idle foolishness. The stuff of legend."

"An interesting story, nonetheless," Lazare said. "Like other stories that I've heard since coming to Iberia. The fall of Calatrava, for instance. The retaking of Calatrava. Have you heard that one?"

"I haven't," Ramiro lied.

"No, I don't suppose you would have," Lazare said, sucking on the wineskin. "Hidden away up here in the hills. I suspect you hear very little of the world."

"And see even less," Ramiro said. "Which is the way I like it."

"Of course," Lazare said. "Still, I'm sure you've heard the story about the monster who owned a goat? Yes? Or the one about the half dozen Moors who made the mistake of disturbing a local man in a drinking house not far from here?"

"Why are you here?" Ramiro said, the tenor of his voice making it clear that this was the final time he was going to ask the question.

"Was it really six men?" Lazare asked. "At the tavern in Almuradiel."

"It doesn't matter," Ramiro said. "The stories tell a better tale."

Lazare nodded as if that was somehow the answer he had been hoping to hear, and Ramiro found himself confounded by the man's reaction. His confusion only increased as Lazare smiled and looked at his companions. "I think we've found our man," he said.

"Aye, I think we have," said the one named Ruy. He dismounted from his horse and walked over to Ramiro. "I am Ruy Díaz de Yanguas, master of the Order of Calatrava."

Ramiro was shaken by the realization that he, ostensibly, owed this man his allegiance, even after all this time.

"Welcome, Master Ruy," he said, offering his arm for the other to clasp. "I am a poor host."

"Well," Ruy said, laughing. "It is a good thing we are not here for your hospitality."

✦ ✦ ✦

Ramiro had Fernando bring out food and water from the villa, and as the horses were cared for and the men were fed, he and Lazare and Ruy wandered off to the shade of the orchard to talk.

"I remember you," Ruy said as they walked along the rows. "I was a squire at Alarcos, serving Pedro Ruiz de Guzmán. I was among those who were released with the Lord of Vizcaya. It was because of you and the other knights who stayed behind that I sought out the order."

"You are mistaken," Ramiro said gruffly. "I was not at Alarcos. I am not—"

"You saved my life," Ruy said sternly. "Do not belittle the gift you gave me."

Ramiro shut his mouth and bowed his head. "My apologies," he said. He gestured loosely at his face. "I am a rough beast, and my manners are as equally disturbed."

"You know the Moors are coming," Lazare said. "Miramamolin has more than two hundred thousand men on the other side of those mountains. There is a letter in Toledo—"

"A forgery," Ruy interrupted.

"A forged letter," Lazare corrected. "It claims that Miramamolin seeks to march on Rome. That he wants to do what his forefathers could not. Drive the Christians out of Iberia forever. It doesn't matter if he wrote this boast or not; his men think it to be true. The kings of Castile and Navarre think it to be true." Lazare paused and put his hand on the trunk of one of the apple trees. "He's coming to La Mancha at the very least," he said. "Two hundred thousand men will be on the plain. They will go north to Toledo. They may go east to Valencia. They make even go as far as Barcelona. Who knows? They will definitely spill over into these hills, especially once they hear stories about the Beast of Calatrava—the monster, haunted by revenge, who hunts Moors." He dropped his hand. "It took us only a few days to find you, and there are only six of us. How long do you think it will take hundreds—thousands—of Moors to track you down?"

"It doesn't matter," Ramiro said. "I died a long time ago. My life is insignificant."

Lazare ducked his head and peered down the row of trees. In the distance, a portion of the villa's roof could be seen. "It's not just *your life* that is at stake anymore though, is it?"

"What do you care?" Ramiro said, his hands shaking. "This is not your home. This is not your fight."

"My home is far from here," Lazare said. "That is true. I left behind people I love in order to find a way to help them in their struggle." He shook his head. "I wanted to find a symbol that could give my people hope, and during the time I have spent among the people of Navarre and Castile, I have realized that such symbols do not lie outside the home." He touched his chest. "They're here." He gestured at the tress around them. "And here."

"What do you want from me?" Ramiro demanded.

"We want you to give them hope," Ruy said. "The kind of inspiration no king can command from his people."

"I am a murderer," Ramiro said. "I slit men's throats while they slept. I am not a symbol of hope. I cannot be redeemed by leading an army to victory."

"You don't have to be anything other than a man who seeks to protect his family," Lazare said. "That is, I have come to understand, what binds all of Iberia together."

"Family," Ruy echoed.

"Very well," Ramiro said after gnawing on the scar tissue inside his check for a moment. "You must do something for me first." Ruy nodded. "There is a citadel a half-day's ride from here. Castillo del Ferral. They threaten my family more immediately than Miramamolin."

"If we take this citadel, then you will help us."

"I will consider it," Ramiro said. "But only if *he* comes with us." He pointed at Lazare. "Your arguments may be convincing, but your actions speak more truly. Help me, and I will help you."

"Okay," Lazare said. "I suppose there is a long tradition here of monks becoming knights."

"Aye," Ruy laughed. "There is."

SEVENTEEN

——

They approached the Castillo del Ferral in the late afternoon, when the heat of the day was still heavy about the walls, and the shadows among the trees were getting long. They numbered six—Brother Crespin remained with the horses in a narrow vale a half mile away—and they carefully appraised the citadel's walls and towers. It was Ramiro and Ruy's assessment that not more than two dozen Moors resided inside—maybe half of them would not be combatants. The pair, having had several hours to discuss strategy during the ride from Ramiro's villa to the citadel, were well past the awkwardness of the initial meeting.

The other three knights were professional soldiers. They knew what to do, and Lazare did his best not to distract them while he prepared himself for battle.

He had not been entirely honest with Ruy and the others. While he had spent years pretending to be a Cistercian monk, he had grown up in the green woods outside Yorkshire, where there was no shortage of opportunities for young orphans to learn martial skills. Unlike the other youth, though, he had little interest in becoming a longbowman. He had been drawn to the mysterious associate of Marion, the noblewoman who had been a source of constant consternation for Locksley. He and the other boys had called him *Old Ox*, a childish perversion of the name by which the others knew him—*Audax*. He had once heard Marion call him by a different name, and he had kept that secret to himself—for it meant that Marion and Old Ox had known each other before coming to Sherwood.

Perhaps that was why Old Ox had suggested he spend more time with the Cistercians. Why he had suggested that young Lazare learn not only how to wield a sword, but how to make one as well. And later, when the opportunity arose to travel to France and the center of the Cistercian world, both Old Ox and Marion thought he should go.

He had not had a chance to find a proper hilt for his new sword. The blade was finished, sharp and polished, but the handle was nothing more than two pieces of shaped wood wrapped tightly around the bare tang of his sword and covered with a layer of taut leather cord. The sword squirmed in his grip, untested and unready. Much like he was.

He wore Miguel's hauberk. Miguel was going to cover their assault with the crossbows, and while a padded tunic would not stop a Moorish arrow, they all hoped Miguel would remain far enough away that a hastily fired arrow would be his only concern.

"We can't scale the wall," Ruy was saying. "We don't have the proper equipment. Unless there is another way in, we have to get them to open the gate."

Ramiro nodded in agreement. When Lazare had first seen the man, standing beside the old oak, he couldn't decide which was more gnarled and twisted—the bark of the tree or the man's face. Ramiro's beard—spotty as it was over the scar tissue— alleviated some of his ugliness, but up close, there was no disguising the tortured knot that was the end of his nose or the twisted curl of his lips. Lazare could imagine how much more horrific that face would be if it were seen by torchlight or partially obscured by shadows. No wonder the Moors had been so frightened…

"You should announce yourself," Lazare said suddenly. "Just walk up to the gate and tell them who you are."

"What?" Ruy said.

"You're the Beast of Calatrava," Lazare said. "Famous for killing Moors in their sleep. For strangling children and frightening cattle to death."

"I never strangled children," Ramiro said.

"You're a monster that hides in the shadows," Lazare said, a little disturbed that Ramiro had not denied frightening animals to death. "You don't fight in broad daylight. You skulk in the night. If you simply walked up to the gate and said, 'I am the Beast of Calatrava, and when the sun goes down, I am going to kill all of you,' don't you think they might send out a war party to kill you *now*, instead of waiting for you to catch them all sleeping?"

"They'd have to open the gate," Ruy noted. "If we were all waiting, it might be our best chance of getting inside."

"What if they put archers on the wall?" Ramiro said.

"Don't stand *that* close," Lazare pointed out.

Ruy laughed and looked at Ramiro, who shrugged. "I've attacked a castle with *less* of a plan," he admitted.

◆ ◆ ◆

The Moors responded even more readily than they had hoped. A few minutes after Ramiro had caught the attention of the single guard atop the wall, shouting out a long list of atrocities he was going to perform on all those who resided within the walls, the castle gate shuddered as the heavy bar behind it was removed. Ramiro stood his ground and as soon as the gate was halfway open, a horseman charged out.

The horse barely cleared the shadow of the wall before it was brought down by one of Miguel's crossbow bolts. The archer at the top of the wall fell next. By that time, Lazare and the others were sprinting across the open ground between the forest and the citadel.

The second rider was thrown from his saddle as his horse abruptly changed direction in an attempt to not collide with the first horse that was still thrashing on the ground. Lope killed the fallen Moor with a single stroke of his sword as he ran past, and Hernando paused by the dying horse to thrust his spear into the face of the Moor still trapped beneath it.

The third horseman was caught, framed in the open gate, and with an unholy howl, Ramiro leaped over the downed horse and rider, hurling one of the three Moorish swords he had brought with him. Lazare gaped, unable to believe what he was seeing, and even though the thrown sword hit the Moor like nothing more than a stick bouncing off a wall, the effect of such an unexpected attack was immediately felt.

The Beast had come to Castillo del Ferral.

Ramiro pulled the stunned Moor out of the saddle, hurling him to ground where he beat the man so savagely with the pommel of his sword that blood spurted high enough to mark Ramiro's hair and beard. A Moor charged, and Ramiro threw himself to the side, slashing with his sword. The sword severed the Moor's right leg just below the knee, and the Moor collapsed, screaming and clutching at his blood-spewing stump. Ramiro walked away from the howling man, and it fell to Lazare—his eyes burning, his chest heaving—to put the man out of his misery.

He did the same for the man whose face had been battered in by Ramiro's pommel. As he took stock of the pitched battle inside the gate, he realized that the Moors were ignoring him. Horrified at what he saw happening around him, Lazare understood that his role was to bring mercy to those who had been touched by the Beast of Calatrava.

He threw up after he killed the third mortally wounded man. Wiping his mouth and fighting to keep from vomiting a second time, he desperately tried not to think what this abattoir would be like if none of the Moors were given mercy. How long would all these men scream and wail before they died?

Such was the legacy of the Beast—the horrible truth that none of the stories captured. What really happened when the Beast came was so much worse than any troubadour could dare imagine.

◆ ◆ ◆

"Was it awful?" Crespin's worried face hovered in the moonlight. "I heard so many screams."

Lazare took the offered wineskin and drank heavily from it, washing the bilious taste of the sick from his mouth. "It was," he said after swallowing several mouthfuls of warm wine.

Crespin looked past him, his head bobbing as he counted the returning members of their company. "Who?" he asked when he came up one short.

"Lope," Ruy said tiredly, taking the wineskin from Lazare. "Bastard got lucky." He touched the side of his throat. "Caught him here as Lope killed him."

Crespin gasped as the moonlight revealed the last member of the group, and he closed his eyes until the blood-spattered monstrosity had walked past him. Lazare watched Ramiro stagger past the horses and continue on down the ravine. A mindless revenant, returning to its grave. None of them made any effort to stop him.

"There's a route through these mountains," Ruy said as he handed back the wineskin. "I had forgotten about it until we were at the Castillo del Ferral. We can take the entire army through this pass and be on Miramamolin's forces before they know we are coming." He shook his head. "It wasn't just to protect his family," he said.

"A tactical advantage," Lazare said.

"Aye," Ruy said. "And with him leading the assault, we might have a chance."

Lazare shuddered at the idea of facing a charge of enraged Christian soldiers, the Beast of Calatrava at their front. "More than a chance," he said. He looked for the shadow-shrouded figure of the bloody Beast. "We can't let him fall on the field," he said. "We have to get him home again."

"More than any of us," Ruy agreed. "He has to live."

EIGHTEEN

Fernando and Crespin were waiting for them when they rode up the path to the villa, nearly two weeks after the bloody battle at Castillo del Ferral. Ramiro leaped out of his saddle and walked, stiff-legged, past the pair and into the house. Lazare got down from his horse much more slowly, wincing at the pain such motion caused in his injured hip. Behind him, Miguel and Hernando dismounted much more readily and Miguel took the reins to his horse after Lazare got his footing on the ground.

"It's a boy," Crespin said as Lazare painfully made his way across the lane. "The mother is doing well."

Lazare smiled for the first time since he had killed a man. The motion of his lips felt strange at first, and he was sure it looked more like a grimace than a real smile, but Crespin seemed to understand. Fernando excused himself and went to help the other knights with the horses.

"Ruy?" Crespin asked.

Lazare shook his head, his smile fading. "We won," he said. "Miramamolin was unprepared. It was a rout. Nearly two—" He stopped. The number of dead didn't matter. Too many, he thought. Too many on both sides. "Amairic was there," he said.

THE BEAST OF CALATRAVA ◆ 259

"The battle was barely over and he was shouting about the supremacy of Rome against the infidels." He shook his head. "Iberia, Constantinople, the Cathars in Toulouse. He saw them all as heretics. Rome won, and would continue to win. That was all he cared about."

"But La Mancha was saved. Toledo too," Crespin said. "That is all that matters right now. They defended their homes and their way of life. It is a good victory."

"Aye," Lazare sighed.

The door of the villa opened and Ramiro wandered out, a bundle of cloth in his arms. He wore a bemused expression, the scarred corner of his mouth struggling to turn up. Crespin saw what he was carrying, and he smiled broadly enough for both of them. There were tears in Ramiro's eyes as he raised the bundle so that Lazare could see the tiny face nestled within. "It's a boy," Ramiro said.

"He's beautiful," Lazare said, tears marring his vision. The boy seemed to dance on a series of watery bubbles.

"I am a father," Ramiro said. He looked at Lazare, and through a veil of tears, Lazare saw some of the ferocious madness that was the Beast in Ramiro's eyes. "I am not a soldier anymore," Ramiro said. "I am not a knight. Nor a monster. Nor a murderer. I am just a father. That is the only way I want to be remembered by my son."

Lazare swiped away his own tears. "A worthy goal," he said, his voice cracking. "A worthy goal. Have you given him a name yet?"

"Eleázar Ramirez de Calatrava," Ramiro said without hesitation.

"Eleázar? That is…" Lazare glanced at Crespin who seemed as stunned as he was. "Why…why that name?"

Cradling his son in one arm, Ramiro reached out and laid his hand on Lazare's shoulder. "You're part of my family," he said.

"No," Lazare said. "I…I can't…That is—"

"That is his name," Ramiro insisted. "Iberia had touched you, Lazare. It is just that you be remembered here as well."

"I..." Lazare stuttered to a stop. Swallowing the lump in his heart and nodding, he accepted Ramiro's decision. "I am honored. Deeply."

"He will be a good legacy," Ramiro said proudly. "For both of us."

ABOUT THE AUTHORS

 Linda S. Pearce has worked in the high-tech industry for over twenty years and is active in the animal rescue community. The two met at a Renaissance faire and fell in love immediately. They are now married and live in Seattle with six dogs and two cats.

 Michael "Tinker" Pearce is a world-renowned swordmaker and author of *The Medieval Sword in the Modern World*. He is a student of historic European martial arts and works with Subutai Corporation as a fight choreographer and consultant.

 Mark Teppo is the author of the *Codex of Souls* urban fantasy series as well as *Earth Thirst*, an eco-thriller with vampires. A bibliophile whose interests include historical martial arts and esoteric traditions, he lives in the Pacific Northwest.

 Angus Trim is a skilled swordmaker and machinist who lives in the Pacific Northwest. He is adept in various western martial arts as well as tai chi sword form.

Made in the USA
Coppell, TX
25 January 2021

48786742R00157